A STONE IN THE POOL

A Stone in the Pool rounds off Susan Tweedsmuir's trilogy of Victorian novels. In this book she recreates the life of the last century at various levels: in university society at Oxford, where her heroine, Rachel, grows up in seclusion with her scholarly father; in a shabby-genteel quarter of London, where she goes on a visit; in remote Dorset, where she meets the poor but happy family of Paul Sibley, an unsuccessful suitor; and finally in a large country house, where she goes to live when she marries.

The reader will be fascinated by these glimpses of a vanished age, and charmed by the gentle heroine, first in her early innocent happiness and then in her distress at the wounding coldness with which she is received by her aristocratic new relations.

Those who have read *Cousin Harriet* and *Dashbury Park*, which began the series, will recognise some of their favourite characters as they reappear in Rachel's story.

A
STONE IN THE POOL

A Victorian Story by

SUSAN TWEEDSMUIR

*If a stone is thrown into a pool no one
knows how far the ripples will reach*

GERALD DUCKWORTH & CO. LTD.
3 Henrietta Street, London, W.C.2

First published 1961

© 1961 *by* SUSAN TWEEDSMUIR

Printed in Great Britain by
Page Bros. (Norwich) Ltd., Norwich

To Felicia Seymour Taylor

with gratitude for her help

I must explain to my readers that I have placed Sir William Warren (a character in an earlier book of mine) in Paris as British Ambassador in the '80s of the last century. I apologise to the shade of the real Ambassador at that date.

S.T.

I

As a child, Rachel Barrington had only known two places, Oxford and the seaside. Her mother had died when she was four years old, and an elderly Scotch cousin had come to keep house for her father and herself. She saw little of children of her own age, and her life was spent in playing in the garden of the house in north Oxford, which boasted a large mulberry tree, and a small summerhouse with creaking floor-boards, where spiders scuttled and spun webs and swallows swooped in and out of a nest in the roof. Rachel's dolls were seated carefully upon a circular seat which ran round the little hut, and her minute blue and white tea set was carefully laid out on the table with a mulberry on each plate. Her father encouraged her to read, which enriched each game, and although she had few books she read them over and over again. Kingsley's *Heroes* furnished her with many stories from mythology, and even if it proved difficult to double the parts of Perseus and Andromeda it could be accomplished.

Life in the house in Oxford went on evenly from day to day, week to week, month to month. Rachel met few other girls, and the rare garden party to which she went made her feel awkward and out of things. One or two of the dons' wives tried to be kind to the lonely girl, but their parties were something of an ordeal. Rachel listened a great deal but hardly spoke a word. This was not considered unusual, as young people were not expected to air their opinions when their elders were conversing.

She often found the conversation interesting and liked sitting silent while university topics were discussed. Oxford was very much a man's world in which the dons' wives played an important but quiet part. They attended lectures, listened to sermons and not only echoed their husbands' comments but made shrewd and trenchant remarks of their own. The academic world rarely lacked drama. Controversies raged about religious and scholastic opinions against a background of greatness and pettiness, intrigue and bitterness, shot with kindness and a real selflessness practised by those capable of such virtues.

The young men poured through Oxford and its ancient buildings like heady new wine in old and solid bottles. They were the *raison d'être* for this old town placed by waters and surrounded by low quiet hills.

Just before the vacation the university blossomed into a flutter of muslins as sisters and their friends stepped into the dingy gloom of Oxford station, to be borne down the steep slope into the town seated precariously in hansom cabs. The river was alive with gay parasols, young men punted and rowed, and vast quantities of food were consumed, after which the young ladies and their chaperones returned to London, heartfree or not, no one could say.

All this was outside Rachel's life, and as she grew up her father looked at her sometimes with a puzzled stare. He had always dreaded her growing up. Women's higher education was in the air, and she could perhaps go to Somerville or Lady Margaret Hall, but he did not feel anxious for this to happen, though she might perhaps go to the lectures arranged for Oxford ladies. He had set her some essays, which he corrected with care. They were promising, but he had felt bound to warn her not to jump to conclusions and always to be scrupulously accurate rather than to make any attempt at picturesque writing.

Her cousin, like all Scotch people of her date and age, had a great (if unwilling) respect for learning. She regarded it as a mysterious vocation entered into by men. It was not well paid and was in fact a much less profitable activity than the other professions. She taught Rachel to sew and to mend linen, and though she showed only a very ordinary aptitude for this household craft, she developed a talent for embroidery. Her work avoided strident colours and ugly designs and had its own delicacy and charm.

The house had steadily burning coal fires, shining grates and fire irons; the food was plain but well cooked, and its routine was that of a well regulated clock. Rachel took refuge in dreams.

2

This kind of life might have gone on much longer if Rachel under pressure from her father had not accepted an invitation to tea from Mrs. Neville, the wife of the head of his college. This gave Rachel no expectation of pleasure, rather that of dread and apprehension.

She was not alone in these fears. A tea party at Mrs. Neville's was regarded as a penance by many of those invited to it. The house was chill and forbidding, the tea black and tepid, the cakes crumbled to sawdust on plates, and the chairs were a menace to the spine. But owing to her husband's position as Vice Chancellor of the University her invitations could not be disregarded. The reason for Rachel's inclusion at this unfestive board was that Mrs. Neville had a niece staying at the Master's Lodgings who was the same age as Rachel.

Rachel had demurred at going, but her father and cousin had taken no refusal, and she found herself in the quadrangle of one of the larger colleges a few minutes early. As she stood looking at the door of the Principal's Lodgings, at the graceful lines of windows above the green turf, steps approached, and a tall undergraduate with two books in his hand ran up the three steps from the middle of the quadrangle and came to stand beside her at the door. Rachel looked up at him and had the impression of gaiety suppressed into momentary seriousness.

'Are you going in there?' he said, indicating the door of the Lodgings with a wave of his hand.

'Yes, I've been asked to tea,' said Rachel.

'Oh dear, rather an ordeal,' he said, and seeing her face fall he added, 'I expect you will be all right.' Then he said breathlessly, 'I say, would you be very kind and take in these books with you and leave them on the hall table? I've written a note—it's inside this book—if you would just give them to the butler.

I'm in a tearing hurry—it's very kind of you. Mrs. Neville lent them to me, they were such dull books that I've only glanced through them.'

'What name shall I say?'

'Richard Gervase,' he called as he cleared the three steps with a flying leap.

Rachel turned to the door and rang the bell. It was opened by a butler who had such an air of frigid dignity that for a moment Rachel almost gasped as he confronted her. She looked down, and then looked up at the butler.

'Mr. Gervase gave me these books.' His face did not relax.

'He was returning them to Mrs. Neville,' she faltered, 'and he handed them to me on the doorstep.'

The butler took the books from her and laid them on a marble-topped table. He managed to convey that it was odd, to say the least of it, that this should have happened. Nice young ladies in his opinion did not carry messages from undergraduates.

Rachel advanced to the drawing room, which seemed both high and long. She threaded her way between small tables loaded with bric-à-brac and between footstools treacherously placed in front of sofas.

Mrs. Neville rose majestically from behind a round table, her figure darkly outlined by the stained glass window behind her.

'You are the first person to arrive,' she remarked. Rachel felt relegated to the inferior position of an over-eager guest. Then a door near Mrs. Neville opened and a girl came in. She stared at Rachel with round, startled eyes.

'This is the Principal's niece, Emily Deering,' said Mrs. Neville, with the air of one who disclaims all responsibility. 'This, Emily, is Miss Barrington.'

The two girls shook hands and stood speechlessly beside the tea table. Rachel turned her head to look at Emily and met Emily's glance. They both looked away.

At that moment the door at the far end of the room opened, and the butler announced several names. Mrs. Neville marshalled the ladies round the table, and their smiles seemed a little set as they awaited her commands.

'Mrs. Maxwell, will you sit by Miss Barrington?' The youngest of the ladies seated herself next to Rachel, who, paralysed with shyness, dared not look at her.

While Emily handed round the tea cups, Mrs. Maxwell handed Rachel a plate of bread and butter. Rachel took a piece and laid it on her plate, and then looked up at her companion's face. The gaze bent on her was so mild and benevolent that some of her shyness vanished.

'I'm Mrs. Maxwell, and you are Miss Rachel Barrington. I know your father; my husband is a don at this college.'

Emily planted a cup and saucer smartly beside Rachel. The cup heeled over spilling its contents into the wide saucer.

Rachel, utterly dismayed, tried to right it, but it was lifted off the table and replaced by a full cup by her neighbour.

'Don't say a word,' whispered Lucy Maxwell, 'I'll manage this.' She glanced rapidly at her hostess, who was fortunately engaged in a stately gossip with the imposing lady on her right, whose ample form masked the affair of the tea cup from Mrs. Neville's glance.

'You are kind,' said Rachel looking up at Lucy.

'Nonsense,' said Lucy, 'I used to upset tea cups when I was your age and still do sometimes.' She had tipped the contents of the saucer back into the cup and taken a sip of tea.

'But won't your tea be quite cold?' whispered Rachel.

'It will be that anyhow,' whispered Lucy, smiling at her. 'Just behave as if nothing had happened.' She turned to her next door neighbour and Rachel drank her bitter tea in silence.

Emily plumped herself down beside her. Conversation rose jerkily around them, but there was sufficient noise for Emily to say to Rachel, 'Sorry about the cup, but I thought my aunt's eyes were on me and it makes me so nervous.'

She glanced quickly at Rachel and then darted a look at Lucy Maxwell, who turned smiling to the two girls.

'Have you been here long?' she enquired, looking at Emily.

'No.' Emily glanced over her shoulder at her aunt, who had turned her attention to her other neighbour, a small woman with a pointed nose, and lips which she licked every few minutes. She looked obsequiously up at Mrs. Neville's imposing bust and shoulders.

Emily heaved a sigh, 'Well that's over,' she said, 'until they all want second cups.'

'It must be nice for you to be here on a visit,' said Lucy.

Emily made a slight grimace, and Lucy laughed.

Mrs. Neville darted a glance charged with suspicion. Laughter was seldom heard at her table. Lucy composed her features, looking solemn though a smile lurked on her lips.

Emily said, encouraged by the smile, 'I know there is lots of sightseeing to be done, a lot of old churches and colleges, but I don't see many people. I never see anybody young.'

Lucy's eyebrows rose in surprise. 'But what about the under-graduates?' she asked.

'I'm never allowed to talk to them. If one of them comes to dinner, Uncle Henry takes them away and talks to them.'

Mrs. Neville rose to her feet and led the way into another room.

'Emily, you and Miss Barrington can go and sit on the window seat.'

From where the two girls were sitting they heard lowered voices.

'Let's meet again,' said Emily. 'Can I come and see you one day? Can I come tomorrow?'

The tea party was broken up by the principal guest rising to her feet. Lucy Maxwell lingered for a moment to speak to Rachel.

'Perhaps you will come and have tea with me some day and meet my husband. I will write to you—Oh, there he is.'

Rachel saw a man with a very erect carriage coming towards them, his rather austere features relaxed as he smiled at his wife. As he came up to them Lucy said, 'This is Miss Barring-ton, Mr. Barrington's daughter.'

George Maxwell looked into Rachel's small face with interest.

'I know your father well,' he said, 'and Lucy, what was your tea party like?'

'Nicer than usual,' she replied. 'I sat by Miss Barrington.'

Rachel lifted her eyes to George's face. 'Mrs. Maxwell was so kind, my tea cup was upset—so she helped me with it.'

'My wife's grand at helping,' he said, 'so there was no tea-cup storm?'

'Luckily Mrs. Neville didn't notice,' said Lucy. A look of gaiety and confidence passed between husband and wife.

'Well, Lucy, we must be getting home,' said George.

'I shall write to you about a day for coming to tea. I do hope you can come. Goodbye.'

She slipped her arm through her husband's and they walked away together.

Two days later Emily came to see Rachel. She seemed out of breath and fanned herself vigorously with her handkerchief.

'I stepped out,' she said, 'while my aunt was busy with the store cupboard. She wanted me to help, but I hate it, and when she was taking down some jam pots she wasn't thinking about me and said 'yes' over her shoulder, so I came out of the house quick with Jane, the second housemaid. She's got a brother who is a scout at the college. He lives somewhere at the back of your house in some sort of lane.'

She sat bolt upright in her chair her eyes taking in the details of Rachel's bedroom. As they sat facing each other, one each side of the mantelpiece, a silence fell. Neither knew where to begin.

Rachel's bedroom was a pleasant room, though shabby, furnished not with any method but with a table here, and a chest of drawers there which did not match in design. The chairs in which they sat had faded chintzes with different patterns. A large tree overhung the garden outside the window, its branches tapping on the window.

'Well,' said Emily, 'that was an awful tea party.'

'Yes, I was so frightened,' said Rachel, 'except for meeting Mrs. Maxwell.'

'Yes, I like here,' said Emily, 'she's one of the few people Aunt Sarah doesn't say anything nasty about. She might like to, but she doesn't dare because Uncle Henry likes her and her husband so much. My aunt doesn't much like anybody.'

'How dreadful,' said Rachel, who found it easy to like people, though she knew very few people to like or dislike.

'Yes it is,' said Emily nodding her head. 'But don't let's talk about my Aunt Sarah, let's talk about us.'

'You begin,' said Rachel.

Emily leant forward in her chair. 'Well, I live in a square in London. My parents are always talking about being poor, and we haven't got much, and I have to get my clothes made by little dressmakers, and I can't take cabs when I want to, and

I don't get asked to the big balls, only small dances. What about you?'

'I've never been to a dance or a ball.'

'Oh but aren't there any here?'

'Only at Commem. and sometimes one in Eights week.'

'Oh dear, this place must be awful,' and Rachel suddenly seemed to see Oxford slipping into a yawning abyss of dullness.

'Oxford is a place to learn, not for dinners and things like that,' she said.

Emily tossed her head. 'I can't understand that. There are plenty of young men here.'

'I never meet any of them. Sometimes one comes to see my father, but they seem very shy, and my father takes them away into his study.'

'But don't you ever meet them outside?'

'No, I only see them in the distance.'

'But look, that's not true, my dear,' said Emily. 'You know Richard Gervase. Aunt Sarah's butler said you had brought some books from him, so you must have been seeing something of him.'

Rachel's face flushed. 'But I was only waiting on the door step to come into tea, and this man, Mr. Gervase, asked me to give them in at the Lodgings as he wanted to return them. I don't know him and had never seen him before.'

'Aunt Sarah will never believe that,' said Emily with a little laugh. 'She thinks you must know him very well, and she wondered how you came to know him as he is rich and smart—he belongs to Bullingdon and all that.'

'I have only seen him that once.' said Rachel stiffly. 'I couldn't refuse to take the books, could I? As a matter of fact, he didn't want to return the books himself. He said they were dull and he didn't want to talk about them—your aunt had lent them to him.'

Emily laughed. 'That I can believe. If I were you, I'd try and meet him again.'

14

3

THE promised tea with Mrs. Maxwell happened a week later, and Rachel found herself ushered into a narrow hall and then into a small drawing room. Through the windows she glimpsed a little walled garden. The welcoming look on Lucy Maxwell's face gave Rachel a feeling of confidence. There were no footstools to trip over, and there were books and papers on two tables. Some of them looked new, and one had a paper knife stuck between its pages. Rachel wondered if she could take a look at the books after tea.

'I see that you are looking at our books,' said Lucy. 'They invade every corner of this house, and George has even suggested putting them on each side of the staircase—on each step I mean. I have so far persuaded him not to do this, as I can't see how we should ever get them dusted, and the children would play with them and tumble over them.'

'What did your husband say?' asked Rachel.

'Well, he has promised to try and keep his books within bounds at the moment,' said Lucy.

Suddenly an irregular tattoo was beaten on the door, and two children came in. They looked at Rachel with the air of those who find an obstacle in the path to pleasure and shook hands with her reluctantly. Lucy took no notice of this hanging back and going over to a cupboard produced a Noah's Ark.

'Could you help me push back the chairs?' she said. A space was cleared in the middle of the floor, and Lucy and Rachel knelt down and helped the children to make a procession into the Ark. The paint was flaking off some of the animals, and from hard usage they had become bipeds instead of quadrupeds. Rachel proved to have great skill in propping them up, and she was just considering how to insert a giraffe, which had lost two legs beside a tuft of carpet, when the door opened and a young man came in.

'Hello, Richard,' said Lucy rising from her knees as she smiled up at him. The two children after a hostile stare at the newcomer averted their heads to continue their game. Rachel tried to rise but found it difficult encumbered by her long skirt. Richard held out his hand and drew her to her feet.

'Mr. Gervase, Miss Barrington,' said Lucy.

They confronted each other across the Noah's Ark animals and the children's bent heads.

'We've met before,' said Richard, 'on the door step of the Principal's Lodgings. You very kindly took the books I wanted to return.'

'Sit down both of you,' said Lucy smiling, 'I want to hear more about this.'

Lucy and Rachel watched as Richard gravely helped the children, who, also grave and absorved, bent their heads and with their small fingers assembled the motley collection of beasts.

Then there came a knock at the door, and Nurse, inexorable as fate, stood in the doorway.

'Put the Noah's Ark away,' said Lucy.

They tumbled the animals back into the Ark.

The children having left the room, Lucy said, 'Thank you so much, Richard, for playing with the children.'

Richard had collapsed into a chair. 'They're easy to play with,' he said.

'They're very good,' said Rachel.

'They can be very naughty,' replied Lucy, 'they can scream, scratch and even, I am sorry to say, bite, but they behave passably well downstairs, and anyhow when they see you, Richard, they know that you will have a game with them.'

Richard settled himself more comfortably in the armchair. 'Yes,' he said, 'I enjoy playing. I am supposed to be seeing your husband, but I always come early for a game.'

He glanced at Rachel, who sat forward in her chair, her face a little flushed, her hands clasped. Her lips were parted over her small even teeth. He saw her clearly for the first time. She always looked people straight in the face. Her father had told her that she must never let shyness interfere with this.

16

Lucy rose. 'I must go and say goodnight to the children,' she said. 'Don't go, Richard, George will be here any minute, and please don't go, Miss Barrington, we have hardly had any talk.'

Rachel, who had never been alone with a young man, tried to think of something to say which would bridge a gulf of silence, when Richard remarked, 'It was kind of you to take those books into the Principal's Lodgings.'

'The butler looked rather astonished,' said Rachel.

'He lives in a perpetual state of gloomy astonishment,' said Richard. 'I believe he was in service before with a Bishop, and apparently life was more exciting and more lavish at the Palace than in Oxford. I had to submit to a cross-examination about the books, and of how they came to be returned by you. Mrs. Neville is so inquisitive and won't let anything alone.'

Richard smiled as he continued, 'I just told the truth for once, but she's got that very tiresome way of looking as if she couldn't or wouldn't believe a word you say.'

Rachel laughed and felt at ease.

George Maxwell came in saying, 'How do you do, Miss Barrington. Sorry I'm late, the college meeting dragged on so long. Come along, Richard.'

The day outside waned gently and Rachel found herself listening for the first time in her life to someone near her own age, as Lucy continued questioning her quietly about her life and circumstances. It had never occurred to Rachel that anyone could want to hear about her own affairs.

Later, when Rachel got home, her cousin Mrs. Cunningham inquired about the tea party. Rachel described the house. It had, she said, a William Morris wallpaper in the drawing-room, a pattern of leaves, pale green on a white ground. There were blue and white jars on the mantelpiece and coloured prints of Italian pictures on the walls.

'It looked very light and pretty,' Rachel said, glancing round at the bulky mahogany and the heavy curtains which darkened the room in which they were sitting.

'And did you get a good tea?'

'I didn't really notice,' said Rachel. 'I was more interested in talking to Mrs. Maxwell, and then an undergraduate, Mr.

Gervase, came in and we played at Noah's Ark with the children, and then he went away with Mr. Maxwell, and Mrs. Maxwell and I talked again. She is so kind.'

Mrs. Cunningham looked at Rachel. She saw that Rachel's face and figure looked pleasing, and although she was not given to using the words handsome or beautiful, the word bonny did occur to her.

She sighed. Rachel was growing up. What a pity that children did grow up. She had been such a dear little girl, and now—neither Rachel's father nor she would be able to manage the life of a grown-up girl. Oh well, perhaps it would be all right and easier than she thought—but perhaps not.

A few days later, when Rachel was leaving the house, she came on a man trying to unlatch the little iron gate. It was not an unusual latch to undo, but his mind seemed to be elsewhere. Rachel advanced towards him and opened the gate from her side.

'It is rather a difficult gate,' she said.

'Not really,' he replied, 'only I'm bad at gates.'

He was a tall young man, and as he removed his cap his unruly hair sprang up.

'I live here,' said Rachel, 'and know its ways. Did you want to see my father?'

'Yes, please, I do. Is he at home?'

'No, but he will be in half an hour.'

'Then I'll come back.'

'No, please come in and wait in his study. I know he will be in soon. He sometimes forgets but I don't think he will today.'

The two young people walked along the mossy tiled path and stood under the sombre porch of the house.

'By the way my name's Paul,' he said, 'Paul Sibley.'

Rachel led the way through the little drawing-room into the study. It was a scholar's room. Books lay open on a large writing desk, pens were strewn casually here and there, the quills looking like the discarded feathers of untidy hens. Books had also invaded the window seats and the floor, and dust lay thick on some large volumes piled in one corner. Rachel glanced at them.

'My father won't allow any of his books to be touched,' she

said. 'My cousin who lives with us can't move him an inch about this. He just won't let anybody come in here except very occasionally, and then for weeks he says he can't find anything, and that the books are put in back to front and in the wrong order.'

She glanced up at Paul, who laughed.

'I am just the same,' he said, 'it's so easy to lose a train of thought if you mislay a book and can't find a quotation you want.'

'Do sit down,' said Rachel. She stood looking uncertain and then turned to leave the room.

'Won't you sit and talk to me while I wait for your father?'

He waited till Rachel had sat down in an arm chair, then seated himself in another one so abruptly that it gave an ominous creak, and a slit in its leather back burst open and exuded a puff of stuffing.

Paul did not notice. He crossed his long legs and settled himself back in the chair. He went well with the room, Rachel thought. His angular form and careless pose seemed to suggest an inability to cope with the difficulties of daily life, while the broad forehead and keen grey eyes and the firm, well defined lines of his mouth hinted that in the sphere of the mind there was little that he could not understand and interpret.

She found herself talking easily. He asked her what books she liked, and they plunged into that subject, so absorbing when two book-lovers meet, of tastes and feelings and fine shades of meaning. They found that they agreed, and Rachel was startled when she heard the front door slam and rapid footsteps crossing the adjoining room.

Her father entered, looking apologetic, and then, when he noticed his daughter, perplexed.

'Sorry to be late,' he said, but Paul had uncoiled himself from the armchair.

'It doesn't matter a bit, sir,' he said. 'Miss Barrington and I have been having a delightful talk'

Mr. Barrington looked at his daughter. 'I am glad,' he said, 'but we must get to work now. Run along, my dear.'

Rachel caught a glance of amused sympathy from the young man. She left the room with slow steps, her head high. At the age of eighteen dignity is a fragile thing and hard to maintain.

4

EMILY found the atmosphere of the Principal's Lodgings oppressive and inimical to her ideas of amusement. She came as often as she could escape to visit Rachel. Rachel did nothing to prevent her coming and in fact up to a point enjoyed her visits. But Emily had a way of inserting a sudden prodding question into an ordinary conversation which she found disconcerting.

'I hear that you met Richard Gervase at the Maxwells.'

'Yes, I did. I went to tea with Mrs. Maxwell, and he came in and played with the children. They seemed very happy to see him. They are such a nice little boy and girl.'

Emily let this pass. To her, children were supers in the drama of existence.

'Did you make friends?'

'Oh no', said Rachel, 'nothing like that. We just talked a little, that's all.'

'Well, I must say you are in luck. I never get a chance to talk quietly to a young man, especially what my father would call a gilded youth like that. The mammas in London will be after him for their daughters when he leaves Oxford.'

'I don't know what you mean,' said Rachel, her colour rising a little.

'My dear, don't be silly. We girls must look after ourselves, especially when our elders are useless. My mamma and papa are no help. He grumbles about being poor, and my mother just bursts into tears, and your cousin and your father are, I should say, no good either. You don't want to be like one of those deadly dull girls who come to Oxford to study and never speak to anyone.'

Rachel, who liked to study and had thought of asking her father if she might attend some courses of lectures, rose to her feet. Before she could speak Emily began again. She seemed unable to stop herself. 'I think it's a beastly shame,' she said, 'that men should have it all their own way in this world—and we have to wait about and be pleasant and look nice.' To Rachel's horror tears came into Emily's eyes.

'Oh Emily,' she said helplessly.

'You say, "Oh Emily", and that's all the help I get from anybody—"Oh Emily",' she mimicked Rachel's voice.

'But I can't help you, I'm afraid,' she said reasonably, 'about young men, I mean. We do very little entertaining and it's mostly my cousin Louisa's and my father's friends. Father just thinks I'm still a child—the other day when a young man was here he told me to run along.'

'A young man. Who was it?' Emily pounced.

'A Mr. Sibley.'

Emily's eyes opened widely.

'Paul Sibley,' she cried, 'why, he's Richard Gervase's great friend—you could get to know Mr. Gervase if you know him. Why are you looking so cross?'

'I'm cross,' Rachel replied, 'because I think this is all so stupid.' She stamped her foot. 'Let's talk about something else.'

She looked at Emily, who gave her a sidelong glance, penetrating and sly. 'Very well my dear,' she said, 'time will show which of us is being stupid.'

One evening as George laid down his book and looked at her with a smile, Lucy said,

'I feel we ought to ask that girl Rachel Barrington to dinner one evening. She has such a quiet life and never sees anybody of her own age. Could we get one or two young men to meet her, perhaps?'

George Maxwell lit his pipe and threw the match into the fire.

'If you wish it, dearest,' he said, 'we could make it the occasion to ask the new don and his wife, or would that be too many?'

Lucy's serious expression amused him as she looked at him.

'We could put eight round the table,' she said, 'and Annie could manage it all right.'

'You look very grave,' he said, 'Is it too big an undertaking? But why do you say eight?'

'Because,' said Lucy, 'I think we ought to ask Mrs. Neville's niece too, and to get a young man to make us even numbers.'

'Did you like her that day at tea at her aunt's?'

'I hardly talked to her. She didn't attract me like Rachel Barrington did. She looked a little pert I thought, and I should say she might be very observant of one's shortcomings.'

'Not a very interesting dinner party for the new don and his wife, but I daresay they won't mind,' said George.

Lucy smiled. That familiar sentence was as far as George would go in his estimate of a social gathering. Enjoyment was something that he ruled out. His idea of pleasure was an evening alone with Lucy, or a dinner in college, where the discussion of some historical subject had proved interesting and provocative.

Emily and Rachel both accepted the invitation in their different ways—Rachel timidly deprecating her dress and her conversational powers and Emily with pretended alarm at the probable cleverness of her fellow guests.

'People in Oxford aren't clever,' said Rachel, 'they are learned, which is different.'

'Oh rubbish, there's no difference.'

'My father despises mere cleverness,' said Rachel. 'He says it's easy to be clever. Anybody can be clever, but you've got to be much more than that to be any use.'

'Well, I expect your father is right about Oxford,' said Emily. 'In London it's considered a very good idea to be clever. But do look at my sleeves—do you think they are set in properly?'

The two girls were sitting in Emily's bedroom at the Principal's Lodgings, with Emily's dinner dress spread out on the bed.

'My aunt is sending me in a cab to the dinner party,' said Emily. 'I'll come and fetch you and bring you back. I shall take some lavender water for my handkerchief as that old cab smells so mouldy—you can have some of it if you like. Stingy old thing—she might have let me have the brougham.'

'Well, it will be nice to go in the cab,' said Rachel soothingly. 'My father was going to hire one, and now he needn't, and it will be so nice too, if we can go together.'

The evening came. Lucy dressed in an evening gown from

her modest wedding trousseau, and George, with the set face of a martyr to duty, looked austere and handsome in his evening clothes.

Lucy was walking about the dining-room with some sticks of smoking lavender in her hand. She pushed them amongst the coals and they gave out a soft fragrance.

'Just to make sure that there isn't any smell of cooking,' she said.

The door bell rang and Mr. and Mrs. Westwell were anounced. They were both tall and thin, and in Mrs. Westwell's case this was accentuated by the shapeless garment that hung loosely on her bony frame, while her hair fell lankly on each side of her hollow cheeks. She was, thought George, an admirer of William Morris and the Pre-Raphaelites. She should have harmonised with the Morris wall paper and the blue and white china pots on the mantelpiece, but somehow she did not. He averted his gaze from her abruptly and drew Mr. Westwell into a corner of the room. Lucy and Mrs. Westwell seated themselves on the sofa near the fire.

The door opened and Miss Deering and Miss Barrington were announced. Emily came in with a slightly exaggerated timidity of manner, while Rachel, inwardly frightened, looked outwardly composed.

Mrs. Westwell shook hands limply, the door opened again, and Mr. Gervase and Mr. Sibley were announced.

At dinner, George found Mrs. Westwell rather hard to get on with. He was not at all given to small talk, and Mrs. Westwell's rather flat replies to any conversational approach resulted in silences. He turned with relief to Rachel and asked her a question about her father, and soon they had found subjects in common.

Mrs. Westwell had been asking Paul what exactly he was studying. She hoped he was not wasting his time like so many young men. Paul, who was a very hard worker and had to make his own way in the world, intercepted a laughing glance from Richard, who was engaged in many of the less serious pursuits which Mrs. Westwell was denouncing in her level and unemphasised tones.

'I always study for part of the day,' she remarked. 'I am on the early Popes at the moment.'

Paul, a little at a loss, glanced across the table and saw Richard turn to Rachel, while Mrs. Westwell engaged George Maxwell's polite but reluctant attention.

Lucy smiled at Paul, and drew him into talk with Emily and Mr. Westwell. She so much wanted her dinner party to be a success. They rarely had one, and like many hostesses through the ages she wondered why she had embarked on this particular enterprise. But Emily was sparkling with smiles at Paul and seemed ready to be amused by anything. Paul responded, and even Mr. Westwell's ponderous face relaxed into an occasional smile. Lucy sent a glance down the table to George, who was listening with grave attention to what his neighbour was saying, while Rachel was listening with a different kind of attention to Richard's account of a day's hunting, her eyes fixed on his animated face. She much preferred listening to talking and Richard's vivid description of his latest day's sport held her spellbound.

'It is going better than I feared it might,' thought Lucy.

When the ladies rose and left the dining-room the two young men thought how much they wished they were alone with their host. They liked him, and he did not intimidate them.

Lucy led the ladies upstairs. Mrs. Westwell adjusted her dress and fingered her lank hair, and the two girls peeped speechlessly into the mirror. They passed the nursery and saw the two children asleep in a dark room where a fire glowed and a night light flickered. Lucy paused for a moment by the half open door. Mrs. Westwell made no remark, and she and Emily rustled quickly down the staircase. Rachel lingered for a moment, and Lucy slipped into the room and adjusted a blanket which little George's out-flung arm had disturbed. Then she tip-toed out of the room thinking how lucky children were to be asleep with no obligations to make a dinner party pass off well. She smiled at Rachel and Rachel smiled at her.

Emily and Mrs. Westwell were standing some way apart in front of the fireplace. A card table had been put out at the further end of the room.

'I thought we might play a round game,' said Lucy.

'I do not play cards,' said Mrs. Westwell, but Emily's eyes sparkled.

'But round games are quite easy,' she said.

At that moment the gentlemen came into the room. After a few exclamations and withdrawals Mrs. Westwell consented to seat herself at the card table. Emily, sitting between the two young men, was in her element. She gave small giggles and squeals of laughter, dropped her cards, picked them up again. George Maxwell, thankful not to have to converse, entered into the spirit of the game. Mr. Westwell, similarly glad not to have to dredge the depths of his mind for conversational pearls, unbent, and Paul and Lucy helped Rachel. Her shyness vanished when she saw that Paul didn't take the game in the least seriously. His long fingers clasped the cards tightly, and he often forgot when his turn came to play.

Richard and Emily made a fair amount of noise between them. Mr. Westwell though more silent seemed to find Emily engaging and occasionally exploded into a good laugh. Mrs. Westwell handled her cards as if they might carry some infection. Then she stared fixedly at an Arundel print of a Madonna on the wall opposite, but George with firm determination drew her attention to the game.

The evening passed quickly, and Rachel was amazed when the parlour maid came in and announced that the two cabs were at the door. The Westwells and the two girls made their farewells, and Lucy parted from her guests saying that she hoped to see them again.

George remarked, 'I don't feel as if I ever want to see the Westwells again. I shall have to meet him of course, but I would call her a pretentious fool.'

'Yes, but the evening went well I think,' said Lucy. 'Richard and Paul were so nice and easy and the two young ladies looked so pretty.'

5

Mrs. NEVILLE was finding Emily useful to her, being too obtuse to see that the girl was laughing at her behind her back and was also being indiscreet about her economical habits and her other foibles. Emily had a youthful callousness about her aunt's problems and a lack of understanding that, having little private means, provision for old age in a small house in Oxford or in the country was a matter of concern and calculation to Mrs. Neville. Emily had never known the grace and comfort of a happy home and was always on the fringe of London society, to which the entrée was restricted to those who had powerful family relationships or a solid backing of money. So when her mother accepted Mrs. Neville's invitation for her to stay on in Oxford she was on the whole pleased and acquiescent. Oxford to her was no lovely city set in hills but a mere stodgy mass of masonry, only of interest because for part of the year it housed undergraduates who might always be observed at street corners and with whom she was able to have a quick word occasionally at the Principal's Lodgings. This might lead to something more perhaps—a meeting in London later, an invitation to dance at one of the few London balls to which she was asked.

Rachel was glad when she heard of Emily's continuing stay in Oxford although Emily's conversation tore gaps in her cocoon of dreams. Emily never read a book, her reading consisting of turning over the pages of a ladies' magazine of fashions. She sewed and was always making alterations to her meagre wardrobe, but being young and light-hearted she taught Rachel to laugh at the comedies of every day life. Emily slid into Rachel's house, carefully avoiding Mrs. Cunningham and her friend's father as much as possible.

Mr. Barrington did not notice that Paul Sibley came a little

oftener than before to ask advice about his work. Nor did he
realise that Paul often came a little before the appointed time,
and he was astonished one day on returning early to hear a
man's voice in the drawing-room. He went in to find Paul
seated between Rachel and Mrs. Cunningham, all laughing
at some joke that Paul had made.

Mr. Barrington drank his tea with rapidity and saying over
his shoulder, 'Come along Paul,' left the room. He reached his
study and started to fill his pipe. He looked round for Paul.
Through the open door he heard him ask Mrs. Cunningham if
she would bring Miss Barrington to tea in his rooms, and Mrs.
Cunningham saying in a precise if startled voice that she
thought she could. Mr. Barrington went back into the drawing-
room and saw that Paul was standing looking down at the two
ladies. Rachel was flushed and looked happy, and Mrs.
Cunningham was looking down with a reserved expression.

'Yes,' she said, 'that will give us both great pleasure.'

'Come along Paul,' said Mr. Barrington, 'we've no time to
waste.'

'Then that's settled,' said Paul, and followed him out of the
room into the study.

That evening, when Rachel had retired to bed, Mr. Barrington stared at his cousin, who was methodically folding up her
needlework preparing to insert it into her workbag, and
remarked, 'There is no need for you to go to tea with that
young man if you don't wish to.'

Mrs. Cunningham looked at him. 'I am not going for my
own pleasure, Arthur,' she said, 'but it will be nice for Rachel
to go.'

'Young men are not here to give tea parties but to get on
with their work,' was the austere reply.

'Aye,' she said slowly, 'but a wee bit of pleasure does not
come amiss to young people, and Rachel's life is a quiet one.
You may not remember, Arthur, but you were young once.'

With that she put her needlework into the bag and after a
brief goodnight left the room. Mr. Barrington was left with
what to him was an unwelcome thought, that his child had
turned into a grown-up person. Rachel should no longer be
regarded as someone who did lessons and received an absent-
minded pat on the shoulder, but as a young lady who was

emerging into a new world. He resumed his book with a frown of impatience, quite unconscious that his feelings were familiar to parents through the ages.

Rachel was eagerly looking forward to the tea party, but was worried that Emily had not been invited. She considered mentioning the subject to her friend, but shrank from Emily's curiosity and her probing questions. Emily would be sure to find out about it, but Rachel could not see that there was anything she could do to secure her an invitation. When she said to Mrs. Cunningham, 'I wish Emily had been asked too,' the latter replied, 'No pairson has any control over another pairson's invitations.'

'But I am sure she would like to go,' Rachel persisted.

'That may be'—a remark which effectively closed the subject.

But Mrs. Cunningham had reckoned without Emily, who appeared in the house two days later saying that she had met Paul Sibley in the street as she came out of a shop, and he had said that the two ladies were coming to tea and 'he asked me if I would come too. You sly thing, you never told me you were going to tea with him,' she said later to Rachel.

'I meant to tell you when I next saw you,' said Rachel, making a slight compromise with her conscience.

'Well anyway, I'm coming,' said Emily.

The day arrived. Emily met them, and they progressed silently together—Emily venturing a remark that it was a fine day, to which Mrs. Cunningham replied briefly, 'Aye, that it is.'

Paul met them at the foot of his staircase. Climbing the stone steps to his rooms, they held up their skirts a little above the steps coated with the dust of many years. As Paul pushed open the door and stood aside to let them enter, Richard Gervase skirted an arm chair and came forward to shake hands. Mrs. Cunningham saw behind him Lucy Maxwell, who rose to her feet to greet them smiling. (There was no need for me to come, thought Mrs. Cunningham as she shook hands with Lucy, they already have a chaperon.)

A low table was spread with solid-looking bread and butter and sandwiches flanked by a muffin dish. A short confusion ensued while Paul invited Mrs. Cunningham to pour out tea. Lucy sat beside her on the sofa, while Rachel and Emily perched themselves on two stark-looking chairs. Paul provided a rush-bottomed chair from his bedroom and a stool on which he and Richard severally sat down. Mrs. Cunningham gravely wielded the heavy metal tea pot. She never talked while she was pouring out tea; she regarded it as too serious a matter to be interrupted by trivial conversation.

'What on earth shall I talk to her about?' thought Lucy, but Mrs. Cunningham, after accepting a muffin from the dish and drinking a sip of tea, turned to her: 'You have children have you not, Mrs. Maxwell?'

'Yes I have,' said Lucy. 'I have two.'

'Dear wee things,' said Mrs. Cunningham.

Lucy looked up, uncertain what to say next, and her eye caught some peacocks' feathers standing in a tobacco jar on the mantelpiece.

'How pretty those are,' she said.

'Yes,' said Richard, 'we have peacocks on the terrace at our house—they are very noisy.'

'Do they really foretell rain?'

'Well, it seems to me that they screech whether it is going to rain or not. Our visitors complain that they wake them up at all hours of the morning. We have got far too many, but my mother liked them and so my father is loth to get rid of them.'

'Some people think it is unlucky to bring peacocks' feathers into a house,' said Mrs. Cunningham.

'My father never listens to that; he is not superstitious,' said Richard.

Paul stole a look at Rachel. She was sitting bolt upright in the bony-looking worn chair, her hands one on each of its wooden arms, her feet barely touching the ground. She looked amused but a little apprehensive. Mrs. Cunningham took a surreptitious glance at the clock. Unfortunately a peacock's feather from the neighbouring tobacco jar had flopped across its face and she was unable to make out the time.

Paul said, 'My old nurse would never let me look at the new moon through glass. I could never peep out of a carriage window on a fine night, and had to hurry upstairs with my head averted in case I caught sight of the new moon through a staircase window.'

'My nurse never allowed me to walk under a ladder,' said Richard. 'That is supposed to bring specially bad luck.'

'Do you have many of these superstitions in Scotland?' asked Lucy.

Mrs. Cunningham prepared to rise. 'These and many more,' she said. 'The countryside is full of them; they come down from heathen times. Clever people in Edinburgh do not believe them, although the great Professor Murchison was nearly run down avoiding a ladder in George Street.'

'Well, clever or not clever, I expect it comes to the same thing with all of us,' said Richard.

'We have many ghosts in houses in Scotland,' said Mrs. Cunningham, 'and queer things happen'—she paused and said to Richard, 'Can you tell me the time?'

He took a gold watch out of his pocket, snapped it open and showed her its face. Opposite was a brilliant little picture of a woman, young and lovely.

Mrs. Cunningham rose to her feet. 'We must be going,' she said.

'Oh no,' cried Paul, 'not yet.'

Mrs. Cunningham sat down reluctantly. 'Well, we can stay just a wee bit longer.'

Emily craned her neck as Richard was about to close up his watch. 'Can I see the picture?' she asked.

Paul frowned, and Richard without a word gave her a brief glimpse of it and snapped the watch to. He returned it to his pocket.

'My mother,' he said curtly, and turned to speak to Lucy, enquiring where she and her husband were thinking of spending the vacation.

Paul talked across the tea table to Rachel. He rose and bent over her shoulder to show her a book. Mrs. Cunningham sat in silence, and Emily stared round her conscious that she had made a blunder. Richard looked for a moment at Rachel who was glancing up at Paul and responding to something he said with a laugh. 'She is pretty,' he thought.

Then Mrs. Cunningham rose with an air of determination and said they really must go. She and Lucy walked down the staircase followed by the two girls and young men.

They said goodbye to Richard who walked quickly away across the quad, and Paul said in a low voice to Emily and Rachel: 'The portrait is of Richard's mother who died—she was killed in a hunting accident three years ago. Richard never mentions her, and I never ask him about her.'

'I'm sorry I asked to see the portrait,' said Emily.

'You couldn't know, could you?' said Paul.

6

THE term ended. The gowns were gone, and the town resumed its usual activities unassisted by the presence of the young gentlemen. The learned young ladies, few in number and carefully unobtrusive in their ways, silently vanished.

Richard went home and Paul to a reading party with some other undergraduates. Emily returned to London to her parents, and Rachel was invited to stay with them for a few days. She offered to refuse this invitation on the ground of the spring-cleaning, an affair which was taken with deadly seriousness by her cousin; but Mrs. Cunningham would have none of this.

'No, Rachel, I shall do better without you. I have asked your father to go away, and he fell in with my suggestion.'

Spring cleaning was sacred to Mrs. Cunningham, a stern almost Calvinist necessity. So he bowed his head, took a room near the British Museum and prepared to depart.

Rachel and her father arrived in London, and their luggage was piled on the top of a four-wheeled cab. The traffic entertained Rachel, but her father was impatient to get on. He sat with his hands clasped round his knees while the ancient cab rattled its way along. He was annoyed at being chased away from Oxford, and frowned at intervals. They made their way through some small streets into a square. He handed Rachel some silver and a five pound note.

'This should be enough for you,' he said, 'Buy your Cousin Louisa a small present to take back, and don't forget to go to see some pictures and museums, and St. Paul's and Westminster Abbey.'

'Yes, father.'

'This is my address. The day you can come to the British Museum, I will spare an hour of time and show you round.'

She dismounted from the cab. The Deering's house was small. Inside a green railing, bushes which had very little resemblance to their cousins in the country waved their spotted green leaves in the spring breeze. The door remained shut; the door knocker and handle were streaked and unpolished. Rachel looked at her father, who was showing signs of impatience.

'You didn't ring properly,' he said, and he pulled the bell so vigorously that it nearly came off the wall.

The door was opened by a parlourmaid dressed in black with an exaggerated cap and apron—at least it seemed exaggerated to Rachel, accustomed to the more homely parlourmaids in Oxford. The four wheeler man carried Rachel's small trunk up the steps, and her father said goodbye and drove off. Rachel, feeling oddly deserted, stood in the hall, and opened her mouth to speak, but at that moment Emily came tempestuously down the stairs, her skirts flying. She flung her arms round Rachel, and the next few minutes passed in a cloud of enquiries and explanations.

'Come upstairs,' said Emily. 'My mamma's in the drawing-room.' She flung open a door and ushered Rachel into a room darkened by lace curtains and blinds half drawn down. Mrs. Deering rose from an armchair. She was an older edition of Emily, except that Emily's mouth curved upwards while hers turned down. Emily wistfully sought gaiety, while her mother sought slights and grievances. Rachel felt that Mrs. Deering welcomed her with polite words but with caution.

There was a silence while the parlourmaid, her cap streamers flying, brought in tea and put the tray crookedly on a small and shaky-looking table. She then returned with a tiered cake-stand. Mrs. Deering poured out tea and drank her cup with her little finger genteely curled. She looked at Rachel's quiet clothes, and Rachel wondered if she should also curl her little finger when she drank her tea. Was it the right thing to do in London? But she decided not to change, and clasped her tea cup firmly and ate a dry piece of bread and butter and a slice of gritty cake.

'Come upstairs to your room,' Emily said. 'May we go mamma, please?'

Once on the staircase Emily took Rachel's hand, and they mounted quickly to the next floor.

'Let's unpack,' she said.

They laid Rachel's clothes out on the bed.

'How neat and tidy they all are,' said Emily, fingering them.

'I'm not really tidy,' said Rachel, 'but Cousin Louisa won't allow any untidiness. She doesn't even like me to lay a parcel down on the drawing-room table. Do tell me more about living in London.'

'Oh, London,' said Emily, 'there's not much to say about it. It's dull and dirty, and if you aren't rich and can't ask people back they don't want you. I'm not allowed to go about alone— at least I'm not supposed to, but sometimes I slip out and go and look at the shops when Mamma thinks I'm in my room. I am glad to say that you and I can walk about together, and the shops don't mind if we look at things and don't buy anything.'

'But can't we do other things?' said Rachel, 'There are shops in Oxford.'

Emily gave a little crow of laughter. 'Yes, there are one or two, but they're not good shops, they are pretty old fashioned. The shops here have the latest fashions—wouldn't you like to see them?'

'Yes, I would, but I would like to see some pictures too, and my father wants me to meet him at the British Museum.'

Emily shrugged her shoulders. 'Well if that's what you want to do of course we shall do that. I wish we could go to the play, but it costs so much.'

'But I've got five pounds,' said Rachel. It seemed to her like the wealth of Eldorado. 'I can pay for the seats.'

'Oh, well, at that rate we can go,' said Emily. Then her face clouded, 'but we can't go alone. Mamma and Papa will have to come, and . . .'

'Of course,' said Rachel. 'When I go to a Shakespeare play in Oxford my father always comes and my cousin too. She generally falls asleep, which is rather a waste of a ticket.'

'Well I'll leave you to dress. Put on something ordinary as we are alone.'

Emily's father came in, rubbing his hands. 'Well, young lady, welcome to the modern Babylon. Have you ever been here before?'

Rachel shook here head.

'Well, that's a pity. You must get married, young lady, and come here on your honeymoon.'

Rachel coloured and looked down at her plate, and Emily's father turned his attention to his roast mutton. Silence fell. There seemed nothing to say.

Mrs. Deering said, in a voice that at once demanded and repelled sympathy, that she had got caught in the rain on her way back from having luncheon with Mrs. Gibbs. Mr. Deering listened without interest; he only gave perfunctory attention to his wife. He looked across the table at Emily, who smiled at him as she recounted her small doings of the day.

After dinner Emily asked if she and Rachel could go up to her bedroom and talk. Mrs. Deering said she thought they might like a game of cards and seated herself at a baize-covered card table, while Emily dealt the cards for Beggar my Neighbour.

Presently Emily yawned. 'May Rachel and I go to bed. I think she is tired after he journey?'

Mrs. Deering looked a little like a disappointed child.

'Couldn't we play one more game?' asked Rachel.

'Yes, my dear, we will play another round.'

When the door of Rachel's bedroom had closed Emily flung herself down on the bed.

'You see what it's like here, what my life's like night after night. Nothing happens.'

Rachel seated herself on a chair. 'But my evenings are very quiet too,' she said. 'Cousin Louisa sews, and I read, and my father works in his study.'

'Yes, but you don't mind. You don't feel that things are going past you, that all sorts of things are happening outside in London.' She flung out her hand towards the window, outside which the traffic came distantly to their ears like an animal softly growling to itself.

Rachel looked at her with a puzzled frown. She liked Emily

34

but found her baffling. 'Couldn't you read more or have lessons in something—the piano perhaps?'

'No, I hate the piano. I don't mind making clothes—that's the only thing I like. By the way, that gown of yours wants some stitches in the waist.'

They talked for a little before Emily took herself off to bed. Rachel pulled back the curtains, opened the window and stared out into the square. It looked silent and enclosed under a sky where the moving clouds revealed the moon for fleeting instants. There was nothing much for the moon to illuminate but a small square of houses, dingy bushes and trees, and pavements still shining with damp. Rachel pulled the curtains and retreated to bed.

———— 7 ————

Breakfast was a silent meal. Mr. Deering ate his food with concentration. At the end of it Emily said, 'Rachel would like to take us to the play.'

'What's that?' said Mr. Deering.

Emily repeated it.

'Please I should like to,' said Rachel, 'it is so kind of you to have me to stay. My father gave me some money.'

'Very handsome of him to be sure,' said Mr. Deering, 'very well let's go. What would you like to see? Let me know this evening and tomorrow one of the men in my office will get seats.'

He left the house banging the front door, and Mrs. Deering poured herself out another cup of tea.

'I wish your father wouldn't bang the door it shakes the house and the hinges are nearly broken.'

'Why don't you get it mended?'

Mrs. Deering cast up her eyes to the ceiling, which had a dark crack running across it. 'You know as well as I do,

Emily,' she said, 'the builder won't come again till his bill has been paid.'

Emily looked at Rachel, who was staring down at her empty tea cup to avoid looking at her friend's cross and embarrassed face.

'Well,' said Mrs. Deering acidly, 'I expect Rachel has heard of unpaid bills before, haven't you, dear? Your father isn't a rich man, is he?'

Rachel, embarrassed in her turn, did not know where to look or what to answer. Her father was certainly not rich, and Cousin Louisa, she always understood, had been left badly off by her husband. But no bills were ever mentioned in their household, and her cousin had said to her once when she was growing up, 'Remember, Rachel, what you can't pay for you cannot have,' and she had accepted this unquestioningly.

'Can we go out, Mamma?' said Emily, abruptly changing the subject.

'Yes, you can get me half a yard of ribbon, but remember'— then followed a great many explanations and discussions, and the morning had already advanced before the two girls stepped into the street, Emily closing the front door cautiously and quietly behind her. Rachel put the argument at breakfast out of her mind and tried to enjoy the bustle of carriages, hansom cabs and four-wheelers as they walked along and entered a shop. She wandered from counter to counter as Emily tried to match the ribbon, a rather sickly mauve, and the woman brought out rolls of ribbon pinned onto white paper. At last she concluded her purchase and they left the shop. Carriages drew up at the door, and from neat broughams ladies alighted and rustled into the shop without haste. Emily turned away, and they walked back almost in silence to the square and into the dark little house. Rachel's spirits, usually even and cheerful, experienced a drop as they did so. She went up to her room and, opening a book she had brought with her, tried to immerse herself in it. She heard voices in the next room, and snatches of irritable talk seeped through the walls.

Rachel opened the window a little and pulled aside the curtains. The outlook was not encouraging; a drizzle of rain was falling, and somewhere a barrel organ played a mournful tune. She stared at the houses opposite; they were also heavily curtained and the square seemed enclosed and dead.

Emily came in. She pulled the lace curtains together with a jerk. 'Mamma likes to keep the curtains closed. She says the people opposite stare so much at this house, they would like to see inside it. Do you mind keeping them closed?'

Rachel apologised, but to her it all seemed silly. No one in that silent square was anxious, she thought, to pry into anyone's house, and besides, what was there to see? A bed, an armchair, some worn carpet, a wardrobe all smeared with dust, and some china animals, of which a dog had lost an ear and the cow a horn, while the cup lettered 'A present from Bournemouth' had a jagged chip in it.

Over the boiled mutton, tough and underdone, Mrs. Deering complained about the price of meat and the ribbon Emily had brought her, and Emily and Rachel were perforce silent. Emily's young face took on a sulky look and Rachel tried to listen sympathetically and to make a few remarks out of politeness.

The afternoon and evening passed heavily, but the next day the weather improved and Rachel persuaded Emily to go to a picture gallery. Rachel studied the pictures carefully, but Emily was only interested in those of the anecdotal kind which told or tried to tell some story. She said she was tired and sat down on a seat. Rachel could, if she chose, go round and look at everything. Rachel agreed and went from room to room consulting her catalogue continually. She returned to find Emily exchanging remarks with a man who had seated himself beside her. Rachel approached timidly. She imagined that he was a family friend met by chance, but as she came nearer he laughed loudly, rose to his feet, said goodbye and walked off to join an overdressed lady who had just come in through the door. As they passed the two girls she gave them a sharp glance, and they heard her say, 'Who's that girl?'

'Only someone who spoke to me.'

Rachel's face grew hot. Emily remarked airily, 'He spoke to me first, that's all I can say.'

Rachel was silent.

'I suppose you thought it was vulgar of me to speak to a man I didn't know. I knew you might be shocked but I thought there was no harm in it.'

Rachel proposed no more expeditions to picture galleries.

Mr. Deering brought back a list of plays. 'Now which do you fancy?' he said.

Rachel very much wanted to go and see Henry Irving and Ellen Terry and said so. But the Deerings and Emily exclaimed that they never went to the play and would of all things like to see a comedy. Rachel yielded the point at once. After all, she reminded herself, she was giving them a treat in return for their hospitality. She produced her father's five pound note and handed it to Mr. Deering to pay for the tickets. She was conscious of the concentrated glances of the Deerings and Emily as the small crackling square of paper was handled carefully by Mr. Deering and stowed away in his wallet.

'I shall bring you the change, Miss Rachel,' he said. He gave her a side-long glance. 'I expect you see many of these in your home.'

'I've never had one before,' said Rachel.

'Nor have I,' said Emily. 'Aunt Sarah never lets me have any money. If she sends me out to buy anything in Oxford she makes me note it down in a book, and if I am a halfpenny short, I am bullied till I find it.'

'Ah, money, the root of all evil,' said Mr. Deering.

Emily's eyes filled with tears. 'It's not money that's the root of all evil—it's not having any that matters.'

Mr. Deering pushed his chair back violently as Mrs. Deering put her handkerchief to her eyes.

'It's no use you and Emily snivelling,' he said to his wife. 'I give you all the cash I can and there are endless bills when I come back and tears and complaints. It's enough to drive a man away for good,' and in a moment he was gone, slamming the door with a violence which made the house shake.

'What will the neighbours think?' wailed Mrs. Deering, and indeed several curtains in the square moved from side to side, and faces looked towards the Deerings' house as its master, with flying coat-tails and uttering a shower of oaths, rushed along the pavement.

Rachel sat as if turned to stone. The maid with a glance at once inquisitive and careless, brought in some letters.

'Who are they from?' asked Emily.

'Mostly tradespeople,' answered her mother briefly, and without opening them rose and put them into an escritoire.

8

THE two girls retreated upstairs. Rachel felt her little bed-room unbearably dark and stuffy. I really must open the window, she thought. As she drew the lace curtains back the spring sunshine came dancing into the room. Emily made no objection and subsided limply on to the edge of the bed. She dabbed at her eyes.

'Now you see what my life's like,' she said. 'This goes on all the time. You see why I'm glad to come to my aunt's. She's a selfish, stingy old cat, but at any rate we never have this.'

Rachel sat down beside her and put her arms round Emily's shoulders. 'But couldn't you do something about it?' she said. 'Move into a smaller house?'

Emily looked at her sideways. 'But this is a respectable neighbourhood. If we moved, we might be in a slum—you don't know what you are talking about.'

Rachel desisted, privately thinking that unpaid bills were the kind of respectability which she would most dislike. Surely anything, even a slum, would be better than that. She suggested a walk and the two girls went out together into a nearby park. Rachel's spirits rose a little at the sight of the children bowling hoops, the proud-looking young riders, and the fine carriages. Emily brightened up and looked eagerly around her.

They went to the shops in the afternoon. Rachel looked about for a little gift for her cousin. She counted the money in her purse but did not have much in it; the five pound note which her father had given her should have supplied enough for a present. She fixed her affections on some fine lawn handker-chiefs and told the assistant that she would return and buy them.

'Why didn't you get them?' asked Emily.

'I can't until I get the change from the five pound note,' said Rachel.

Emily looked at her a little oddly, she thought.

That evening when she went to bed she heard heavy foot-steps on the stairs and sounds as if someone had knocked against the bannisters of the staircase; then Mrs. Deering's door was opened and an altercation began. She pulled the sheet over he head and tried to sleep.

The next evening they were to go to the play. At breakfast Mr. Deering, whose eyes were puffy and his expression sulky slapped his pocket and said, 'I've got the tickets and I have ordered a cab to take us. I thought Miss Rachel would like to do the thing in style.'

'Can Rachel have her change?' said Emily.

Her father looked a little confused and said, 'there isn't much left. I will give it you before you leave.'

'But she wants it now,' said Emily, and a hard look came into her eyes.

'I went out with some fellows last night as a matter of fact, and I had to pay for some—well things, but she shall have it.'

'She must have it,' said Emily.

'That's no way to speak to your father, Emily,' said Mrs. Deering.

'Oh, please,' said Rachel—'I—'

Emily stood up, and she and Rachel left the room.

'Emily's becoming a little spitfire,' they heard Mr. Deering say as Emily closed the door with something of her father's violence.

They went up into her bedroom, and Rachel sat down feeling sick and shaken. There was a knock at the door and the maid came in bearing a salver with a letter on it. Her cap was askew and the salver yellow with lack of polishing.

Rachel took the letter and recognised her father's hand-writing. She found that it contained only a few lines. He was coming to fetch her the following morning and take her to the British Museum. He added briefly that he was obliged to go back to Oxford a day and a half earlier than he expected and that she must therefore curtail her visit to the Deerings. Rachel felt a rush of joy and relief, until Emily came in and her face clouded over.

'I can quite understand you're glad to go,' Emily said. 'This household isn't a nice one to be in, but I shall miss you.'

'But you'll be back in Oxford and then we can see each other.'

'Nobody really wants me there,' cried Emily, 'and I can see your cousin doesn't like me.'

'Now listen,' said Rachel, grasping the arms of her chair, 'you've got something to do there. I know running errands for your aunt isn't very interesting, but you are helping her and you don't have to worry about money and she will be entertaining in the summer term.'

'Yes,' said Emily reluctantly, 'I suppose you're right. There's nothing for me to do here. Mother doesn't let me do anything but this eternal sewing. I mend the linen, which hardly holds together, while she potters round all day complaining and grumbling and getting in the way.'

In the evening the two girls were ready in very good time and waited until Mrs. Deering trailed slowly into the drawing-room. Mr. Deering came back just in time, and they packed into a musty-smelling cab. Rachel tried to enjoy the sights of evening London. Mrs. Deering sat upright fidgeting with her gloves, and Emily stared out of the window.

They found their seats in the dress circle. Rachel tried to lose herself in the delights of anticipation, and when the curtain went up she was taken into another world.

The curtain had hardly gone down before Emily stood up and stared at the inhabitants of the boxes and down into the stalls.

'There are some very grand people here tonight,' she said. 'Look at their clothes and jewellery.' A tall girl was sitting at the side of a box, and in front of the box was an imposing dowager who scrutinised the stalls through a lorgnette. Some one evidently entered the back of the box. The girl turned her head with alacrity.

Mrs. Deering pulled Emily back. 'Oh for goodness sake, child, sit down. People are beginning to stare at you.'

At the end of the performance they joined the stream of people and found themselves in the foyer. Rachel, her mind moving in a dream of the play, came slowly behind them, one hand holding up her skirt and the other clasping the neck of her cloak.

'It's raining,' said Mr. Deering, 'I'll try and get a cab.' He disappeared, leaving the ladies of the party in a crowd of people, some of whose more fortunate members had carriages waiting for them outside.

Rachel was startled from her dream by Emily whispering in her ear, 'Look, there's Richard Gervase.'

As if he had heard her Richard turned round. He looked puzzled for a moment, then smiled formally, hesitated and came a few steps towards them.

'I didn't expect to see you here,' he said, but feeling that he had perhaps been clumsy, added, 'I hope you enjoyed the play.'

Rachel's face lit up. 'Yes, I did, she said, 'I've never seen anything like it before.'

He stared at her for a moment. In this crowd of people, some bored and blasé, some merely there to talk about the performance afterwards, she seemed as fresh and unsophisticated as a wild flower in a steamy hot-house. Emily started to speak to him, but at that moment he was tapped on the shoulder by the lorngette of the dowager they had seen in the boxes.

'James says the carriage is there, and we can't keep the horses waiting.'

Richard turned with an almost imperceptible movement of impatience. 'I must run,' he said, and went out through the door, piloting the dowager through the crowd and followed by the tall girl who had been sitting in the box.

'Who was that girl?' asked Lady Wentmore as the carriage moved away.

'Miss Barrington, I see a lot of her father in Oxford. He's a great scholar,' he replied.

Lady Wentmore, who had imagined Oxford as an exclusively masculine place peopled by teachers and undergraduates, said nothing more. She glanced at her daughter, who began to talk to Richard about the play. Richard agreed with some of her strictures. But a thought crossed his mind that it might be pleasant to go with someone whom a play made completely happy.

9

Mr. BARRINGTON duly called for his daughter the following morning.

'We will walk part of the way,' he said, 'and take a cab for the last bit.'

Rachel's mind was a turmoil of worry and unhappiness. Mr. Deering had not given her back the money at breakfast, and Emily had not mentioned it. They progressed along at a quick pace. She was accustomed to adjusting her steps to her father's long stride. He said little, only glancing down at her from time to time.

In the echoing halls of the British Museum he showed Rachel a bewildering number of busts and they finally came to rest in front of the Elgin marbles. Mr. Barrington was a good teacher, accustomed to expounding decidedly and clearly, and Rachel listened entranced to his history of the marbles, their transportation from Greece and the tale of how they had finally come to a resting place in the Museum.

When they left the museum Mr. Barrington put his arm through his daughter's and pulled her along across crossings, and up and down side streets, till they reached a small French restaurant where they sat down opposite each other.

After their food was ordered he asked Rachel if she was enjoying her stay in London. Rachel hesitated. She looked at her father and saw him as he sat, his back to a brown panelled wall, in an unaccustomed setting. Hitherto she hadn't really looked to see what he was like. He looked at her, too, with a fresh interest.

She saw a tall man who had disposed his long legs with difficulty under a marble topped table, his hands grasping its sides. His face was set in lines cut deep between nose and chin. There were furrows on a wide brow, dark eyes under bushy eyebrows, and a strong mouth under a nose which jutted out. She noticed, too, a slight carelessness in his clothes, neat and well brushed as they were, and felt herself in the presence of a man who cared little for worldly success and was dedicated to the dream of a classical world, someone who had escaped from the sordid troubles of every day.

He saw a quiet girl, plainly dressed, with soft long-lashed eyes, straight features, and mouth which showed firmness and sweetness.

This scrutiny of each other only took a moment of time; then Mr. Barrington repeated his question. To his surprise, Rachel's face clouded; the light went out of it. She put her two hands on the table as if to steady herself. She looked at her father and read astonishment and concern in his eyes.

'What on earth is the matter?'

Rachel drew a long breath and told him about the five pounds, how she felt sure she was not going to get the change, and in halting words about the household in which she was staying. His eyebrows drew together in a frown.

'But surely you will get what Mr. Deering owes you?' he said.

'I don't believe I shall,' she replied. Nothing had been said about it, and from Emily's silence she was certain that nothing more would be said.

'I never much liked the look of that girl.'

'But, father,' said Rachel in great distress, 'Emily's nice, she's good, and she has such an unhappy time of it.'

He was still frowning, and she continued bravely, 'I can't give up seeing Emily—she is unhappy and even her aunt isn't very kind to her. Please, father, don't make me give her up.'

The stern features relaxed. 'Well you can see her from time to time in Oxford—I don't imagine her life in the Principal's Lodgings is a bed of roses. But you can never again go and stay with her.'

'Oh, I don't want to,' cried Rachel.

'And now about the money,' her father went on, 'I haven't got a lot to throw about. Have you any left?'

'Only a few shillings, and I must give the maid something when I go.'

He pulled a leather bag out of his pocket and counted out some money.

'And I've seen some handkerchiefs Cousin Louisa might like for a present.'

'Well buy the handkerchiefs and tip the maid, and there will be a shilling or two left over.'

Rachel put her bag, which had been her mother's, on the table; it was old and shabby, and the clasp did not work easily. She carefully laid the silver coins into its depths.

'Don't mention that I have given you any money,' said her father. 'Just put your bag away when you get back. I had no idea that you were with that kind of person, or I should not have allowed you to go there.'

'But it isn't very nice being poor, father,' she said.

'My dear child I have never been anything else but poor in the eyes of the world. Dons are not rich people, but I've kept out of debt and paid my way, helped by Louisa, who is a model of care and economy. Learn from her about this. When your mother and I married we had very little to live on. Now I have a bit more, but you will never have much. I advise you to fix your mind and thoughts on the things of the mind and find your riches there.' He pulled out his watch and looked at it.

'Now I must go back to the Museum. I will fetch you the day after tomorrow in the morning.'

'Father, you have been kind,' said Rachel.

'Well, it isn't your fault. I should have been more careful to find out what those people were like.'

He smiled a little and added, 'the sight of ready money in the shape of a five pound note in a household like that is a temptation,' he said. 'We won't speak of it again.'

He put her into a four-wheeled cab, and she sat clasping her bag looking out into the busy streets. The cracking of whips and the noise of shouting and grinding of wheels, combined with the rattling of the cab, gave her a headache; but her spirits had risen, and she felt that her father had not only been kind and wise but had treated her for the first time not like a child but like a grown up person.

Emily wept when Rachel left, and Rachel, distressed and heavy-hearted, climbed into the cab.

Her father remarked as they drove to the station, 'Well, I'm sorry for that girl.'

Rachel was glad when they reached Oxford. The gate of the house squeaked in its familiar way. Mrs. Cunningham seemed pleased to see her and, like a general after a sweeping victory, triumphantly showed her the results of the spring-cleaning. The house smelt of soap and bees' wax, the clean curtains stirred in the breeze, and her little bedroom seemed a haven of peace and cleanliness. Mr. Barrington had a suspicion that some of his books had been moved, and came into tea with a furrowed brow.

'Nothing has been touched except your carpet, which was taken up, and your chair covers, which have been washed and mended,' said Mrs. Cunningham placidly as she handed him his cup of tea.

His face cleared. 'Perhaps there are worse things than one's books being touched,' he said to Rachel with a smile, and she smiled back.

She told Mrs. Cunningham a little about her visit and about the incident of the five pound note.

Mrs. Cunningham remarked evenly, 'No wonder the man takes a drop of drink married to a handless fushionless body like that. That poor girl, it's a fine thing that she can sew well— she could take some in to do and get paid for it. Well, well, we'll see.'

Rachel felt happier about Emily coming to the house. Her cousin was kind-hearted under her austere exterior, and if Emily could be classed as an object for her pity she would be more welcome.

Rachel wrote a letter to Mrs. Deering thanking her for the visit, and her life started again on its usual way.

The flowering trees, laburnum and may, came into bloom in a sudden burst. The skies cleared, the sun shone, and the soft air was full of bird songs. Rachel cheerfully performed household tasks, read the books her father gave her, did some necessary shopping in the dark little shops in a nearby narrow street, and brought bunches of spring flowers into the house.

Paul Sibley came back to do some extra work a few days before term started. He called to see Rachel's father, who asked him to come and dine one evening.

'Have you made progress with your studies?' asked Mrs. Cunningham.

'Yes, some progress,' said Paul with a side glance at his tutor. 'We shall see what Mr. Barrington thinks about that.'

After dinner Rachel sat down to the piano and played softly to herself. She was not a great performer but had a light touch and a good ear. She never played to an audience. She was her own audience and played for the pleasure it gave her. Mrs. Cunningham occasionally asked for a Scotch air, but otherwise she hardly listened and often fell quietly asleep.

This evening she had nodded over her sewing when the door opened and Paul entered. He came quietly up to the piano: 'I didn't know that you were a musician.'

'I'm not,' said Rachel, 'I only play to amuse myself, never for other people.'

She closed the piano. Paul leaned against its side and looked down at her smiling. They began to talk in lowered voices. He told her about his work and his ambition to be a lawyer.

'Some day you will be famous.'

'I'm afraid that's a long way off. There will be a long time when I shall be just a briefless barrister living in lodgings in London.'

'Where do you live? I mean, where is your home when you aren't at Oxford?'

He briefly described his home in a parsonage in Dorsetshire where his father had a small congregation. He had three sisters younger than himself, and his parents were very busy with the parish and their parsonage.

'My father gave me all my first lessons in Latin and Greek; he is a good scholar, wasted in a way in such a rustic parish. My mother is always busy with sick people and teaching in the Sunday School, and my sisters are picking up as much education as they can get.'

Rachel listened entranced and drew him on by asking questions. Paul made her feel at ease, her shyness forgotten for the moment. Mrs. Cunningham woke up, saw the two young people at the piano, and resolutely closed her eyes again.

10

Emily returned to Oxford, and the two girls began to meet again. Rachel's visit to London was not mentioned between them, except when a passing reference to it cropped up in the course of conversation. Mrs. Cunningham unbent to Emily a little and even asked her advice on the mending of household linen. Rachel had politely enquired about Emily's parents.

'They're much the same,' said Emily. 'Papa is out more and more, and mamma cries and just goes on in the usual way. I don't see how he can want to come home, it's so mournful. I want to make a little cash, Mamma doesn't know about it, but I slipped out and found a dressmaker in a small shop. She wasn't nice and is as sharp as a needle, but I showed her one or two things I had made, and she said I could embroider some initials for her. I don't know how I can do it here. It wouldn't do, for Aunt Sarah won't like it. If she finds me sewing in my room she'll accuse me of neglecting my duties and talk about ingratitutde.'

'You could come and do your sewing here.'

The upshot of this was that Emily was allowed to use the little sewing room at the top of the house. There was a dummy figure in one corner, a hard chair, a table, and a view of the garden through the branches of a mulberry tree. The handkerchiefs were for a trousseau, and Emily had been given time in which to do them. It was a start on the road to some kind of independance. She could never get away for a long time from the Principal's Lodgings, but the work progressed nevertheless.

The term went on and the spring was replaced by summer. Pavements showed soft patches of rose colour, white and yellow, where pink and white may and laburnums had drifted down and shed their petals. The low hills round the town were veiled in a transparent haze.

One fine morning Rachel was carefully selecting a bunch of roses in the garden. She concentrated on her task as there were not many in full bloom. She was walking round the flower bed snipping with her scissors here and there, when a confused noise arose in the road. There was a clatter of hoofs, loud and startled exclamations, the noise of a fall. She ran to the gate.

Repairs had for several days been done to the road, and a steam roller, squat and black, was finishing the job. Rachel opened the gate. She saw that the steam roller had stopped a few yards away on the right. On the left was a trembling horse and near it a figure which lay stretched out on the ground. A small crowd of errand boys and passers-by was collecting. Rachel stood rooted to the ground as a shift in the crowd made a gap through which she saw that the recumbent figure was Richard Gervase.

At that moment she was pushed on one side by her father, who, followed by Mrs. Cunningham, had come out of the house. Mr. Barrington bent over Richard, who lay white and motionless. He stood up and said to a strong-looking man beside him, 'Help me to bring him into the house.' He elbowed the crowd aside as he lifted Richard up by the shoulders and the man took his feet. Between them they slowly and carefully bore him up the staircase to the spare bedroom.

'Fetch some sheets and blankets from the cupboard,' said Louisa Cunningham, and Rachel, white-faced and trembling, obeyed.

'Is he dead?' was her thought as she fumbled along the shelves of the cupboard. Her agitation had a depth hard to measure. As she came along the passage with armfuls of linen, Mrs. Cunningham took them from her. She ran back for the blankets. When she returned Mrs. Cunningham had pulled the window blinds down.

'Is he dead?' whispered Rachel.

At that moment Richard opened his eyes and then quickly shut them again.

'Dead, no,' said Louisa Cunningham, 'he's concussed, I think. Your father has sent the man for Doctor Wilkins.'

She came out of the room, leaving the door slightly ajar.

'Run down to the kitchen, Rachel, and tell Lizzie to heat a

kettle of water in case the doctor needs it. We will make up the bed later.'

Mr. Barrington emerged from the study with a telegraph form in his hand. He gave it to Rachel and told her to go to the Post office. Rachel put on her outdoor cloak and ran quickly out of the house. A man, obviously a groom, was leading the horse away to the livery stable.

'This 'orse never could abide these things. 'E must have shied when he saw it coming,' he was saying.

As she sped past she heard the steam roller man, who was climbing back to his seat on the engine, shaking his head and shouting after the groom, "E reared right up, the 'oss did, and the young gent fell off and 'it his head against the kerb.'

Rachel flew on, her feet hardly touching the pavement, in so great a turmoil of mind that she was nearly run over by a dray, which pulled up just in time. She ran down the little street to the small, dark post office. She handed the form over the counter, and the old man looked at it through his steel-rimmed spectacles.

'Never can make out your father's hand, Miss,' he said.

Mr. Barrington's handwriting was not an easy one to read, but his daughter was used to the crabbed characters in which he wrote.

Rachel took a telegraph form and copied it out in a round hand. The address was Gervase Priory, Woollington, Dash-shire.

'Gervase Priory, so that's the name of Richard's father's house,' she said to herself.

II

THE rest of the day passed slowly. Mrs. Cunningham came and went into Richard's room. A telegram arrived saying that Sir Edward Gervase would arrive about four-thirty. The

Principal of Richard's College came to make enquiries and was closeted with Rachel's father in the drawing room.

About five o'clock a cab drew up at the little gate. A man walked up to the door and, seeing a notice on the knocker, entered the hall with no further ado. Mr. Barrington was in his study and there was no sound in the house. Hannah emerged carrying a tray of tea, and Rachel came down the stairs. Sir Edward Gervase stared at her.

'Did you want to see my father?' she said.

'Yes, yes, if you please,' he replied impatiently.

Rachel walked past him down the hall and found her father in the study deep in a mass of papers. Recalled from these labours he looked at his watch, sprang to his feet and was through into the hall in a minute.

Rachel heard the sound of the two men going up the stairs, the door of the spare bedroom being softly opened and as softly shut, and her father descending into the hall. Presently she heard the sound of a heavy stread downstairs and went out into the garden; the birds were calling to each other all round in the trees. There was a fresh scent of flowers, and a bee was working busily on the flower beds. Very little traffic passed. Rachel drew a long breath. She went back into the house.

'Come in and have your tea,' said Mrs. Cunningham as she passed the drawing room door.

'My daughter,' said Mr. Barrington.

A tall man rose to his feet and shook hands with her. He looked dusty, and his face was set in lines of worry and anxiety. He sat down again and took up his tea cup, spilling a few drops on the table cloth.

'Oh dear,' he said.

'It is of no consequence at all,' said Mrs. Cunningham.

'Upon my word I don't know how to thank you, ma'am,' he said, 'for taking Richard in.'

'Never heed it, we could do nothing else,' said Mrs. Cunningham.

'Richard's my only child,' he said.

Mr. Barrington was listening gravely. 'I do not think you need be unduly anxious, Sir Edward,' he said. 'Our doctor was reassuring about there being no bones broken, and if

Richard can be left quiet for a few days there should be no ill effects.'

Sir Edward frowned and said into his tea cup. 'Richard is a careless horseman.'

'The livery stable man came round to say that the horse your son was riding always rears when he sees a steam roller.'

'Eh, what? Yes I expect that's it, that's the reason.'

He looked across the table at Rachel, who was nervously crumbling a scone on her plate, and continued,

'Yes no doubt that's the reason. But we have put you to a lot of trouble, I fear.'

'We do not grudge trouble in this house,' said Mrs. Cunningham, 'and I am accustomed to nursing.'

'You are very good.' His eyes strayed round the room and rested again on Rachel.

At that moment the doctor entered the room. As Rachel slipped away she heard the doctor say, 'Well he's better, you can set your mind at rest.'

She went softly upstairs. As she passed the door of the room where Richard was lying she heard her name called, and she turned and stood shyly in the doorway. The blind had been half pulled up, and the late afternoon sun touched the carpet by the window with a slanting ray. Richard was lying with his hands locked behind his head—staring at her.

'Are you feeling better?' she said.

'My headache's nearly gone but I feel a little muzzy. I hope that old doctor will let me get up. I say, you have all been kind.'

'It's nothing,' said Rachel confusedly.

'If I come downstairs, will you come and talk to me?'

At that moment voices were heard in the hall and Rachel sped away from the doorway and shut herself into her room. She paced up and down and gazed into the garden. When she went downstairs, tiptoeing by Richard's room she heard Mrs. Cunningham's voice.

'You can get up and sit quietly for half and hour.' The tone of her voice was kind but firm.

'Can't I come downstairs?'

'The doctor said not today, but tomorrow if your headache has gone you can come down to the drawing-room for a short while—but only if your headache has quite gone.'

Richard gave a sigh. 'Has my father left?'

'Yes, his man got rooms at the Mitre. Sir Edward will be round in the morning.'

The evening meal was a silent one. Mr. Barrington had regarded the day's interruptions to his work as a necessary consequence of being the tutor at a college. Although he much preferred teaching young men to getting entangled in the ups and downs of their lives, he had a broad humanity and kindness which made him much liked by the undergraduates, and if he returned from their everyday troubles to the world of ancient Greece with a sigh of relief no one found it in their hearts to blame him for this. He ate his dinner as rapidly as he could.

'I shall be working late,' he said. 'I'll look in on Richard before I go to bed.'

'Better not. I will see now that he is settled for the night. Rachel, you had better go early to bed. I shall need you for a lot of things tomorrow.'

Rachel escaped thankfully to her own little room, glad to have time to think over the events of the day, which seemed to have lasted for an indefinite stretch of time. She clutched the end of her bedstead with tight fingers as she recalled the sight of Richard lying in the road, white and still. She had thought him dead for some minutes, and the shock remained with her. Then the bustle of the day, the doctor, Richard's father's arrival, his anxiety and his lack of ease in their house, and Richard calling her into the bedroom.

She walked to the window. A bat swooped by. She closed the curtains and went to bed. Her thoughts for some time came between her and sleep. Only a wall separated her from Richard. As sleep approached and made her thoughts inconsequent and vague she remembered her father's telegram which she had copied out. The address was Gervase Priory. 'What a pretty name,' she murmured as she fell asleep.

12

Richard woke up early the first morning after his return home. He had forgotten where he was. He stretched to feel the length and comfort of his bed. The light coming in through the tall window struck harshly on his eyelids, and he winced and burrowed his head into the pillow. Then with an impatient movement he sat up and saw not the shabby austere bedroom in his college, but a spacious room filled with well-polished furniture with shining brass handles. The leaves of a tree moved outside the window in a light wind, and he remembered that he was at home.

This thought gave him only a modified pleasure. It was a bore to leave Oxford several weeks before term was ending, a bore not to feel too well, a bore to be restricted in what he wanted to do. He dressed and went downstairs to the dining-room, where his father was sitting at a small table by the window.

As Richard went to the sideboard and uncovered a heavy silver dish, his father asked him if he had slept well. He said he had. As a matter of fact he had been restless and had had uncomfortable dreams.

'I have had a note from Victoria. She is down here for a few days. She wants to come to luncheon tomorrow, and bring Mary too.'

Richard nodded briefly. 'That would be nice,' he said non-committally.

His father glanced at him. 'What are you going to do today?'

'I may go and take a look at the river.'

'You won't find any fish. The May fly rise is over.'

Richard said impatiently, 'Well I shall take my rod all the same and try.'

He went into the gun room and looked for his fishing rod. The sun was bright, but a north-westerly wind was blowing. On the river bank covered by overhanging trees Richard found his way to a gap, pushing aside a bush starred with wild roses. The river took a slight turn at this point and there was a pool and an eddy below some stepping stones.

The fish were not interested in his bait and although he saw several rises he caught nothing, but the casting and reeling in of his line, and the complete quiet, soothed his restlessness.

He sat down on the bank with his rod beside him; the water flowing gently along in its easy, effortless way made an unexacting background to thought. It was living its own life, it seemed to say, through meadows and past woods, under bridges near hamlets, paying no regard to the creatures that wriggled and spawned in its depths—or the swallows that swooped across its surface.

Richard walked back home along a path bordered with bushes. The house had the balanced look of the century in which it was built. Its length, from where Richard could see, was perfectly matched by its height. The orangery at one end completed the symmetrical effect. Roses blossomed on its walls, and a magnolia spread polished leaves under a window which was closed and across which the curtains were drawn—his mother's bedroom, kept by his father's orders just as she had left it. Nothing in it had been touched since the time when she had been brought home and laid on the bed to die. The cupboards were locked, and the head housemaid only allowed on sufferance to dust and air the room.

Richard frowned and abruptly tried to change the current of his thoughts. He felt more tired than he would have cared to admit, and yet longed for action, the action and excitements of Oxford—the jokes with his fellow undergraduates, even the lectures which he often forgot to attend, and his books. He had brought some with him, but had been told by the doctor not to do much reading, but to stay out of doors as much as possible. The silent house and his father's company seemed like a sort of imprisonment, an imprisonment with comfort and beauty thrown in.

That evening they played a game of cribbage and went early to bed, candle in hand up the curving staircase.

'Are you feeling all right, my boy?' There was a note of wistfulness in Sir Edward's voice.

'Yes, thank you.'

Both doors shut simultaneously.

The next day dawned fine. A light mist rose from the river, birds sang and twittered, and a climbing rose tapped gently against Richard's window. It was hard not to feel a rise of spirits. Richard opened the window and cut off the rose with his nail scissors, placing it in the button hole of his jacket.

His father, always crochety at breakfast, briefly acknowledged his greeting. As he rose from the meal he said, 'You remember that Victoria and Mary are coming to luncheon today?'

'I'm not likely to forget,' thought Richard. 'Life here is not all that full of engagements.'

When Lady Wentmore and Lady Mary Tyrrell were sonorously announced by the butler, father and son were waiting for them, and Richard who had been staring out of the window, his hands jingling the coins in his pockets, turned to meet the two ladies.

'My dear Edward—and Richard,' said Lady Wentmore, 'this is an unexpected pleasure. My dear boy, how are you? What an unlucky accident. How did it happen?'

'The horse I was riding shied at a steam roller and threw me off.'

'And you were taken in to a house?'

'Yes, Mr. Barrington took me to his house.'

'Does he live alone?'

'No, with a cousin, Mrs. Cunningham, and his daughter. They were very kind.'

'Yes, kind people,' said Sir Edward. 'The cousin is Scotch, a nice lady, very good to Richard, and Mr. Barrington a clever fellow, knows a lot about ancient Greece, but couldn't have been kinder.'

They moved into luncheon and sat at the round table beside tall french windows. Mary and Richard fell into talk about hunting, the London season and other topics, while their elders talked about politics and country topics, crops and grass land.

After luncheon Sir Edward said to Richard, 'Take Mary to see if the peaches in the kitchen garden are ripe, and ask Macandrew to give you some.'

'Well, your peaches are always better than ours,' said Lady Wentmore, 'We shall enjoy them.'

When Mary's and Richard's footsteps had died away, Lady Wentmore said, 'I brought Mary down here for a few days. She has had so many balls that she was really getting tired, and I thought she would enjoy the others more next week if she had a rest.'

Sir Edward appeared quite satisfied with this explanation, but he suspected that the reason for their return to their neighbouring country house was not unconnected with Richard's convalescence at the Priory.

Mary and Richard walked along in companionable silence. They had known each other since childhood and played together in their respective nurseries, chased each other, played hide and seek, ridden their ponies side by side.

'How's the season going?' asked Richard.

'Much as usual,' said Mary. Her second season was proving unrewarding.

'You don't sound as if you were enjoying it much.'

'Oh yes, I am, but it's not as good a one as last year's, though there have been some good balls, and Mamma likes garden parties and we go to all of them. And then we give dinner parties, and the conversation is sometimes so stupid, and I wish I was back down here. And the dogs miss me so much, but Mamma wouldn't hear of my missing a single thing until now, when she said that a few days' rest in the country would make me enjoy it all more. I shall hate going back.'

They went into the kitchen garden and inspected the peaches ripening slowly in the sun, and Richard opened the door of a greenhouse, where a peach tree spread its branches flat against a white-washed wall. The head gardener, who was tying up some plants, received Sir Edward's order for a basket of peaches for Lady Wentmore in silence. He was not enamoured of picking over much of the fruit in the garden except for the needs of the house, but he reflected with satisfaction that his fellow gardener at Wentmore Chase would be annoyed at the glimpse (which he would no doubt be given in the kitchen) of a basket of peaches so much superior to those of his own growing.

13

THE two older people sat on wicker chairs on the flagged path beside the house and looked down over the garden. Lady Wentmore put up her parasol, and they sat in silence. Both had troubles and difficulties which they were uncertain of putting into words to each other, although they were distant cousins and had known each other all their lives.

Lady Wentmore had been very good-looking in her youth and she had become an imposing dowager who inspired awe rather than any warm feeling among the people she met. Her blue eyes looked steadily at the world, but also coldly and appraisingly. At a ball or a party in London she had a way of greeting her friends which was firm and decisive. Her acquaintances were always doubtful as to whether they would be honoured by a handshake or not. She knew the temperature of the social world of London in which she moved, and no rise or fall in it went unmarked by her.

As a young and untried girl she had married her distant cousin Lord Wentmore. He was attracted by her stately good looks, and having had a wild youth wanted to settle down. The attraction lasted for only a short time, and Victoria found herself the helpless spectator of his vagaries in the shape of extravagances and debts. She also had to keep a brave face and an appearance of serene calm when hints of his infidelities reached her ears. The Wentmore marriage, which had been hailed by Victoria's relations as a brilliant match for a penniless girl, became a series of shifts and humiliations.

There were two children, Ronald and Mary, and Victoria early made up her mind to bring them up strictly in the paths of good behaviour and care about money affairs.

When her husband died in his middle forties the whole burden of debts, mortgages and extravagances fell on her shoulders.

She rose to the occasion, and although quite untrained in dealing with business she worked early and late, grasping, through hard and painful labour, the intricacies of estate management. She sent away the agent, who had muddled along for years very comfortably, and threatened to leave the sleepy firm of family solicitors who had mismanaged the Wentmore estate for over fifty years. She let the London house furnished on a lease, closed up the larger part of the Chase and lived with the two children and their nurse and a few servants in a small wing of the house.

Her days were spent in a round of seeing her tenants and writing difficult business letters, and the children could never think of their mother as someone with any kind of restful leisure on her hands. She was always pre-occupied and frowning over some knotty point.

They played endless games together and were allowed dogs and a pony. Their friends were gardeners and grooms and the family servants. They were allowed by the head housemaid to go sometimes into the shut up part of the house under strict surveillance. They were awed and interested by the ghostly look of the shrouded rooms, the pendant chandeliers enveloped in holland bags, the discoloured squares and oblongs on the walls where the pictures had been taken down to be laid carefully under the dust sheets which covered the sofas.

The situation of the Wentmore family underwent a change for the better when Mary was sixteen. Victoria's parents died within a year of each other and left more money to their only daughter than she had dared to hope for. They had consistently 'talked poverty'. Her mother spent a great deal of time hoarding pieces of string and brown paper from incoming parcels, using ends of candles and sticks of sealing wax down to the quick, and substituting cheap and wholesome puddings for the more palatable and expensive suggestions of her cook. An uncle also died, leaving Victoria an unexpectedly handsome legacy, and the estate, at last cleared of debt, showed sometimes even a small margin of profit.

At the moment when Lady Wentmore and Sir Edward were sitting on the terrace at the Priory, Ronald was travelling on the Continent with a tutor, a man of austere principles but little aptitude for jokes. Victoria Wentmore was doubtful about sending Ronald to Oxford or Cambridge. She regarded these establishments with suspicion as places where young men wasted their time and their parents' money and in return learnt very little (or possibly a great many useless things) which could only be necessary to them if they went into politics or to the Bar. The Brigade of Guards also held dangers in the way of extravagance. A good regiment chosen on the advice of an important military friend would be a soberer choice. Victoria had no idea of relinquishing to her son the reins of management of the Chase.

Mary must marry, and marry well and suitably. Her portion would not be large but it was something, and she had youth and good looks to recommend her. She rode well, looking her best on horseback. She also danced well and did not lack partners at balls.

Victoria Wentmore moved her parasol to shade her face from the sun. Sir Edward and she both sat up straight in their wicker chairs and gazed at the flowers and the grassy slopes beyond which wound the river. They talked as old friends are apt to, with long pauses and spurts of conversation.

When they broke the silence, it was to speak of landowners' problems, difficult harvests, repairs to farm and cottages, thieving gypsies, and sometimes of the gossip of their neighbours and the prospects of hunting the following winter. Then Sir Edward broke off the conversation by saying, 'How do you think Richard is looking?'

'A little pale, I think.'

Sir Edward sighed. 'He seems rather restless. This isn't a very cheerful house to come to now, I fear.'

Lady Wentmore gave him a glance and then she looked straight in front of her. 'You must try and rouse yourself, Edward. You can't go on sorrowing like this year after year.'

Sir Edward's lips tightened into an obstinate line. 'My dear Victoria, one can't help these things.'

At that moment Mary and Richard came walking across the lawn. Mary ducking her head to avoid a low-lying branch of the cedar tree which spread its dark bulk to their right.

Her mother rose and asked if Richard would send for her carriage, and then said, 'Edward, do let Richard come over to us as often as possible, and please come too. We won't let him get tired. I will ask Frederick to come if you are there—he wants to see you. Mary and Richard can play a game of croquet if he can't do anything more violent.'

After the ladies had departed Sir Edward went back into the garden. The blackbirds and the thrushes were calling to each other from the trees and shrubberies. The flowers threw out waves of scent from the stored up warmth of the day. No sounds came from the house, only a vague murmur from the direction of the stableyard could be heard, which soon faded into the evening hush. He walked up and down the flagged terrace, soothed by the quiet scene, when a peacock which had flapped upwards on to a low branch of the cedar tree gave a startlingly harsh cry.

Sir Edward turned and went into the house.

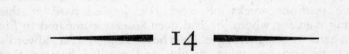

14

RICHARD arrived back in Oxford when the days were lengthening into high summer. He found his friends busy and preoccupied, and those who were in their last university year haunted by the stresses of their final Schools. There was so much to hear and Richard felt he had so little to tell on his part. But his college engulfed him. He met Paul Sibley on the first day of his return, crossing the college quad. Paul had a collection of books under his arm, which all slipped and fell to the ground as he greeted Richard. They picked them up and walked off together discussing matters of importance to them both.

'Are you going to any of the Commem. balls?' asked Richard.

'No,' said Paul, 'I'm no dancer.'

Richard said nothing. He had guessed something of Paul's poverty and his desire to cost his parents not one farthing more than he could help, and Commem. entailed expense. Richard felt completely disinclined for these festivities himself, his head ached, and bright lights still hurt his eyes. He had been offered by an Oxford friend the chance of going to Norway to fish. This promised a complete change and a reason for not going back to the Priory. He felt slightly guilty but salved his conscience by thinking that he would spend part of his vacation at home. His work had suffered considerably from his enforced absence from Oxford, and he could work there. In a mood of gloom and annoyance he walked along to see Mr. Barrington, knowing that it was not only his fall from the horse but his lack of concentration that had retarded his work. As he walked along the tree-lined road and saw the green fields beyond his mood lightened, and he approached the Barringtons' house with a smile on his face.

He walked along the path to the front door. It was ajar. Rachel, who was carrying a vase tightly packed with flowers into the drawing-room, started when she saw Richard and some water from the vase dripped on to the floor.

Mr. Barrington laid down his writing and bent his attention to his pupil's needs. He was sorry for Richard, who had lost some precious weeks of work. He looked hard at this young man for whom life had been so easy compared to his own hard-working struggle. Then he remembered Sir Edward's black tie and mourning tie-pin, and recalled hearing that Richard's mother had died. The boy must have suffered from shock and sorrow, and that was probably what made his mind work so unevenly.

His face softened a little. He took up a quill and pulled its feather up the wrong way, then laid it down with a slight sigh, and bent his mind to help Richard.

Soon afterwards Richard emerged into the hall to find Mrs. Cunningham and Rachel descending the stairs dressed for going out. Mrs. Cunningham was taking Rachel to a tea party of some of her own friends. Rachel was going with little expectation of pleasure but with an outward acquiescence to please her cousin.

Richard walked along a little way between the two ladies and he asked Rachel if she was going to the Commem. balls. She shook her head gravely.

'Nor shall I,' he said. 'I shall probably go off to Norway to fish on the last day of term.'

Rachel felt that the balls to which she would have liked to

62

go were suddenly less desirable and exciting. She looked up at Richard. She had only the vaguest ideas about Norway. As she was growing up she had read *Feats on the Fiord*, and there her knowledge ended. She asked him if he had read it, and he said no and on an impulse asked if he might borrow it. Then he turned to Mrs. Cunningham and asked her if she and Rachel would lunch with him in his college two days later. 'I will get Paul to come,' he added.

Mrs. Cunningham accepted his invitation with unusual promptitude, for she was usually apt to ponder at length over any social invitation. He added that he would be glad if Rachel would bring the book with her.

Two days later Richard showed himself a good host, and he and Paul kept the conversation going between his guests. The room was warm and the windows were open, and the sound of voices drifted up, thrown back by the walls into a sort of hollowness.

Luncheon finished with the sweet which was the famous college chef d'oeuvre. It was pale brown in colour and had a castellated appearance. Richard attacked it with a spoon, but when it showed signs of resistance and then disintegration, Mrs. Cunningham asked if she could help, and the pudding was restored to order. The young people were too much aware of each other to be much interested in food, but they left nothing on their plates.

Paul's face showed a fine-drawn student's pallor. He had worked unobtrusively but nevertheless at high pressure while his contemporaries cherished the idea of doing little work in the term but catching up with it in the Long Vacation. The claims of Paul's home were too strong for him to work much there, where he was expected to help with the overgrown garden and neglected orchard in his father's parsonage. He liked outdoor work but it conflicted with his books.

Richard teased him about his studious habits, remarking, 'You are one of those dreadful men who really like work.'

'I don't really think that anyone likes work for its own sake,' Paul replied, 'but if your work is interesting and really holds your attention you don't find it easy to stop doing it—what do you think, Miss Rachel?'

'Yes, I agree,' she said after a startled pause, looking down at her plate and then up at Paul. 'When I am writing an essay my father sets me it seems just a task when I start it, but it gets more interesting as I go along.'

'There, you see, Richard,' said Paul. He abruptly changed the conversation by asking Mrs. Cunningham if they were going away in the Vacation.

'I think Mr. Barrington should go away,' she replied, 'he never stops working. He might be persuaded to go to Scotland or to the Lake District. He likes to walk and it is the best change he can get.'

'And you both?' asked Paul.

'I am giving the subject my serious consideration,' said Mrs. Cunningham. 'Perhaps Rachel and I might go over to the sea, but I am not sure where to go.'

Paul sat back in his chair and then leant forward with clasped hands on the table.

'There is a pretty cove about two miles from where we live,' he said. 'My mother knows a woman who has a little house and keeps lodgings in the village near the cove, and you could come over to see my parents and we could come and show you good picnic places.'

Richard looked at Rachel. It was hard to know what she was thinking, but she smiled and her shyness seemed to have evaporated. He walked to the window saying that he would show her the buildings, which stood up dark against a sky bright with sunshine which threw long shadows on the grass where young men walked. Richard pointed out the chapel and the buildings which flanked its tall sides. He was more interested in the fact that he had successfully climbed many of the roofs than in their history, and Rachel, leaning her elbows on the windowsill, looked up from time to time into his face as he warmed to his subject.

Meanwhile, Mrs. Cunningham and Paul discussed the possibilities of a visit to the seaside. Mrs. Cunningham was evidently taken by the idea of going to the village he described, and she asked some searching questions. When she rose to leave, Paul promised to write to his mother that evening.

Rachel opened her reticule and laid *Feats on the Fiord* on the table.

'I shall enjoy reading it,' said Richard, 'and will bring it back next term.'

15

AFTER Richard's luncheon party a correspondence ensued between Paul's mother and Rachel's cousin. It concerned the possible dampness of beds, and the necessity of conveying Mrs. Cunningham's own sheets to the cottage by the sea.

Mrs. Sibley's replies were reassuring on these matters, if a little criss-crossed in the matter of handwriting, and vague about details. Eventually Rachel and her cousin found themselves comfortably installed in a rose-covered cottage with a welcoming landlady. A garden posy was standing in a china vase on Mrs. Cunningham's dressing-table and propped up against it a note from Paul.

Rachel stood entranced by the scent of flowers which came in through the window and the distant murmuring of the sea, while Mrs. Cunningham reassured herself that the beds had no suspicion of dampness.

All her life Rachel was to remember her first walk to the sea, down a lane which led to a sandy cove. The little waves lapped on the shore, the lazy sea and the flower-decked lane gave her a sensation of peace. Her thoughts were unshadowed—in fact she had no thoughts at all.

Walking up the lane serene and happy, she started and flushed as she saw Paul advancing towards her. He was looking a little anxious.

'Mrs. Cunningham sent me to find you,' he said, 'she feared that you might have fallen into the sea.'

'I'm very cautious,' said Rachel.

Paul looked down at her and said, 'I should have thought that you were the sort of person who could take risks.'

Their eyes met. 'Well I haven't taken many so far.'

'My mother is here to see that you are comfortably settled,' said Paul.

They found the two ladies sitting on the sofa of the crowded little sitting-room. Pampas grass waved dustily in a tall jar, spiky-looking rose-coloured shells brought by the landlady's seafaring nephew from foreign parts menaced the milder shapes of china cows and sheep.

Mrs. Sibley's clothes gave the impression of having been assembled from a rag bag, so little relation did they bear to each other in shape or pattern. But in greeting her Rachel saw that her visitor's face was so finely chiselled and her blue eyes so mild and kind beneath her rusty black head-gear, that whoever she spoke to would quickly forget her witch-like appearance. Mrs. Cunningham's plain snuff-coloured dress provided complete contrast.

By dint of moving one china animal behind another, Paul found a corner on the velvet-draped mantelshelf on which to rest his elbow. He looked down on the three seated ladies and his tall form seemed to dwarf the room.

'Paul, do be careful of that fire screen,' said his mother, as that object painted with water lilies swayed ominously behind him. 'You had better sit down.'

'I'll be careful,' he said, as he moved the screen further back into the fireplace and gingerly re-adjusted his elbow on the mantelpiece.

'Will you come over and see us tomorrow,' said Mrs. Sibley, 'and take tea with us? My daughter Anne will come for you in our pony cart.'

Mrs. Cunningham thanked her and agreed after a short pause.

'It's a pretty drive,' said Paul.

'Yes,' said his mother, 'and my husband would much like to meet you.'

When mother and son had left Mrs. Cunningham remarked to Rachel that she was not very fond of driving. Horses and ponies were unreliable creatures. They bit, they kicked, and, worse still, they shied on the smallest provocation—or on no provocation at all, she added darkly.

'Richard Gervase would never have had that accident if he hadn't been riding a horse.'

Rachel to her annoyance found herself flushing. 'But Richard Gervase enjoys riding,' she said. 'He has ridden all his life.'

66

'That may be,' said Mrs. Cunningham, 'but it's a dangerous occupation all the same.'

The next day dawned fine. Mrs. Cunningham made herself ready in good time and sat on the sofa, her gloved hands folded in her lap. Rachel stood gazing out of the window, and saw a little pony cart turn into the lane and drive up to the door. Its occupant, a slight girl, threw the reins on to the pony's back and came quickly along the little flagged path framed by lavender bushes. Her face was freckled and sunburnt, and she held a pair of driving gloves in her hand.

'I'm Anne,' she said. 'I wonder if you would like to come now, as Tommy our pony doesn't go very fast.'

Anne and Rachel both felt shy and smiled a little uncertainly at each other.

'We are quite ready,' said Mrs. Cunningham.

When they went outside Tommy, the pony, was busily cropping the roadside grass. The trap, more properly called a tub, was nearly circular. There were faded cushions on the seats. Anne got into the cart and grasped the reins, and Mrs. Cunningham surmounted the little step and seated herself opposite to her. After Rachel had got in and closed the little door Anne gave the reins a shake. Tommy, torn from his luscious meal of grass, moved reluctantly forward. Mrs. Cunningham glanced at him. She saw that he was stout and moved slowly and was therefore unlikely to indulge in any alarming antics.

'I'm afraid he's rather lazy,' said Anne.

'I would prefer him to be slow,' said Mrs. Cunningham. 'Could I put my parasol up or would it alarm him?'

'Oh no, he's quite used to it. Mother often has a parasol.'

Anne gave the reins another shake, and Tommy broke into a trot and then relapsed into a walk. Mrs. Cunningham's parasol tilted perilously near Anne's face, and so she closed it with a faint sigh. Anne, looking slightly flushed, drove on in silence, and long strands of greenery brushed their hats as they went round corners. Mrs. Cunningham sat silent and rigidly erect. Rachel was also silent but happy and amused as she looked about her. Anne turned the little cart between two crumbling stone gate posts, and Tommy, happy at the thought of his stable, pulled hard on the reins. The inmates of the cart clutched its sides as they went towards the house. By tugging hard on the reins and showing unexpected firmness, Anne manoeuvred the pony alongside two stone steps before the doorway of a long, low house.

Paul, who was standing on the top step, handed the two ladies out. His mother stood behind him smiling a welcome, and Mrs. Cunningham was escorted into the drawing room. Paul lingered for a moment as Rachel looked about her at the grandfather clock and the staircase with shallow steps which wound its way to the landing above.

Then they went into the drawing room in silence. It was a long, panelled room with windows at each end. On the garden side the ground sloped down to some willow trees which fringed a small winding stream. There was a low table spread with tea things.

'My husband had an unexpected call to a parishioner,' said Mrs. Sibley, 'but he will be back soon.'

Mrs. Sibley grasped the handle of the large brown tea pot with a worn hand. She wore no rings except a narrow wedding ring which slipped up and down her thin finger.

The tea was excellent with a loaf and a pot of honey, a jar of home-made jam, and a sensible-looking cake. There were sounds of scurrying feet in the passage and children's voices in the passage. Rachel looked around her. It was a homely room. The walls were panelled, and the paint, once white, had mellowed to an indeterminate yellow which blended well with the pale water colours hanging closely together on the walls. The china on the tea table had obviously seen long service. This showed itself in faint cracks on the sides of the cups and chips at their edges. Mrs. Cunningham and Rachel were given unchipped cups with a pattern different to the rest and of a more elegant shape. The room had a lived in look about it. It had obviously been romped in by children, and grown ups had sat there to read and talk, to sew and to make music. Its carpet was faded, and the chintzes, with patterns slightly blurred by age and use, had been patched, while the curtains, warped by long years of sunlight, hung unevenly on the poles.

Mrs. Sibley talked to her older visitor of Oxford which she had known in her youth.

'Has it changed much?' she asked, and was told that some new houses were being built.

'The essential Oxford doesn't change,' said Paul, 'it just goes on in the same old way.'

At this moment the door opened and a tall man came into the room. He shook hands with the visitors, and his wife poured him out some tea in a large cup.

'My husband likes his tea drowned in milk,' said Mrs. Sibley.

Mrs. Cunningham looked interested. She had been brought up as a Presbyterian and she regarded the Anglican clergy as inexplicable people with a Romish taint clinging to them.

'Do all your clergymen favour weak tea?' she asked.

Mr. Sibley's dark eyebrows shot up on his forehead. 'I don't really know,' he said, in a voice as measured and deliberate as her own. 'It may be general among my clerical brethren, but if so I am not aware of it.'

There was a silence and Mrs. Sibley said, 'Anne, why don't you and Paul take Miss Barrington into the garden?'

'A good idea,' said Paul, and the three young people went out through the french windows into the warm afternoon. The garden sloped down from a narrow terrace. It was edged by flowers fighting a losing battle against encroaching weeds. The roses, climbing up the walls of the house, flung out long branches in every direction. They walked down a moss-grown path in silence and on to an uneven stretch of grass. A stream pushed its way through reeds and flowers, gurgling and eddying in the little pools at its edge, while swallows swooped back and forth over it.

'How very pretty,' said Rachel.

'Yes,' said Paul, 'it's pretty and I like it. It knows its own mind. Rain or shine, flood or drought, it just goes on its way. Now, human beings rush in every direction and change their minds, but this stream never does that.'

'But father says that it has altered its course even since he first came here,' said Anne, whose mind was a literal one.

'It may have,' said Paul, 'but I still maintain that it's got a purpose and knows what it's doing.'

'Let's sit down,' said Anne, and she seated herself on a willow branch which leaned sideways away from the stream.

Meanwhile, the two older ladies sat on by the tea table. Mrs. Sibley asked Mrs. Cunningham whether Mr. Barrington was pleased with Paul's work. Mrs. Cunningham replied that she had every reason to suppose that he was. Paul's mother said with a little sigh, 'He works very hard and sits up till all hours of the night with his books.'

'He should succeed in life,' was Mrs. Cunningham's cautious answer.

Mrs. Sibley looked at her. 'Success isn't everything,' she said, 'I want him to be happy too.' She stared in front of her for a moment, then she rose to her feet. 'Would you care to see the house or go out into the garden?'

'I would prefer to see the house,' said Mrs. Cunningham.

They went up the staircase and on to a landing. Rooms with doors ajar or flung wide opened out of it, and a faint scent of old rose leaves came from a blue and white bowl on a table.

'This is the schoolroom,' said Mrs. Sibley, pushing open a door. 'Come and shake hands, children—this is Susan and this is Mary.'

The two children, who had been eating bread and honey, advanced towards the visitor; the stickiness of their hands made a slight rasping sound when they encountered Mrs. Cunningham's kid glove. They were cleanly if shabbily dressed and their hair hung tangled over their eyes, but they had a look of vitality and intelligence. A pile of lesson books had been flung down haphazardly on a deep window seat alongside an open paint box and a jam jar full of muddy paint water. In the middle of the room stood a table with two plates and mugs and a loaf of bread.

16

THE days succeeded each other, going happily by, with quiet hours, small comings and goings. Plans could be arranged and carried out, although a difficulty had arisen when, after their tea at the Vicarage, Mrs. Cunningham told

Rachel that she would prefer not to drive in the Vicarage pony cart again.

Paul had driven them back to their lodgings and had swerved round corners in a way which she thought highly unsafe. Tommy, unable to loiter or browse, had shown his displeasure by shying at an old woman who was picking up sticks by the roadside. Mrs. Cunningham remarked that she did not possess a nervous disposition, but that she must, none the less, draw the line somewhere, and she drew it at pony carts.

It was left to Rachel to give Paul's mother a rather lame explanation of this. The whole thing was difficult, as she did not feel that she could leave her cousin alone. Mrs. Sibley was instantly sympathetic, and the problem was quickly solved. There lived, Mrs. Sibley said, in the next village, an old man who had an ancient vehicle described as a fly, although its mode of progression suggested nothing more aerial than a hearse. The tired horse seldom went beyond a foot-pace. It could, however, take the Oxford ladies to some nearby spot. So Mrs. Cunningham travelled majestically in an atmosphere of moth-eaten felt and was deposited at the rendezvous for the picnic.

Picnics through the ages have a certain sameness. Some people hold that food tastes better when eaten in the open air, some maintain that food tastes basically the same wherever it is eaten, and others say that they prefer to have their food on plates and their knees under a solid table unplagued by flies and wasps, wandering breezes, or sudden showers.

Rachel loved picnics. She had been to so few of them and her enjoyment helped to make them agreeable to her companions. Paul and she made a fire with sticks and drift wood, and even Mrs. Cunningham, seated bolt upright by the outspread table cloth, relaxed and tried her best not to notice the admixture of sand which had found its way into the food. Mrs. Sibley cut the cake. It was a plain one with currants widely spaced.

'We call it "shout cake",' said one of the children to Rachel. 'The currants are so far away from each other that they would have to shout if they wanted to make each other hear.'

'Don't talk about food, Mary,' said Mrs. Sibley, 'you are very lucky to have food at all when so many people have to go without—and currants are dear,' she murmured under her breath.

Paul pulled his sister's pigtails and engaged her in an amiable fight. Rachel looked on with amusement, entranced by a family life such as had so far been a closed book to her. This give and take of outspoken criticisms in good part delighted her. No one answered irritably, and arguments broke up in laughter.

They went to church, and church-going seemed to be a part of life, not a mere formality. In spite of the age and infirmities of the harmonium, Anne's playing showed a firmness of tone and a sense of harmony, and the singing, in spite of the nasal voices of the school children, and the off-key sounds made by some of the older members of the congregation, held sincerity and charm.

The service was plain, Mr. Sibley's sermon was suited to the needs and comprehension of his congregation, and Mrs. Cunningham found nothing to object to on the grounds of Popish leanings.

At first sight it seemed as if life at the Vicarage went on without any directing hand. Mrs. Sibley constantly mislaid her spectacles. She also put letters into unexpected places. They were returned to her from the backs of cushions on the drawing-room sofa, they protruded from underneath the ornaments on the mantelpiece, and were usually recaptured by Anne. Sometimes one of the children came dancing in, waving a letter retrieved from the garden or in the hen coop. In spite of this loose grip on her correspondence, to any discerning observer Paul's mother was the directing force in the household. She spoke quietly to the two village girls, whose heavy footsteps could be heard throughout the house, and gently corrected their mistakes and shortcomings. The cottage people came to her for advice and sympathy and their endless troubles of leaking roofs, rheumatism and children's ailments. Her household revolved round her. 'Where's Mamma?' was the cry most frequently heard on the staircase and in the passages.

Paul's relationship to his mother was on the surface a matter of light jokes and allusions to family foibles, but underneath this Rachel, who observed them quietly but closely, realised their deep devotion to each other.

Mr. Sibley pursued his parish work without heeding any

72

family turmoil. His sermons occupied most of his time. He also had a secret passion for architecture and corresponded with other enthusiasts. He neither fussed nor raised his voice, and appeared to be unsurprised when his family differed from him in an argument.

The days passed fast and happily for Rachel, and Paul, who sat up late at night, felt little fatigue and a sharpened awareness of life.

The last Sunday of their visit was spent at the Vicarage. After church Rachel and her cousin returned there to spend the remainder of the day. After luncheon Mrs. Sibley excused herself, as she had to take a Sunday School class. Before she went out she established Mrs. Cunningham in a wicker chair on the small terrace outside the drawing room windows. That lady then leant back in the chair and closed her eyes. At first she considered knotty problems of her return to Oxford. She was chiefly concerned about whether the strip of carpet on the top landing would last for another year. It had shown signs of disintegrating in spite of careful repairs. Her thoughts grew vaguer, and she closed her eyes and dozed, waking occasionally to the pleasant sound of a sonata being played softly by Anne in the drawing room.

Paul and Rachel were left together, and after a desultory conversation he suggested a walk, and they descended the incline towards the stream. They walked to its verge in silence and Paul said, 'Let's go on a little further.' They came to the edge of a little wood. Paul opened a gate and they found themselves in a small clearing, in the midst of which stood a bench faded to the colour of the rest of the wood.

'Let's sit down,' said Paul. 'My father had this seat made years ago by the village carpenter. My parents used to come and sit here, but they don't often come now they haven't much time. I sometimes bring a book here, and the children play games. You get a good glimpse of the stream.'

Rachel saw in front of her that the wood sloped gently down to the edge of the stream, the trees thinning as they went. She seated herself and Paul leant against a tree.

'Have you enjoyed your time here?' he asked.

Rachel smiled up at him. 'Every minute of it,' she said. 'You've all been so kind to us.'

'It's easy to be kind to you,' he said.

'Thank you,' said Rachel, a little nonplussed.

Paul hesitated as if he were going to make some remark, then thought again and remained silent. Rachel suddenly felt embarrassed and did not know what to say next. She looked upwards into the branches of a tree.

'There's a squirrel,' she said, as a whisk of russet-coloured fur showed itself moving swiftly up a tree tunk. The squirrel poised itself on a branch, a nut between its paws.

'I suppose it's beginning to collect its winter hoard,' she said.

Paul looked upwards. 'Yes, he's a lucky fellow. By hard work he can collect enough nuts to last him through the lean months of winter.' His voice shook a little, and he added with vehemence: 'We men have to work for years before we can do that.'

Rachel stared at him with surprise.

'I can't afford to ask anyone to marry me,' he went on, 'not until I have got a sure footing at the Bar, and I ought not to ask any girl to wait for me till I get that—it wouldn't be fair to her.' He paused, and his next words came out with a rush, 'Rachel, if you are still free, could I speak of this to you again?'

There was a silence, broken only by the snapping of a twig as the squirrel made his way from branch to branch. Rachel stared down at the glade in front of her without seeing it or the twinkle of running water between the branches. She raised her head. 'I don't know,' she said unhappily, her voice sounding strained and a little harsh. She glanced at Paul and looked away again. His face was paler than usual and his pose more rigid.

'Well, we won't talk about it now,' he said. 'I—I didn't mean to speak of this to you till later. Let's go back to the house.'

They returned there in silence, to find Mrs. Cunningham and Mrs. Sibley sitting at the tea table while Anne brought in the tea pot.

'We thought we would have tea early, Rachel,' Paul's mother said, 'as Mrs. Cunningham feels that you must get back to finish your packing.'

She glanced at Paul as she said this, and then looked down

74

at her cup. Paul excused himself and left the room. Mrs. Sibley did not look at Rachel but continued a conversation with her cousin. But somehow Rachel was unhappily conscious that Paul's mother suspected his feelings towards her, and was allowing herself to wonder what had been said that afternoon.

Paul did not reappear until they had almost finished tea. He looked and spoke as usual, and rescued with a smile his mother's spectacles from under a sofa cusion. All the same Rachel's heart was heavy. She felt that for her there would never again be that carefree atmosphere at the Vicarage.

Mrs. Cunningham and Rachel left early the following morning to return to Oxford.

17

Rachel could never remember much of the rest of that Oxford vacation. It went by in a dreamy way, and she enjoyed dreaming.

One morning she received a letter from Emily, saying that she was coming down from London to Oxford, as her aunt wanted her help in getting the house ready for the autumn term. Rachel looked forward to seeing Emily, and suggested a day for her to come to tea.

Emily arrived early and they sat in the garden. Emily poured out her grievances. Her father, she complained, went out more and more and, she suspected, took more to drink, and her mother was more querulous and complaining than ever.

'I've done some more embroidery and it's brought in a little money, but my father doesn't know about it. I give mother a little to help her. Most of it went on stockings and a pair of shoes, but I've put a bit by for a new dress.'

Rachel listened and sympathised, trying to stave off the question she dreaded, Then it came.

'Now tell me,' said Emily, fixing her with a shrewd glance, 'about your time at the sea side. Did you see much of Paul, and what is his family like?'

'They are very nice,' replied Rachel. 'We went to tea with them and to picnics. It's a lovely place, the cottage we were in—'

But Emily was not to be deflected. 'And Paul?' she enquired, cutting Rachel short.

'He was working very hard, but he came on some picnics and expeditions. His mother was so kind, and he has a very nice sister who is musical.'

'What's their house like?'

'Oh, long and low and covered with creepers.' As she spoke she saw the long drawing-room with its windows opening on to the sloping garden, the little hill opposite and, below, the willow-fringed stream.

Emily recalled her to reality by asking her, 'Have they any money?'

'I don't know,' said Rachel, 'I never noticed.'

'But you must know from seeing how they live—unless you went about with your eyes shut. Parsons are usually as poor as church mice.'

Rachel recalled the slits in the curtains and the patched chintzes in the Vicarage drawing-room, but she was determined to say no more; she found Emily's remarks inquisitive and a little vulgar.

'Didn't they ever talk about money?'

'Never,' said Rachel with emphasis, 'it was never mentioned once.'

A faint embarrassment seized her. She knew she was not being quite truthful. Paul had indeed spoken about money when they watched the squirrel in the wood. At that moment it was tea time, and Rachel thankfully remembered that she and Emily would be expected in the drawing-room on the stroke of five.

Richard started his term at a disadvantage as far as his studies were concerned. This did not worry him unduly— although it concerned his tutors, who were interested in his doings and his work. He came one evening near the end of

October to see Mr. Barrington and found Rachel just opening the gate in front of the house. He helped to push it, and then they both paused and looked at each other.

'I expect you have come to see my father?' she said.

'Yes, but can't I say a word to you too? I haven't seen you since last term.'

He stooped and picked up a horse chestnut that was lying on the ground. He peeled off its wrinkled spiny covering and held it in the palm of his hand. He smoothed its polished surface on the sleeve of his coat.

'Did you like chestnuts when you were a child?' he asked as he held it out to her.

'Yes I did like them,' she said as she took it. 'We have always had heaps of chestnuts from our tree, and I used to put them on my dolls plates and pretend they were buns and cakes.'

She glanced down at the round object on the palm of her hand and then raised her eyes to Richard's face.

'The sad part is,' she said slowly, 'that they don't stay shiny like this. They get dull and dry and you have to throw them away, and then after a while you can't find any more.'

'I wish you could see them at my home,' said Richard. 'We have an avenue of them.' A thought shot through his mind, that it would be pleasant to walk with Rachel in the autumn woods near his home.

There was a brief silence which Rachel broke by saying, 'Are you enjoying the term?'

'Well, it's been nice seeing people in college but I'm behindhand with the work. I don't seem to be able to concentrate.'

'Do you still have headaches?'

'Just a bit, nothing to speak of. I'm riding again and keeping very clear of steam rollers.'

'Are you sure the horse won't shy at drays and other things?'

'Oh no he won't, and if he does I shall stick on him all right. I must have been absent-minded the day he threw me. I don't usually fall like that.'

'I am glad you are going to be careful.' She looked down at the chestnut in the palm of her hand and smiled a little.

'Are you?'

Richard seemed to be about to speak when Rachel's father emerged from the front door. He frowned a little.

'Hullo, Richard, you are a few minutes late.'

Richard sprang forward to shake hands with his tutor. 'I hope to see you again soon,' he said over his shoulder to Rachel.

Rachel's fingers closed over the chestnut, then she slipped it into the pocket of her gown and made her way upstairs.

She then opened her writing desk and dropped the small round object into a beaded bag. She stood dreaming for a moment and wondering if she could plant it in a bowl or in the garden where it would perhaps grow into a shady tree.

Richard looked to see if she was in the drawing-room or garden when he left, but she was nowhere to be seen.

 18

Rachel had gone one evening to dine alone with Lucy Maxwell as George was dining in college. Mrs. Cunningham and Mr. Barrington, seated in the drawing room near a small fire, were silently pursuing their usual avocations, but Mr. Barrington's book did not appear to hold his attention. He turned a few pages and then put it down again, rose and poked the fire, which in Mrs. Cunningham's view was doing nicely and only needed to be let alone. He then relit his pipe and stood looking in front of him.

Finally after a quarter of an hour had passed Mrs. Cunningham raised her head and looked up at him. She laid her embroidery on her lap and smoothed it down with outspread fingers.

'Have you anything on your mind?' she asked. 'You seem troubled.'

Mr. Barrington pushed his spectacles up on to his forehead as he stared at Louisa for a minute. She looked so calm and unflurried. He hardly knew where to begin.

'I wanted to speak to you about Rachel,' he said.

Mrs. Cunningham sat bolt upright in her chair, and her embroidery slid down on to the floor. 'Rachel,' she said, 'what about her?' as she picked it up. 'Are you not satisfied with her?'

'In most ways I am.'

'I should think so,' said Louisa, as colour mounted to her face, 'Rachel's—'

'I know you love Rachel,' he said, 'and care for her so excellently.'

'Well what is wrong?'

'There is nothing wrong, but well—Richard Gervase and she were talking in the garden.'

'Well there's no harm in that that I can see,' said Mrs. Cunningham. 'Rachel had been on an errand to the post office for me. I was sending off some old clothes to poor Jessie in Fife. If Mr. Gervase was coming in at the gate it was only natural that he should stop and have a word with her. Paul Sibley comes in and out, and stops and has a word with us but he once stayed to tea. What ails you about this, Arthur?'

Mr. Barrington made a quick irritable movement and nearly upset a small table. 'Paul Sibley is a different matter. Whatever happens Paul will never be distracted from his work by anything. Richard is different, everything distracts him and my daughter shouldn't help in this. There's nothing between Rachel and this young man is there, Louisa?'

Mrs. Cunningham looked up at him. 'He was in this house for some days after his accident and she has therefore seen more of him, a bit more that is to say, than she has of any other young man, and they are on friendly terms.'

'But she is much too young to be thinking about such things.'

'Rachel is eighteen,' said his cousin calmly. 'Many girls are married at that age.'

'Bless my soul—so she is,' he exclaimed. 'So she is,' he repeated.

'I cannot perceive,' said Mrs. Cunningham, 'what is worrying you, Arthur. If Rachel sometimes speaks to one of your pupils there is no great harm done on either side.'

Mrs. Cunningham was not being strictly truthful about this. She suspected that Paul had a more than casual interest in Rachel, and she liked Paul.

'What ails you at Rachel?' she went on. 'She has sense and

decorum. She lacks friends of her own age certainly, but Mrs. Maxwell is very kind.'

'You must realise, Louisa,' said Mr. Barrington, firmly pursuing his own train of thought, 'that Richard Gervase belongs to a different world to ours, a world of wealthy landowners who go to London and meet and entertain in each other's large houses, and whose life is lived on a scale we can hardly imagine. Debts and gambling come into this life. I have not had a generation of young men through my hands without knowing this and knowing something of what goes on.'

'But I can't see,' said Louisa, 'how this affects Rachel.'

'They were standing with their heads together and she held something in her hand. Can't you see, Louisa, how much I should dislike any young man who came to me as a pupil getting entangled with my daughter.' He paused.

The slight jar of the front door was audible.

'There comes Rachel,' said Louisa, 'do not let her see that we have been discussing this.'

'I will go into the study,' said Mr. Barrington. He had pushed his spectacles further and further up on to his forehead till they met and mingled with his mane of thick grey hair, and Mrs. Cunningham was thankful when he closed the door of his room.

She was looking down at the magenta flowers with their vivid green foliage set against a black background, destined to cover a footstool, when Rachel came in.

'Did you have a nice evening?' she asked.

'Yes, I did,' said Rachel. 'Lucy and I sat by the fire and talked. She's asked me to call her Lucy. She is so nice and kind. She's asked me something else, she's going to some lectures and she asked me to come with her, do you think father would let me go?'

Mrs. Cunningham reflected for the space of a moment or two.

'I'm not saying that he wouldn't,' she said. 'I would think myself it would give you an interest outside this house. The ladies who go to these lectures speak well of them, and I am sure Mrs. Maxwell will chaperone you.'

'Yes she would, she says she would,' said Rachel eagerly, 'and she even thinks I might study for an examination and live at home.' Mrs. Cunningham looked rather taken aback by this. 'There's something,' Rachel went on eagerly, 'called the "Association for the Higher Education of Women" which has been started, and there are a few students at Somerville Hall and Lady Margaret Hall. I don't want to go and live in a Hall but I should like to study.'

Mrs. Cunningham rose. 'Well dearie we will think about it. Mind you, I'm not against the idea for you. You've had a good training in household matters, and the two servants and I can do what's necessary.'

'Oh I can help you and study too.'

'Well, speak to your father about it. I think he might say yes.' At this moment I think he certainly might, she added to herself but not aloud.

The next day to Rachel's surprise he agreed and after a few slightly derogatory remarks on the doubtful use it would be to Rachel to pursue the course she suggested, gave his consent. Rachel did not know till much later that he had done so in the hope that this might prevent her having an entanglement with one of his pupils.

19

MEANWHILE Richard received a letter from Lady Wentmore saying that she and her daughter would like to come down for the day to Oxford. The late October weather seemed to her set fair for sunshine and lack of rain.

Richard replied that this would give him great pleasure. He was disinclined for work, and this would give him the excuse for a day's idleness. He wondered if he should ask anyone to meet the two ladies, and he decided to invite a cousin of his from another college, a cheerful young man named Roger who could be counted on to rattle away either to Mary or her mother. He did not invite Paul, who belonged to a different part of his life, the life of learning and discipline which half attracted, half repelled him.

They lunched in Richard's room. Mary and the young cousin talked about hunting, the cubbing season had begun and Richard had been out with a hunt near Oxford. Lady Wentmore listened indulgently. She had hunted in her younger days, and she knew its importance, its shibboleths, and its expertise. Her eyes strayed round the room. She noted the peacock feathers in the tobacco jar, the sporting prints, the small portrait of Sir Edward hanging over the mantelpiece, and a mezzotint of a man dressed in hunting attire standing near a table crowned by an impressive inkstand. There was a tall window behind him, and he was depicted as pulling on a pair of gloves, and in fact waiting for his real life, lived out of doors, to begin. His hunting crop was tucked under his arm. The significance of the picture was nothing to Lady Wentmore. She just saw a reproduction of the portrait of someone she had known as an old man in her younger days.

'You are rather like your grandfather,' she said to Richard.

'Yes I am supposed to be,' he said. 'My father always says I am, at any rate. I've got an album here with a photograph of myself in it which he says is more like my grandfather than like him.'

There was a revolving bookcase standing beside the chair on which Lady Wentmore was sitting. It contained very few books, but two photograph albums lay on its top shelf. As Richard took hold of one of them he gave the bookshelf a sideways twist and a small book fell out on to the floor. It was *Feats on the Fiord*; it fell open and Lady Wentmore stretched out her hand and picked it up. It opened on the fly leaf with the words Rachel Barrington in the centre of the page.

Lady Wentmore looked at Richard as Mary peered over her shoulder.

'Who is Rachel Barrington?' Mary asked.

'My tutor, Mr. Barrington's daughter,' said Richard.

'Oh, that was where you stayed after your accident?'

'Yes,' said Richard, 'and she lent me this book to take to Norway with me.'

Mary took the book out of her mother's hand. 'Is it good?' she asked.

'Yes, very good,' said Richard. He looked slightly embarrassed and shut the book and returned it to the shelf.

'I've met that young lady for a moment at the Maxwells. She doesn't say much, but she's pretty,' said Roger.

Richard changed the conversation abruptly by asking Lady Wentmore if she would like to take a look at the college.

Lady Wentmore would have much preferred to go on hearing more about this Rachel Barrington. Her attitude to Oxford was one of condescension. It was a phase which young men went through, an inevitable progression from school to the wider world. A place where certainly friendships could be made useful or tiresome to members of the family later in life.

Her heavy skirt dragged round her feet and her thick velvet coat pressed on to her shoulders. Her boots pinched her feet and the unusual mildness of the October day made winter clothes a burden. But she walked along with her head high and a firm step in spite of a painful corn. She saw Mary and Richard in front of her talking happily together and this sustained her. Half-way across the spacious quadrangle a tall man was seen walking towards them.

'There's Mr. Maxwell,' cried Roger who was finding conversation with Lady Wentmore rather heavy going. They were having the sort of talk which consists of questions of which the questioner already knows the answers, and the questioned is aware of this.

George Maxwell looked as if he had decided to walk away from the approaching group of four people. He was not at the moment prepared to converse with any one. However, he paused and his face set into lines of grim politeness as he was introduced to the two ladies and gave a greeting to the two young men.

Lady Wentmore was not easily awed. She inspired awe but seldom felt it, but she was for the moment tongue-tied, when Richard broke in saying,

'Mrs. Maxwell was Miss Lucy Taynton, Ludovic Taynton's cousin.'

Lady Wentmore felt that she was on firmer ground and they discussed the Dashbury family for a few minutes.

'Is Richard showing you the sights of Oxford?'

Lady Wentmore suppressed a shudder. She had caught

glimpses on her drive from the station of churches and colleges in, as it seemed, an endless succession down a long street.

'I am afraid we shall only have time to see Richard's college before we return to London,' she said, smiling with becoming regret.

'I fear I must leave you then,' said George. 'Do not forget to show Lady Wentmore all the pictures in the banqueting hall,' and with that he raised his hat and walked off with long strides.

'Lucy Taynton is some sort of poor relation of Hugh Dashbury's is she not?'

'Mrs. Maxwell is one of the most charming ladies that I know,' said Richard with asperity, 'and her husband is one of the coming men in Oxford. They are very kind to me and we all like going to their house. Here we are,' he added, as they entered through a door. 'May I give you my arm up these stairs?'

Mary looked at the pictures without any comprehension, but with a suitable show of interest. When Richard escorted them to the station and the train slowly swung into action, he turned away and walked back to his college in the gathering dusk feeling relieved that the day was over. There was a scent of a bonfire somewhere in the air, and the sky was luminous behind the crockets on the roof of a great church. The cupola surmounting a college gateway stood out with two arched black shadows under its small dome. Richard had little eye for architectural beauty. To him the Oxford of history was a background and setting for his undergraduate life, but he felt calmed by the beauty of the scene.

Lady Wentmore in a first class carriage on the way to London also felt relieved that the day was over, but not particularly pleased with everything about it. Mary said nothing but stared into the gathering dusk at the passing fields and hedges.

20

LADY WENTMORE on her return to the Chase wrote a line to Sir Edward asking him to lunch with her. She chose a day when Mary was out hunting and they could be alone together.

Sir Edward came in due time, and while the servants were in the room they talked on indifferent topics, but afterwards when they found themselves in Lady Wentmore's sitting-room, seated by the fire, a short silence fell.

Sir Edward said, 'You went down to Oxford the other day. How was Richard?'

'He seemed well,' and she paused.

'What do you mean, Victoria, seemed well? He is either well or he isn't.'

'He looks well,' but for once Victoria Wentmore hesitated. 'He appears to be seeing something of a girl called Rachel Barrington. Do . . .'

'I saw her,' said Sir Edward, 'when I went to her father's house after his accident.'

'Richard must have seen a good deal of her when they were in the same house.'

'What are you hinting at, Victoria?' said Sir Edward irritably.

'I am not hinting at anything,' said Lady Wentmore. (This was untrue and she knew it.) 'I am just suggesting to you that perhaps it is not very sensible for him to become friendly with a young girl who might perhaps think that his attentions meant something.'

Sir Edward looked at her and looked away again. He puffed at his pipe; he had a great respect for Victoria's judgment in the matters of every-day life, but he wished she would leave Richard alone.

'He's too young to be thinking about paying attention to any young lady,' he said.

'Young men have made unfortunate entanglements before now, when they were very young. Look at Robert.'

'But dash it all, Robert got entangled with a barmaid. This girl is a lady, and her father, though he's not a man I could ever get on with, is a gentleman, and the cousin who lives with them is a nice quiet body. These people—'

'Yes, but Edward, you wouldn't want Richard to marry someone who isn't in society. After all someday when Richard brings back a wife she will have to take her place in the county.'

Sir Edward bent forward and knocked the burnt out shreds of his pipe onto the edge of the fire.

'My dear Victoria, who is talking about marriage? You run on as if you thought—I mean I don't suppose such a thought has even entered the boy's head.'

'No, of course not, but it might. How much longer will he be at Oxford?'

'Two more terms after this one.'

Sir Edward rose to his feet.

'Must you go?' said Victoria.

'Yes, I'm afraid I must.' He glanced at the clock but perhaps feeling that it would be discourteous to leave so soon after luncheon, he sat down again. He made an enquiry about one of the Wentmore farms, and when they had discussed this and the topic dropped, asked about Lady Wentmore's son.

'He doesn't write many letters,' said his mother, 'but I hear from his tutor who writes long letters about the sights that they are seeing. They are in Paris now and seeing something of the Embassy people.' She sighed. 'The bother is that I don't quite trust Mr. Murphy, at least I'm not sure about him. He has excellent references and he is not talkative, but I don't somehow quite trust him.'

'Well look here, Victoria, I know the Ambassador, it's William Warren. His father and I, we were at Eton together. I hadn't seen him for a year or two, when I ran into him at the club in London, but he's always very friendly. Shall I write to him and ask him to tell me what he thinks of the tutor and the boy too?'

'Yes, that would be a great comfort to me,' Lady Wentmore said. She looked suddenly discouraged, and the lines on her forehead deepened. This only lasted a moment, however. She rose to her feet and said, 'Well I mustn't keep you, my dear Edward. It was indeed good of you to come—and if you would write to William Warren I should be very grateful.'

As Sir Edward drove himself back to the Priory his thoughts were distracted by keeping his young horse gently trotting while guiding him past obstacles on the road, to which he might show his dislike by shying. But when he had reached home and had interviewed his bailiff, he sat down in a leather armchair at his writing table, and after a good deal of thought and lighting and re-lighting his pipe, he composed a letter to the Ambassador.

The letter written, Sir Edward rang the bell and gave it to the butler.

'Leave the curtains for a little,' he said.

Lamps were brought in while he still stared out at the landscape which darkened softly and imperceptibly. Then turning, he went to his table, took up a letter and a newspaper and sat down.

He felt disquieted by Victoria's remarks though he had pooh-poohed them. He thought she was making a great deal out of very little. Richard couldn't be thinking seriously about this girl at Oxford, he was much too young to think seriously about any girl. He moved restlessly in his chair, the newspaper fell off his knee on to the ground, he did not trouble to retrieve it, but continued his train of thought. Of course Victoria had a reason for alarm, if any alarm there was. She had set her heart on Richard and Mary making a match of it. He had always thought that this might be a good idea. Mary was a nice girl, a good girl of breeding and manners. She treated him with charming deference and she was a good rider and a sound judge of a horse. A thought flickered across his mind. He had once come across her scolding her maid in the passage outside her bedroom. The cross look on her face was smoothed out when she saw him walking towards her, but she was flushed and angry, he could see. But ladies were apt to scold their maids; his own wife, a paragon of perfection, had scolded her own maid, who had rewarded this treatment with a blind and unquestioning devotion.

How still the house was. In earlier years his wife would have come rustling in in a silk dress, bringing with her her small embroidery frame, and they would have talked of the happenings of the day. Then she would have gone to rest, after which they would have dined by candlelight. He sighed, loneliness must be his portion. It might be mitigated by Richard's marrying, and perhaps children's voices would bring the house to life.

Resolutely he took up his lawyer's letter and applied himself to mastering its contents.

<hr />

21

RACHEL enjoyed the lectures and the intellectual life. Paul said to her one day, 'I think you are right to do this, I wish my sister Anne could do something of the kind, only in her case it would be music lessons, but my parents live in too remote a place and can't afford them anyway.'

Rachel found that having to listen gave her mind a sort of discipline, but always at the back of it was Richard's look, and in her ears the echo of the warmth of his voice, the moment of emotion being cut short by her father's words.

Paul came and went. He behaved just as usual and they might never have had an intimate word together. He had in fact resolved not to speak of his love for Rachel again, at any rate not for the time being. She felt slightly disappointed by his apparent forgetfulness of all that had passed between them, but relieved because she would not have to face Emily's prying questions. But it is dull, to say the least of it, when a young man has declared his love for you, to feel that he has put this out of his thoughts or has decided to place the matter away on some shelf in his mind.

Sometimes she went off into a dream, a habit of which Mrs. Cunningham had tried to cure her by saying sharply, 'Don't dream, child,' and then putting her to some useful task.

One day as Rachel was emerging from a lecture, notebook in hand, she met Richard in the street. He was in riding clothes and there was a splash of mud on his cheek.

'What have you been doing?' he asked.

'I've been to a lecture,' she replied.

'I didn't know that young ladies went to lectures.'

'But I enjoy lectures.'

He stared at her and there was amusement in his glance. 'Well that's more than I do. Now Paul's the person for lectures if you like.'

Lucy joined them at that moment and looked smilingly at them both. 'We've been improving our minds,' she said as a group of ladies plainly dressed and looking not unlike a flock of doves emerged from an old doorway. 'Are you walking back with me, Rachel?'

'Yes, please,' she said. 'Well, goodbye, Richard.'

He turned to Rachel saying, 'I shall come and see your father soon.'

Rachel received a note from Lucy on the day of the next lecture saying that she had caught a bad cold and could not go out, and suggesting that Rachel should go with a don's wife who lived near the Barringtons' house.

Rachel felt shy and uncertain about this, but Mrs. Cunningham said, 'Tuts, that's silly. Just go and ring her door bell and ask her to let you go with her. She won't eat you.'

Rachel went off to do this and was suddenly confronted by Richard's tall figure.

'Where are you off to?' he asked.

She explained what had happened.

'Come for a walk with me instead.' He took her notebook out of her hand and slipped it into his pocket. 'Lectures don't matter,' he said, 'lots of them are pretty dull. Come along, please.' They turned down a lane behind the house which led into fields.

Rachel felt guilty but happy, and looked up into Richard's face.

'I'm unhappy,' he said abruptly. 'I can't concentrate on my work and I get more and more bored with it, and then when I go home I feel I must stay with my father, he is so lonely and miserable since my mother's death. The house used to be full of people coming and going, and now nobody much comes. I don't know if I ought to leave Oxford and go and live with him, but it's no fun living at home.' He went on in this strain until they reached a stile in a field.

Rachel listened silently, her eyes fixed on his face. People had always found it easy to tell Rachel of their troubles. She stayed so still while she listened, with such absorbed attention to their narrative.

As Richard's confidences poured out he found that he was telling her things which he had told no one else.

'Don't go yet,' he urged, after some time had elapsed. 'Have I bored you? I must have, with all my talk about myself.'

The autumn afternoon was quietly progressing, the light from the soft even sky pressed down upon the landscape, and indifferently the trees shed a few leaves. Both young people were leaning against the stile when they heard a voice behind them say, 'I say, can I pass?'

They both started violently, looked up and saw Mr. Westwell standing on the other side of the stile. There was a gleam of amusement in his eyes which was highly unwelcome to them both. As he surmounted the stile he remarked,

'I've been for a country walk, good for the health, I find.'

Richard who had muttered something under his breath, recovered himself and said politely that it was indeed a fine afternoon and Miss Barrington and he were also enjoying the fresh air in a walk.

'Yes, but don't stand still or you will catch cold.'

He raised his hat and walked away at a brisk pace.

When his footsteps had died away Rachel raised a dismayed countenance to Richard.

'Do you think he will tell his wife, she is supposed to be an awful gossip.'

There was so much concern in her voice that Richard's heart melted. He knew little of the rigid proprieties of Oxford life, but he had heard many jokes about the young ladies who wished for higher education, and how much on probation they were by many of the authorities. He had also heard of the strict system of chaperonage to which they had to submit, and jokes had been made of their enforced unobtrusiveness of demeanour. But to Rachel this was emphatically no joking matter. Her eyes had filled with tears, he put his arm round her shoulder.

'Don't cry please,' he said and he kissed her cheek. 'It's selfish of me, I know, but I do like talking to you, you always understand my difficulties.'

He drew back and looked down at her, and a wave of feeling came over him. How good it would be to have Rachel there always listening and understanding. She looked so pretty in her confusion and unhappiness.

'Could you wait for me, Rachel?' he said a little hoarsely. 'Could we some day be engaged?'

Rachel stared at him flooded with amazement and then joy. Was this really happening to her, could the frail growth of hope that she had nourished in her heart have matured into this splendid fruit?

It was a moment with no past or future in it for them both. His father, his relations, his undergraduate youth were completely remote from Richard's mind. He was only conscious of the joy of Rachel's presence, her softness and charm.

Such moments come only in early life, though a deeper and completely different happiness may come later. Youthful lovers live in a rosy cloud too soon to be dispersed in a world of clash and disapproval. If it lasted the world would be a place where lovers would sing songs and talk endlessly about their love for each other and nothing would exist but joy. However, life reasserts itself in this universe, wars are fought, food must be grown, men and women are born and die and sorrow is an intrusive visitor.

But for this afternoon Richard and Rachel were enveloped by the soft cloud. They stayed on talking, and then parted at the gate of Rachel's house. They agreed to tell no one of the afternoon's happenings.

Rachel dreaded questions, but luckily for her her father had gone to London for two nights. The cook, Annie, had been suffering most of the day from a severe toothache and Mrs. Cunningham was preoccupied in administering oil of cloves and discussing with Rachel whether Annie should go to the dentist next day and have the tooth pulled out.

Rachel forced her mind on to Annie's troubles. She went

into the kitchen and found her, speechless, with her head tied up in flannel and giving sudden squeaks every time a jab of pain came from the tooth. She was very sorry for Annie but thankful for her cousin's preoccupation and for her father's absence. She escaped early up to her room—the rosy glow was still round her.

The next day Mrs. Cunningham departed early in a cab to take the weeping Annie to the dentist and Rachel had the house to herself. She moved about trying to dust some china ornaments on the drawing room mantelpiece. She went up to her bedroom and looked for her notebook, to look up her notes of the lecture. She could not put her hand on it. Then she remembered that Richard had slipped it into his pocket.

22

THE rosy glow was fading, with Richard. When he asked Rachel to be engaged to him it seemed the natural outcome of the love he had recently felt for her, the right solution of his difficulties. With her he would have someone who would understand him and whose sympathy would be unfailing.

The thought of his father, however, began to obtrude itself. What would he say? Sir Edward had married when he was young and could not therefore make too many objections on that score. But somehow Richard felt that his father would have other plans for his son's future that would be unfulfilled if he married Rachel.

He put these thoughts as much as possible on one side; his father had always from childhood given him whatever he wished. It would, it must come right. But he felt that it would be best to remind Rachel to tell no one of their engagement. He decided to go and tell his father himself; it would be better than writing to him.

When he had removed his jacket the night before he had

felt a stiffness in the pocket. He had extracted a notebook from it which he recognised as Rachel's. He decided to post it to her, and then another thought struck him. He had still got *Feats on the Fiord* in his bookshelf and he could put the two books together with a note inside.

He posted the parcel and Rachel found it on the hall table the following day. Her father had written to say that he was staying for another night in London. Annie's tooth had been agonisingly extracted, but she was wrapped in gloom as the dentist had said ominously that her teeth were in such a bad condition that some more must come out, and Mrs. Cunningham was completely occupied in trying by every means in her power to allay the cook's mounting hysteria. Rachel slipped unnoticed upstairs.

She carefully opened the parcel and found a letter inside the notebook. It was the first time she had seen Richard's handwriting, widely spaced, large and unformed.

'Rachel dear,

I found your notebook in my pocket, here it is. I meant every word I said, but it is better not to tell your father just yet. I will explain this when we meet. When shall we meet? We had better not go back to the stile. Could you meet me at the University Museum, no one goes there much. I've never been inside it myself. I will be near the door at ten o'clock tomorrow.

Yours,
Richard.'

'Of course I shall meet him,' said Rachel half aloud. She pressed the letter to her lips. 'Of course I shall meet him,' she said aloud again. She wrote him a note and slipped out to the pillar box to post it.

The next day Mrs. Cunningham was taking Annie again to the dentist, and Rachel left the house quickly when they had gone.

The University Museum loomed above her in its varied brick and marble. She scarcely glanced at it as she hurried through the latter day Gothic door. Richard was awaiting for her. He took her hand and drew her along towards a dark corner where there was a wooden bench. Museums held no significance for him. Rachel who had been brought up by her father to revere the past shivered a little as they passed along. What a lot of people had died, she thought, leaving only glass-enclosed relics of their loves and hates.

She had however little time for these reflections as they sat down on the bench and Richard drew her to him, kissed her, then drew away and looked at her.

It did not strike either of them how little they knew of one another, or of the pressures of heredity and environment which formed their characters. A strong attraction held them together. Richard impatient with his home and Oxford life saw Rachel as the embodiment of peace and security, while to Rachel, Richard was the embodiment of a romantic dream come true. Neither of them could see the other in a clear light. The rosy glow had not yet subsided. They heeded the heavy weight of the past all round them no more than two sparrows seeking to make a nest in a convenient hole in an ancient wall.

Richard was more alert than Rachel and some distant footsteps in another part of the building made him withdraw his arm.

'You haven't told any one, about us I mean?'

Rachel looked gravely at him.

'No of course not, you asked me not to say anything to anyone.'

There was no hurt in her tone, only surprise.

'Will your father be pleased?' she asked timidly.

'Perhaps not at first, but he will come round, he may not want me to marry just yet. And what about Mr. Barrington?'

'I don't think he's even thought about it. Perhaps Cousin Louisa does some times.'

'I will go home for a night, I think,' said Richard, 'and speak to my father, it will be better than writing.'

The sound of the footsteps had died away and they sat on entranced till it was time to leave.

Richard went back to his rooms in college and wrote to his father. The rosy dream was thinning for both the young people. Rachel had a growing uneasiness because neither her father nor her cousin knew anything of the engagement. Mr. Barrington had always impressed on her as a child the necessity of keeping exactly to the truth, and Cousin Louisa held accuracy of statement in the highest esteem, and with Scotch literalness refused to take any vague statement on trust, pinning her interlocutor down like a entomologist spearing a butterfly into a case. These two older people, Rachel thought with discomfort, loved and trusted her and she was engaged in deceiving them.

23

RICHARD obtained permission from his college authorities to go home for a night on the ground that his father wished to see him on urgent business. As he moved along their familiar lanes Richard felt a sinking of the heart, and driving through the gates surmounted by stone gryphons and along the avenue to the house his spirits drooped and sank.

He was greeted with obvious pleasure by the butler.

'How is my father?' asked Richard.

'Well his rheumatics don't seem any better, Mr. Richard. He's in the study.'

His father rose from a deep chair. 'I am delighted to see you. I've been rather crippled by an attack of the gout.' There was such obvious pleasure in his voice that Richard was touched by it. 'I don't move about much but if you give me your arm I could walk into the dining room.'

Luncheon went through with mainly questions and answers about the affairs of the estate and country happenings. After they had eaten, Sir Edward rose slowly to his feet. 'The doctor says I must have a short rest after meals,' he said, 'so you go out for a walk, but don't be too long.'

Richard went down to the river, then returned to the house to inspect the fishing rods and guns in the gun room. He opened the door of the library and saw that his father had fallen into a doze, one hand on his walking stick. He looked fatigued and older than when his son had last seen him.

Richard felt the task of telling his father about Rachel

weighing a little heavier on him each moment that passed. He came back into the library later and found a tea table in front of his father.

'I've got into the habit of this,' Sir Edward said apologetically. 'The afternoons are long and the evenings are beginning to draw in.'

Richard drank some tea and helped himself to a muffin from a silver dish. The room was lamp lit and pleasant and Richard glanced at the big ormulu clock on the mantelpiece, its hands were moving inexorably on, faster than usual it seemed to him. But he had said he would tell his father about Rachel and he must start to do it.

'Father there's something I wanted to tell you. I've fallen in love.'

His father who had settled back in his chair started forward and grasped the stick at his side. 'Well that's not unusual at your age,' he said as he eyed his son.

Richard disregarded this and went on. 'You've met her. She's Rachel Barrington. I stayed in her father's house when I had my fall.'

Into Sir Edward's mind a conversation came swiftly. So Victoria Wentmore was right, there was an entanglement in Oxford. He wrenched his thoughts back to Richard.

'Oh, yes, that girl I remember, I hope it's only a passing fancy?'

'No, father, no,' said Richard. His voice had lost its hoarseness and was stronger and clearer. 'No, father, it's not like that, I have asked her to be engaged to me. I won't marry anyone else.'

'Bless my soul,' said Sir Edward, 'you should never have done this, you are much too young, it isn't suitable and I can't allow it.'

'Why not?'

'Because you couldn't bring her to this house; when you succeed me she couldn't take your mother's place.'

Richard looked up for a minute at the portrait of his mother above the mantelpiece. The picture was lit up by branching candlesticks on both sides. Lady Gervase was smiling with pouting red lips. She was wearing a fancy dress copied from a family portrait. Her large black hat crowned chestnut curls and her spreading muslin dress with a fichu crossed over the bosom was confined at the waist by a blue sash. In her hands she carried a bouquet of flowers. Her lovely face looked down at her husband and son with an air of satisfaction and assured pride.

Richard looked at his father who was struggling to say something. Unheeding he cut across this by remarking heatedly, 'Rachel could take her place anywhere.'

'But, my boy, I can't believe that you have been so hot-headed and foolish as to do this. Look here, you don't seem to be getting on well with your work at Oxford. I'll send you abroad, and when you come back you will think differently.'

'I shall not think any differently, father,' Richard said. 'I love Rachel and shall go on doing so.' All the obstinacy of his nature was aroused. His lips hardened into a line.

'Does her father know about this?'

'No, I told Rachel that I would speak to you first before she told him. She agreed, but I shall tell him when I get back to Oxford. I hope he will give his consent.'

'You can be pretty sure that he will,' said Sir Edward, 'you would be a catch for his daughter,' he was going on to say, but he stopped himself in time, checked by the expression on Richard's face, and added lamely, 'it would be a good marriage for his daughter.'

'He wouldn't be swayed by any consideration of that sort,' said Richard, frowning. He recalled Mr. Barrington's austere standards, his worn clothes, his old pipe.

'I don't suppose he would be indifferent to his daughter marrying someone like you. You've got a good deal to offer,' said his father whose temper was mounting.

Richard stood up and walked towards his father and Sir Edward felt a constriction of his heart for a moment, his son looked so like his mother.

'Well,' he said heavily with an accompanying sigh, 'we must discuss this again.' He reached for his stick and leaning on it walked with slow steps to the door. Richard opened it and watched his halting progress across the black and white squares of marble in the hall.

Dinner went by with jerky talk destined to deceive the butler, who having known the Gervases father and son for many years, was not deceived. Their usual easy intercourse had gone and had been replaced by an embarrassed unhappiness.

Sir Edward endured a hard night of pain and sleeplessness, and Richard, who was not apt to be observant of older people's looks, felt his heart smite him.

After breakfast his father said he had some more estate business to discuss. They went into the library where on a large kneehole writing desk a stack of paper was piled. As neither father nor son had really any thought to give to the business it was soon finished, and Sir Edward leant back in his chair and said, 'Richard you are all I have now and I want you to be happy, more than anything else. But I ask you not to do anything in a hurry. I don't know anything of this young lady.'

'But you saw her when you came to Oxford and surely . . .'

'Yes I did but I hardly spoke to her.'

'She doesn't talk much, she's not easy to know, but she is good, gentle and kind and she goes . . .' He was going to say, 'she is clever and goes to lectures.' Then he stopped abruptly, prompted by a sudden thought that it was perhaps better not to mention this fact as his father had a horror of blue stocking women.

At that moment the butler entered bearing a letter on a silver salver. Sir Edward tore the envelope open with a jerky movement, then he adjusted his spectacles and frowned.

'Victoria wants to drive over this afternoon. Ronnie has got into trouble again, he's in a mess of some kind with some woman abroad.'

'I'm sorry,' said Richard then he became silent and stared in front of him.

Sir Edward said, 'Ah, yes, young men get into all sorts of troubles. I dare say this is not a very serious matter and probably some hard cash can settle it,' he stopped.

Richard was frowning furiously. 'My engagement is not a matter which can be settled by hard cash, father, I want to be engaged to someone I love and who loves me and whose father is a very distinguished scholar. I am not asking to marry a foreign actress.'

There was a tense silence, the two men were on the edge of a quarrel. Sir Edward felt a chill of fear at his heart, that Richard should speak to him in that cold hurtful way was intolerable. His world seemed to be crumbling since yesterday afternoon. With an appealing note in his voice he said, 'My boy I only want your happiness, but will you wait a little and come and see me again?'

'I shall have to speak to Mr. Barrington at once, and what shall I tell Rachel? That she is unwanted and unwelcome here?'

'Speak to Mr. Barrington if you must, but tell him please that I urge delay till you are sure you know your own mind.'

Richard stood up. 'Very well,' he said. He looked at the clock. 'I have promised to speak to Jackson about the pheasants.' Richard left the room abruptly, his head high, whilst his father remained a prey to deeply unhappy thoughts. He hated the thought of this girl who had come between him and his son.

Richard went back to Oxford after luncheon, driving himself in a dog cart at a rapid pace to the station. He gave the reins to the groom and jumped down to the ground as fast as possible and was on to the platform well before the train came in.

'Mr. Richard was in a fine bad temper about sum'ut,' the groom remarked to his wife when he returned home.

24

LADY WENTMORE arrived that afternoon to see Sir Edward. She came into the room wearing a look of determination. There was a splash of mud on her skirt, and in clasping her hands too tightly together she had split one glove across the middle. Edward Gervase, his own unhappy thoughts beating a tattoo in his head, noticed neither of these things.

He drew an armchair forward for his visitor, and she sat down more heavily than usual. She looked at her host and saw that his face was ravaged and deeply lined.

'You don't look well, Edward, has the rheumatism been bad?'

'It's not only the rheumatism,' he replied.

Lady Wentmore enclosed in her troubles merely said, 'Oh! I'm so sorry. I am so distracted by worry about Ronnie. You know he never writes letters if he can possibly help it, and I haven't heard from him for some time, but I wasn't worrying much because it's happened so often before.'

She clasped and unclasped her hands and pulled her gloves off so roughly that two buttons fell onto her lap. She put them into her reticule. Then she extracted a letter from inside it, which she tendered to Sir Edward. He took it and read it slowly through.

'This man Murphy seems in a fine taking about Ronnie.'

'Oh, yes, he's proved quite useless, in fact he wants to come back. If it hadn't been for Harriet and William Warren, I don't know what would have happened.'

She opened her reticule again and tendered Sir Edward another letter. It bore the address of the British Embassy in Paris.

'Dear Victoria,

'I have seen your boy Ronnie and I have talked to him and tried to knock some sense into his head. I have even given him some idea of the lady's reputation for having many affairs of the heart. Ronnie listened politely, but I could see that I was making no headway with him. The tutor is no good. He just walks about with a long face. Could you not send out some friend of Ronnie's who could make him see sense? Meanwhile I will do what I can, you may be assured of that. Harriet sends you her love. If there is anyone who you can send, they could stay here.'

Sir Edward lifted his eyes from the letter. 'I am sorry,' he said mechanically. 'I wonder what you can do?' Then his own trouble surged over him. 'I wanted a son and so did you,' he said dully. 'I don't know why we did.'

Lady Wentmore looked up at him, her own troubles forgotten for the moment.

'What is it, Edward? Is it Richard, is he ill or . . .?'

'No he's quite well, but he was here last night and he told me that he has asked this girl in Oxford to become engaged to him.'

Victoria's face whitened and then flushed, she leaned forward. 'You are surely not going to allow this?' she said.

'I don't see what I can do, this girl's a lady and her father is a well-known man in Oxford. It's not like . . .'

'Not like Ronnie's infatuation, you mean,' said Victoria. She was angry, angry with her old friend, angry with Ronnie, and all that she had planned for, worked and hoped for was spoilt. At that moment her heart was like a heavy stone. She felt no pity for Ronnie and only furious disappointment with Richard. Her thoughts darted to Mary.

The silence in the room had lasted some minutes when she spoke. 'I warned you about this, Edward, that there was someone in Oxford.'

'And I told you,' said Sir Edward, 'that it wasn't wise to let Ronnie go off like that with that oaf of a tutor. I couldn't prevent Richard going to Oxford, young men must be educated.'

'But I thought Oxford was like a sort of monastery,' said Victoria. 'I didn't know there were a lot of young women there.'

'You are talking nonsense, my dear Victoria,' said Sir Edward. 'Where there are professors you must expect them to have wives and daughters.'

'And if one sends one's son abroad because it seems a good thing to do, one mustn't be blamed if they get into difficulties.' Victoria's face was doubly flushed, they were dangerously near a quarrel.

'Look here, Victoria,' said her host, 'we have both had a bad knock, and we shan't make it any better by hard words between us.'

Victoria Wentmore was silent for a moment. 'No you're quite right, Edward. I'm sorry for what I said. It is a blow about Richard, I am sorry for you. But is he really engaged to this—this girl?'

'He says so, he seems in earnest about it. He has gone back to Oxford and will speak to her father.'

'Of course her people will jump at it. Oh, Edward, I am sorry.'

'There is just a chance that her father may not.'

'I think that's very unlikely,' said Victoria. 'Richard's a

prize for a girl like that. For any girl for that matter.' Tears rose in her eyes, she was thinking of her daughter Mary.

'I have told Richard to tell this girl's father that I advise delay, and if you delay something it doesn't always happen.'

Lady Wentmore dabbed at her eyes with a lace-bordered handkerchief. 'I'm so sorry, Edward, it's all been rather a shock,' and seeing his face lined and worn she said, 'How could he think of bringing her here to—' she glanced at a miniature of Lady Gervase on the table beside her—'to marry a girl who could never take Marian's place.'

Sir Edward struck his hand on the table. 'We won't discuss this any more. I have done what I could and for the moment there is nothing more to be done about this affair of Richard's. Let's see what can be done about Ronnie.'

He turned away from her and rose, reached for his stick and stared out of the window at the dripping trees and a few late roses pale and sodden clinging to the bushes in front of the house.

He turned to Victoria who was looking straight in front of her. 'Give me William's letter please.'

She handed it to him and he read it through carefully seating himself near her. He laid it down on the table beside him, then took it up again.

'Is there any one you could send to Paris? I take it that you don't want to go yourself?'

'No,' said Lady Wentmore dully, 'it would be no good my going. I've tried so hard with Ronnie but he won't listen to his mother. I've done all I could for my children and Mary realises it a little, but Ronnie takes it all for granted.'

'Yes, yes, I know, Victoria,' said Sir Edward. 'I know how you pulled things round after Ronald's death and the estate was in a pretty good muddle. But if you think it's no good going yourself, whom can you send?'

Suddenly Lady Wentmore said, 'Could Richard go?'

'But, my dear Victoria, he's at Oxford.'

'Ronnie and he have always got on together,' said Victoria, disregarding this interruption; 'he might listen to someone of his own age.'

'But he can't leave Oxford till the end of term,' said Sir Edward. 'I'm sure he would do anything he could to help, but the college authorities would never agree to this. What reason could I give them, it would be no good his going for a few days?'

'It would be some good his going even for a few days, he might make Ronnie see sense.'

Sir Edward doubted this. He knew Ronnie's stubbornness masked though it was by a kind of lazy charm.

'Edward, it would take him away from this girl even if it's only for a few days.' She clasped her hands. 'It might give Richard new ideas going to Paris. He has never been abroad.'

Sir Edward stared at her. 'Well I'll think about it,' he said, 'but mind, Victoria, don't tell anyone about Richard—not even Mary.'

'I shall certainly not tell Mary,' said Lady Wentmore.

25

RICHARD decided to act promptly when he returned to Oxford. He went to see Mr. Barrington in his rooms in college, and found that he had gone out. He went to the house and asked the parlourmaid if the master of the house was at home, then looked up and saw Rachel coming down the stairs.

The parlourmaid disappeared and he said, 'I must speak to you,' and he opened the drawing-room door and she passed through it.

'Can we talk for a few minutes? Where is Mrs. Cunningham?'

'My father will be coming back soon. Cousin Louisa is out for a little while.

Rachel looked strained and Richard put his arm round her and kissed her.

'Your father?' she said.

'Well of course he was surprised,' said Richard, torn between a wish to tell the truth and an even greater wish not to hurt Rachel.

'Was he pleased?'

'No, I can't say he was. He thinks I'm too young to marry yet.'

'Then he doesn't want us to be engaged?'

'Well he wants us to wait.'

'I will wait any time,' she said with a note of finality in her voice, and he saw that she meant every word.

'And I will wait too, but I don't want to,' he said. 'We must think a lot,' he said. 'My father may raise all sorts of objections, but he'll give way. I will speak to your father when he comes in.'

Richard put on a very determined air but he was not feeling happy at the thought of this interview.

At that moment the front door banged, there were footsteps in the hall and Mr. Barrington entered the room.

Rachel jumped to her feet as Richard moved away from her and Mr. Barrington, coming in quickly, paused in the doorway. He adjusted his spectacles, there was something out of the ordinary in the atmosphere of the room which struck him at once.

'Have you come to see me, Richard?' he asked.

'Yes please, sir, can I see you?'

'Come along, then,' he said and led the way.

'Please stay here, Rachel,' Richard said in a whisper as he followed.

Mr. Barrington sat down at his ink-stained desk, pushed some papers impatiently on one side and looked up at him. 'Well, what is it?'

'I've come to ask you if I may marry Rachel. I have told her that I love her and shall ask you for your consent to our engagement.'

Rachel's father stared incredulously at him and asked jerkily, 'But are you serious? I can't believe that you have thought about this. My world and yours are quite separate and different. This must be a passing fancy.'

That is just what my father said, thought Richard.

'Does Rachel reciprocate your wish to be engaged?'

'Yes, she does, and we will wait a little if necessary.'

Rachel's father gave him a long look. He was accustomed to weighing arguments and marshalling facts, but now the keenness of his mind seemed blunted.

'Your father cannot be pleased at your wanting to marry so young.'

'Well he would rather I waited.'

'But does he want this marriage if you do wait?'

Richard, faced with telling a direct lie or the unpalatable truth, took refuge in saying, 'He will when he sees Rachel.'

'Do you mean he's opposed to it?'

An unhappiness and embarrassment came over Richard's face.

'I see,' said Mr. Barrington. 'Your father dislikes the idea, and I feel that there is little to be said for it. How are you going to get over that?'

'My father will come round, sir,' said Richard, 'and I hope you will.'

Mr. Barrington heaved a sigh. He rearranged the pens in the tray before him and there was silence in the room. When he spoke he said, 'I want to be reasonable, Richard, but you must see how much of a shock this has been to me. I am in fault, I have given no thought to Rachel marrying, indeed I have thought of her as a child and not realised that she has grown up.' He threw down the pen he was playing with. 'You do realise that although Rachel will not be penniless, I can allow her very little.'

'That really doesn't matter, sir. I shall have enough for us both. More than enough I should say.'

Mr. Barrington, unheeding, continued, 'You belong to a world of people who have large properties, go in for politics and a life in London of social round in large houses. Rachel's world has been a quiet one among people who have little money and who are concerned with the things of the mind. I am not criticising your world, you didn't make it for what it is. It has produced Cabinet ministers, lawyers, administrators, the people who keep agriculture going; but Rachel will feel lost in it. But all this is mere talk. If your love can stand the test of waiting then I have little to say. Is Rachel still in the next room?' He rose, smiling for the first time and said, 'I've always liked you, Richard.'

'Then may I tell my father that you give your consent?'

Mr. Barrington frowned. 'This is going to be difficult,' he said slowly. 'He is opposed to your marriage. I am only in favour of it if you can show patience and good will.' He smiled again. 'Sir Edward probably thinks that I shall jump at such a matrimonial chance for my daughter. Will you explain to him please that this is not the case, and that I only give my consent to your engagement if I can be sure that your feelings for each other can stand the test of time.'

He walked to the door and opened it.

'Come in here, Rachel, please. Richard has been telling me that you wish to be married. I can only give my consent if I feel that you are both in earnest about this.'

Rachel raised her eyes to his and then looked at Richard who smiled at her.

'Yes,' she said, her voice trembling a little, 'I am, father.' She stretched out her hand and Richard took it.

Mr. Barrington looked at them both. He stifled a pang as he remembered his own engagement to his wife, his long wait for their happiness and their brief happy married life.

At that moment Mrs. Cunningham came into the room. She saw Rachel flushed, her hand in Richard's and Mr. Barrington standing behind his writing table.

'What?' she began.

'Richard has asked my consent to his engagement to Rachel.'

'And what have you said?' she asked.

'His father and I both feel that they must test their feelings for each other . . .'

Mrs. Cunningham with a most unusual demonstrativeness put her arms round Rachel. 'You'll be needing to do your work,' she said to Mr. Barrington. 'Come into the drawing room,' and she drew Rachel away.

Mr. Barrington sat down heavily and stared at his desk as if he had never seen if before.

'You will write to your father, Richard please, and tell him what I have said.'

'Yes, sir.'

'And don't neglect your work because of this.'

'No, sir.'

He followed the two ladies into the drawing-room. Mrs. Cunningham seated herself on the sofa and Rachel after a minute sat down beside her.

'Well now, how did this occur?' she said. The young people seemed struck dumb. 'You have not met much.'

'We've met quite enough to know our own minds,' said Richard.

Rachel nodded her head.

'Can we meet now?' said Richard. 'Can I come here?'

'Yes, if Mr. Barrington agrees. And what about your father?'

Richard frowned. 'He will come round all right, he thinks I'm too young to marry.'

(He thinks many other things as well was Louisa Cunningham's unspoken thought).

She opened her mouth to voice some of the thoughts in her mind and then she saw that Rachel's eyes were ominously full of tears. 'Tut tut, you mustn't cry,' she said rising to her feet. 'I'll leave you for a wee while.'

Left alone the lovers talked together of the things young people in love talk about.

Before he left Richard had obtained permission to come and see Rachel sometimes, but first he must write to his father. This weighed on his spirits as he walked back to his college; it was not going to be an easy letter to write.

Richard posted his letter early the following morning. He was a good deal dissatisfied with his final effort, as he recollected some sentences in it. After it had disappeared into the pillar box he wished he had phrased them differently.

When he came back, he found Paul in his room. An irresistible longing came over him to tell Paul about Rachel, but something, he did not quite know what, held him back.

He had received a message from Rachel's father through Mrs. Cunningham to say that he was not to mention the subject of Rachel and his engagement to anyone; but surely Paul who rarely talked about other people's affairs, and whose discretion could be depended on, was safe to tell.

He mentioned Mr. Barrington, and then he saw just for one moment a flicker of pain pass over Paul's face and a tightening of the lips. It passed almost instantly, but it arrested his wish to confide, and after saying 'There's something'—he stopped.

At that moment his eye fell on a letter which his scout had brought in. It was addressed in his father's handwriting. He reached for it and said to Paul, 'Just look at the newspaper while I read this letter.'

Paul settled himself by the fire, the chair was a deep one and only the back of his head was visible over the top of it.

Richard tore his letter open and read it through.

'My Dear Richard,

This is to tell you that Victoria has just been to see me. She is in great distress about Ronnie. On his way back from his tour abroad with his tutor they stopped in Paris. He went to the theatre and has, as he calls it, fallen madly in love with an actress. He went constantly back stage to see her. He is mad enough to want to marry her. She is, I gather, older than him and is not averse to marrying an English lord. (The tutor is no use at all in controlling Ronnie.) Our cousins, William and Harriet Warren, have been kindness itself, but cannot, alas, make any impression on the boy, who seems to have completely lost his head over this woman, who is far from respectable by all accounts.

'William Warren in writing to Victoria asks if there is no one of Ronnie's own age who could go over to Paris, and try to get him away from this woman. Perhaps she could be bought off with a sum of money which Victoria can spare with difficulty, but she would rather pay cash down than see Ronnie inveigled into a disastrous marriage. He might listen to another young man.

'At any rate would it be possible for you to get leave from your college to go over to Paris? You could say with truth that it is urgent family business. I should be very glad if you could do this. Please write and tell me as soon as you know if you can do this.

'I am expecting to hear from you what Mr. Barrington has said.' The letter ended abruptly there and Richard gave a muffled exclamation as he finished it.

Paul, who had become a little dreamy by the fire, turned his head, 'What's happened?'

'It's a letter from my father. I will read it.'

Paul listened in silence, his brows knitted, and then ran a hand through his hair. 'This is quite outside my experience,' he said slowly. 'I shouldn't have thought you could do much good. Would this young Ronnie listen to you? Is he inclined to take your advice?'

'Well we grew up together and once or twice I've helped him out of scrapes when he was home from school, but that doesn't mean that he will listen to me now, Ronnie's pretty obstinate.'

Paul stood up with his back to the fire. 'I think you'll have trouble with the college authorities,' he said, 'over your work. By the way, how is it going?'

'Not at all well,' said Richard, 'it's so hard to concentrate.'

'I don't suppose that crack on your head did you any good.'

'No,' said Richard eagerly, but he knew that this was not the whole, or anything like the whole, truth. His love for Rachel and his increasing fears and doubts for the future stood between him and any sustained effort of mind.

Paul was frowning. 'I wish my advice was more help to you,' he said, 'but I don't think I know enough about this sort of thing. If you don't think you can help the young man it would be the greatest possible mistake to break into your Oxford term even if you can do it. It all rather depends on how important it is to prevent him making an ass of himself, or if you can prevent him . . .'

Paul was right. Commonsense is so often right in a crisis, and yet the whole thing was beyond commonsense—it was a clash of people living in two worlds. To Lady Wentmore his Oxford studies held no importance, to her and her daughter Mary, Ronnie and his future were everything.

The thought smote him too that going to Paris would mean leaving Rachel, not for long it was true, but the thought of Rachel struck him with a sharp pang and he did not listen to what Paul was saying, until the name Barrington caught his attention.

'You must ask Mr. Barrington about it,' Paul said. 'You will have to see him anyhow, and his advice is sure to be good.'

'I—oh yes, of course I must,' said Richard confusedly. 'I'll go now or tomorrow,' but it was of Rachel he was thinking.

'I must go now,' said Paul. 'I'm afraid I've not been much help, but I am there if you want someone to talk to, and I shall want to hear what Mr. Barrington has said.'

26

Richard found himself again facing Mr. Barrington across the littered desk. He had told the story of Ronnie. Mr. Barrington had listened to it in silence, putting a brief question here and there as Richard paused.

'This is not an easy matter,' he said. 'Let me make it quite clear to you and to your father that I wholly disapprove of your leaving Oxford during the term. Your work will suffer. When you come back the term will be nearly over, and you have only two more terms before you finish Schools. That is my view. As to the rest—' he paused. 'I can form no judgment about this matter. Your father and Lady Wentmore seem to think you could avert this young man's marriage, or that you might have at any rate some influence with him. If you feel that it is your duty to your family to go, I will put the matter to the Principal.'

'I don't want to go,' said Richard. 'I don't want to leave Oxford now.'

'Have you heard from your father?'

'No. I couldn't have done so yet, though I wrote at once.'

'This is an awkward business,' said Mr. Barrington. 'You are awaiting a letter from your father about your proposal to become engaged to Rachel, which is a very important matter to you both and to us all. This business of your cousin cuts across this, and I am put in the position of saying that I do not think you should go to Paris. I know that your father speaks of a few days, but this affair will take longer than that. You might make a momentary impression on your cousin and make him perhaps see reason, but if you leave too quickly and come home again he will slip back to where he was. These things can't be done in the space of five days or so. Apart from this, I am inclined to think that in his reply your father will say that he is opposed to your engagement.'

Richard shook his head.

Arthur Barrington went on unheeding, 'I am inclined to agree with him for other reasons. Could it be that your father, pressed by Lady Wentmore, wishes you to stay on in Paris in order to put off his decision to allow the engagement, and in the hope that you will see things in a different light if you go away?'

Richard stared blankly at him. He had never known his father to be other than completely straightforward in his dealings with himself or others. But a cloud of doubt arose in his mind.

Mr. Barrington recalled him from his confused thoughts. 'Well you must think this over. Come and see me in College when you have heard from your father. Now you can go and see Rachel for a short time.'

Richard thanked him and departed into the drawing room where Rachel was awaiting him.

'You look so worried,' she said.

'I don't want to worry you,' he said.

'But we must share things, worries as well as good things,' she said, 'mustn't we? Is it your father, or has my father . . . ?'

'It's not your father so much,' he said slowly. 'He isn't keen on our marrying but he sees things so clearly somehow. My father's different, he's so lonely and unhappy since my mother died, and he has time on his hands to brood on everything. I haven't heard from him, I couldn't have yet, but I've had a letter about something else.'

He told her the gist of his father's letter about Ronnie. She put her hand in his and he clasped it tightly. Rachel drew in her breath sharply.

'Do you want to go to Paris? I mean do you think you ought to go?'

'I'm really torn to bits. Of course I don't want to go and leave you, and I don't want to leave Oxford, and I don't care if I never see Ronnie again.'

'I wish I knew what to advise you.'

'Don't let's talk about it any more,' said Richard. He took her other hand and clasped both of them in his. 'It will be all right,' he added with a confidence he was far from feeling.

'If we can be together,' said Rachel, 'even a little now, nothing else matters does it?'

Richard felt comforted, as if all the forces of disapproval and difficulty which were converging round them had for the moment become less pressing.

The following morning Richard received a letter from his father which he read with deepening discomfort. Sir Edward asked for an answer about Richard going to Paris. He had seen Victoria Wentmore again. She was getting increasingly anxious about Ronnie. Neither he nor his tutor had written to her. The Warrens had been away from Paris for a few weeks. This added to her anxieties as she felt that as long as Sir William was in Paris she might perhaps receive some favourable news. The letter ended, 'Mr. Barrington seems to take the same view as I do. I am glad to find him in agreement with me. I am sure that in years to come you will see that we are right.'

'He hasn't any thought for me,' Richard said to himself. He crumpled the letter in his hand and then smoothed it out again and made a sudden decision.

He found Mr. Barrington in his room, and produced his father's letter. Mr. Barrington read it and then sat with clasped hands lost in thought. Suddenly he gave a sharp sigh, shook his head and said, 'I think you will have to go—everything points to it. Your father evidently thinks that your work here is of little importance and it is clear that he does not wish you to marry my daughter.' Richard gave an exclamation. 'Please let me finish. Your father is a man of substance. He doesn't consider it a matter of moment what sort of degree you take on leaving here. You will not have to work for your living. He, I understand, left Oxford without taking any degree. In my opinion you should write and say you will go next week. If you do not do this, he will imagine that I have stopped you going and in the future this will make things more difficult for you and Rachel. I suggest that you write to him saying that you can go only for a few days, and then do your utmost to make it clear to Ronnie Wentmore the kind of suicidal act which he proposes to perform. It is just possible, I only say just possible, that you may be able to deflect him from his present course. At any rate you will have done your best. That is my opinion. Rachel,' he paused, 'must wait in patience till you return and you must work in the vacation to make up for lost time here. Do you agree with all that I have said, or indeed any of it?'

'Yes, I'm afraid I do,' said Richard ruefully.

'I understand that Lady Wentmore is your nearest neighbour at Gervase Priory. She seems to have great influence with your father, and if your marriage should take place after you had refused to do this, she might make things no easier for you in future.' He rose. 'I will speak to the Principal. Meanwhile my advice is, prepare yourself for your journey.'

He looked at Richard's harassed face and his gaze softened.

'Well then the decision is made and there is no more to be said. I will explain the matter to Rachel.'

The same evening after dinner Mr. Barrington told Mrs. Cunningham and Rachel about Richard's journey to Paris. He avoided looking at Rachel, but he was aware of her sharp intake of breath.

Mrs. Cunningham remarked, 'Well, you did your best, Arthur, I must say it. But it all seems queer and daft to me. I have little experience of these sort of family troubles.'

Rachel rose and swiftly left the room.

'Poor child, she's gone into a difficult world,' said Mrs. Cunningham.

<hr/>

27

THE day on which Richard and Rachel met for a brief time before he went to Paris, he found Mrs. Cunningham in the hall of their house. She said, 'I will call Rachel in a moment—come in here.'

They went into the drawing room and she put a small leather case into his hand. It contained a photograph of Rachel.

'It was taken some years ago,' said Louisa Cunningham.

'Oh, thank you very much,' he said.

'Well, put it in your pocket—I thought maybe you would like it as a keepsake. I will fetch Rachel.'

Richard departed to Paris. In spite of everything his spirits rose. He forgot Ronnie for the moment and relegated his difficulties to the back of his mind. He enjoyed the journey from Calais to Paris where he had glimpses of châteaux enclosed in trees, and canals gleaming in the wintry sunshine. When he reached his destination he stood bewildered on the platform, jostled by porters, pushed aside by French families shrilly expressing their delight at seeing each other again.

He was approached by a man wearing a sad and anxious expression on his face.

'Are you Mr. Gervase? I am Mr. Murphy.'

It was a relief to hear an English voice and Richard looked pleased. Mr. Murphy however did not respond. His face was set in lines of gloom.

Outside the station, when they had climbed into a fiacre, Richard asked, 'Is my cousin well?'

'Well enough in health although he has a cold in the head,' replied Mr. Murphy. He relapsed into silence, and then cleared his throat. 'I understand that you have come to speak to Lord Wentmore. I have done my best,' said Mr. Murphy, whose long drooping moustache seemed to add to the general gloom of his appearance. 'My very best. I have even appealed to his better feelings and spoken to him of the duties of his position.'

'I am sure you have done all you can,' said Richard, uncomfortably at a loss for words.

'I have also reminded him of Lady Wentmore's anxieties in this matter. But all to no avail. He is now,' Mr. Murphy paused for words, 'like one bewitched. This—this woman holds him in thrall. Often she makes him suffer, but he goes back after they have had a quarrel.'

Richard felt deeply embarrassed. 'Well, I am here to do what I can,' he said, 'but I'm not very hopeful of success, and I can't stay long.'

At this moment the fiacre drew up in a side street and Richard followed Mr. Murphy up a staircase; there was a smell of cooking tinged with gas. They reached a small landing.

'This is your room.' Richard looked round, it seemed clean, but wore no air of luxury.

'Lord Wentmore is next door,' said Mr. Murphy.

Richard knocked and went into the next room, and Mr. Murphy vanished with great celerity down the passage.

Richard stood on the threshold of the room. Ronnie was smoking a pipe and lounging in a chair.

'Well, my dear Richard,' he said, 'I didn't come to meet you, I thought old Murphy would like to get his oar in first. I suppose he's told you what a bad boy I am? He's an old fool who doesn't know anything about life. Well now, I know all you're going to say, my mother and Cousin Edward have sent you to make me see what they call reason. I'll listen if you like, as you have come. But what you say won't make a scrap of difference to me.'

'Now look here, Ronnie,' said Richard. 'I didn't want to come, in fact I've come at great inconvenience to myself. The Oxford people didn't like my going away while term's still on but my father and your mother thought that you and I could talk things over and that you would agree to come home to wait . . .'

'Wait? What's the good of waiting? Marie won't wait, she will go on acting and some other fellow will come along,' he sneezed violently. 'I've caught this cold, it's draughty behind the scenes. Well, go on, say what you've got to say, you're the good boy of the family sent to talk to the black sheep.'

'You take yourself too seriously,' said Richard. 'You are not a black sheep, you've simply got yourself into a mess and don't know how to get out of it.'

'I am not in any kind of mess,' said Ronnie vehemently, 'and I don't propose to get out of anything. I don't want to make what my mother calls a suitable match. Suitable indeed, Heavens, how dull it sounds, and how sick I am of hearing about it.'

He rose and stood in front of the mantelpiece where a small fire, dying from want of attention, gave out a minute heat. 'I suppose you and Mary will marry now. That will be suitable. Money, land, and the joining together of the Priory and the Chase, all difficulties between Cousin Edward and my mother settled about boundaries of the two estates and . . .'

'Shut up,' said Richard furiously, 'leave Mary out of this, or you will be sorry. She's not thinking of me or I of her in that way.'

Ronnie had the grace to look a little ashamed. 'Sorry, Dick,' he said, 'but it's what my mother always wanted.'

'I'm sure she never said anything of the kind to you.'

'It isn't what she's *said*,' he replied, 'but I know it's in her mind. There's talk about it all over the countryside.'

'Well hold your tongue at any rate. Mary and I haven't given this a thought.'

'You may not have, but she has . . .'

'What utter rubbish,' said Richard. 'Don't let's mention it again. I'm here to talk about you. Do you really feel you want to marry this actress? Have you thought about what it will be like if you do? Can you imagine bringing her back to the Chase or her living there with your mother?'

Ronnie's face hardened. 'We can live abroad,' he said, 'it could be managed. My mother must give me some money, after all it will come to me when she dies. . . . It's no good, Dick, my mind's made up. Come with me to the theatre to-night and see Marie for yourself.' He smiled and looked boyish again. 'I'm not sorry to see you, Dick, it was good of you to come, though it's no use you know.'

The two young men dined at a restaurant.

The theatre was extremely stuffy and Richard found himself uncomfortably cramped in his seat. Ronnie, whose cold had become worse, coughed and sneezed before the curtain went up. But when it rose he sat forward and stared at the stage through opera glasses. The scene was a living room and the door at the back opened. Ronnie took Richard's arm in a painful grip. 'There she is,' he whispered with a gasp. Richard stared hard at the actress. She looked demure and charming and a little sly. In the first *entracte* the two young men pushed their way into the foyer.

'Isn't she beautiful?' whispered Ronnie.

'Yes,' said Richard, 'and she acts very well too. My French isn't all that good but I think I caught the gist of it.'

'I've learned a lot of French,' said Ronnie, 'and I've taught her quite a lot of English.'

Presently the signal came for the curtain to go up and Ronnie rushed back to his seat, Richard keeping up with him as best he could. The play progressed and Marie as the adventuress whose arrival disrupted a happy home, acted with spirit and a high degree of skill. Richard tried hard to discern in his mind from the part she was acting what sort of person she really was. Ronnie still sat forward wrapped up in his own dream of longing and admiration.

After the play was over Ronnie said, 'Now come and see her.'

They found themselves in a maze of scenery which smelt of glue, while dust rose round them. Ronnie slipped some coins into the hand of a man in a passage. He then knocked on a door and they were admitted into a dressing-room by a hard-faced elderly woman.

Marie turned round from a low seat where she was putting powder on her face, and Richard had a momentary impression that she was not greatly delighted to see them. But she greeted them with apparent pleasure.

'You were wonderful tonight,' Ronnie said, 'your acting was superb.'

She tapped him playfully on the shoulder and then asked *'Qui est ce monsieur?'*

'This is my cousin, Richard Gervase.'

The two young men sat down uncomfortably on low stools and Marie put the finishing touches to her toilet.

'Can you come out to supper?' Ronnie asked. His voice was anxious.

She shook her head. 'Not tonight,' she said. 'I am tired and shall go early to bed, and you have a cold too and should go back to your hotel. Do you not think so, monsieur?'

'Yes, I do,' said Richard as Ronnie coughed again. 'I enjoyed your acting so much.'

'Thank you,' she said, 'you are very flattering.'

The conversation, which was conducted in a mixture of French and English, gave Richard an odd sensation of unreality. Marie, Ronnie and himself might have been taking part in an extension of the play they had just seen. He studied Marie for a few moments while Ronnie said something to her in a whisper. She was, he saw, not quite so young as she had appeared on the stage. Even the powder and rouge did not completely mask some small lines. Her glance had gaiety but her mouth closed into a thin line.

She gave Ronnie a push. 'You go, *mon cher*, I do not wish to catch your cold.' She smiled at Richard and muttered something to Ronnie in French which he did not catch. 'Go along now, *vite*.'

As the two young men went their way along the passage, dimly lit by a gas jet, Ronnie had a coughing fit which reverberated noisily in the passage. Richard paused till the paroxysm was over, and patted him on the back as he did so.

'Don't do that' said Ronnie crossly.

As he spoke Richard fancied that he heard the door of Marie's dressing room open. He looked back and saw the figure of a thickset man going through it on tip-toe.

Ronnie, wiping his eyes and giving an occasional cough, preceded him down the passage.

When they got back to the hotel Richard said, 'You must go straight to bed, no more talking tonight.'

'But I want to talk,' said Ronnie. 'I want to know what you thought of the play.'

'Nonsense,' said Richard, 'I'm going to bed and so are you—your cold will be worse tomorrow if you don't, and I'm not going to sit up.'

Richard tried to compose himself to sleep, but his dreams were confused. Rachel came into them and vanished again, and through the thin walls of the room he heard Ronnie's fits of coughing. Towards morning he fell into a heavy sleep.

28

HE was roused by a knocking on the door. Mr. Murphy came in.

'Lord Wentmore isn't well, he hasn't slept and has coughed all night. I fear he is feverish. He has refused breakfast although he drank a cup of coffee, but pushed the rolls and butter away.'

Richard flung his dressing-gown round him and went into

the next room. Ronnie was flushed. He was drinking thirstily from a carafe of water beside his bed.

'I hear you didn't sleep.'

'I'm perfectly all right. I've only got a bit of a cough.'

Richard was completely inexperienced in illness, but he felt a misgiving when he looked at Ronnie—there was more to it than just a cough. The boy's eyes were brilliant and his face was flushed.

'Well, just stay where you are,' he said.

'All right. I say, would you be a good chap and get me some cough lozenges, there must be a chemist's shop somewhere. It's no good asking old Murphy about it. He can't string two words together in French.'

Richard went back into his room where he found the tutor gazing out of the window. He turned round with an enquiring look on his face.

'I don't think Ronnie is very well, but he's asked me to go out and get him some lozenges. Can you stay in here?' said Richard. 'I will tell him to knock on the wall if he wants anything.'

'Yes, I will,' said Mr. Murphy lugubriously. 'I think he is far from well and far from comfortable.'

Richard strode into the street frowning and unhappy. He found a *pharmacie*. Any fluency in French seemed to have deserted him, but he managed to buy a box of lozenges and then the chemist explained rapidly that he could make up a '*une bonne medicine pour la toux*' if monsieur would wait.'

He nodded a bald head at Richard encouragingly. And Richard, struck by a sudden idea, said he would return. He had noticed a small jeweller's shop in the same street and he went out quickly and plunged inside the dark doorway.

On the counter was a tray where lay an assortment of small trinkets. He wondered which Rachel would prefer, and after some concentrated thought he chose a crystal locket surmounted by a small and intricate pattern of leaves made up of tiny diamonds set in gold. It somehow seemed to accord with Rachel. He paid for it and returned to the *pharmacie*. On the counter stood a large bottle containing a thick brown liquid.

Richard paid for it and returned rapidly to the hotel.

Laying the lozenges down by Ronnie's bed, he held out the

bottle of cough syrup in his hand; with some difficulty he induced Ronnie to swallow a spoonful.

'Now do try and sleep,' Richard said.

'I can't sleep,' said Ronnie. 'I want to get up.' He moved restlessly about in the bed. 'I want to see Marie. I must see her.'

'Yes, but try and sleep now,' said Richard.

He felt utterly baffled and perturbed. Then a thought struck him. His father had given him a letter to Sir William Warren. He had not meant to present it. He had felt that there was no point in bringing the British Ambassador again into Ronnie's affairs. William Warren had said in his letter to Lady Wentmore that he could do nothing with Ronnie.

As the afternoon wore on Ronnie's fever mounted again. In the intervals of coughing he lay muttering to himself. Richard, increasingly anxious and alarmed, watched by his side. He had advised Mr. Murphy to go out and get some fresh air. When he returned they both stood looking at Ronnie and Richard wavered no longer.

'You stay here and give him water and I will go to the Embassy.'

Mr. Murphy agreed gloomily to do this. He did not like being near any illness which might be infectious, and he had no idea of what to do.

Richard hailed a fiacre and was driven to the Embassy. He noticed little of the streets or the traffic. The imposing butler looked hard at him and Richard tried to compose his demeanour realising that he must look untidy and slightly dishevelled.

He handed the letter of introduction and waited in an anteroom.

Presently the butler came in to announce that the Ambassador would see him. He was conducted into a room where two people sat at a table loaded with tea things.

'Hullo,' said Sir William, 'I got your father's letter. This is my wife.'

Lady Harriet rose smiling and shook hands.

'I will give you some tea,' she said. Richard was aware that his hand was shaking, as he took it.

'You've come to Paris to try and make Ronnie Wentmore see some sense I imagine,' said Sir William.

'Yes, sir, I have, but he's ill now.'

'Have something to eat first before you tell us,' said Harriet. She plied him with bread and butter and cake.

'Ill, is he?' said Sir William. 'Well, well.'

'Yes, he's got fever and never stops coughing, and he isn't getting any better, he's very feverish.'

'Well,' said William Warren, 'the first thing to do is to get a doctor or——'

He walked purposefully over to the writing table, wrote a short letter, rang a bell and gave the note to the butler.

Meanwhile Richard drank thirstily the cups of tea which Harriet gave him. He began to feel as if he had caught Ronnie's cold.

When Sir William returned to the tea table he was frowning. 'I have asked our doctor to go straight to your hotel,' he said. 'This is a difficult business. Hotels dislike illness, it's bad for trade, and it all sounds to me pretty uncomfortable. If the doctor takes a serious view of Ronnie, he will probably want to bring in a nurse and you cannot handle this yourself. I think if he is really ill his mother should be sent for.'

'He won't want to see her,' said Richard.

'That may be. But it's too heavy a responsibility for any one of us to take, if he is dangerously ill. I have had trouble like this before with English people falling ill in Paris, and it's been an added anxiety to my wife and myself in our position here.'

'I'm so sorry,' began Richard.

'It's not your fault, not in any way.' Sir William looked at his wife. 'Harriet, I think I will go to the hotel with Richard, where, with any luck, we may find the doctor. I asked him to go as soon as possible. What do you think?'

'Yes,' she replied. 'I think you should go.' She looked grave and concerned. 'And you could see the hotel people, and if Victoria Wentmore comes to Paris she must come here, unless she would prefer to stay at an hotel.'

Richard looked at Harriet Warren. He had been too much agitated to do so before, but the Ambassador's decisiveness had given him confidence. He had been conscious of her only as a presence in the room. Now as she turned away from him and looked up at her husband, he saw that she was someone to be reckoned with. Someone who had combined a soft beauty of face and form with calmness of spirit. She was not thinking of herself or of any impression she could produce on Richard. She reminded him somehow of Rachel, who had the same kind of serenity and who gave him the sense of calm which is rooted in peace of mind.

'Well, let's go,' said Sir William as he rang for his carriage. While they waited Harriet turned to Richard and asked him about his father, his work at Oxford and George and Lucy Maxwell.

'I hope to see her soon,' she said.

29

THE Ambassadorial carriage nearly blocked the narrow street in which the hotel was situated, and people stopped to stare at Sir William who jumped out quickly. The hall was empty and Richard preceded him up the stairs. When they reached Ronnie's bedroom they went in quickly. A short man was standing beside the bed. He held a watch in one hand and Ronnie's wrist in the other.

He looked grave, nodded silently to Sir William and replaced Ronnie's wrist on to the bed.

'I wish to speak to you,' he said in French.

'We can go into my room,' said Richard and he led the way. Mr. Murphy rose from his chair and bowed to Sir William.

The doctor spoke to Sir William in rapid French, his face grave and concerned.

'Did you understand that?' said Sir William, turning to Richard.

'No, I only caught a word here and there.'

'He says that Ronnie is very gravely ill. There is great cause for anxiety. He has contracted a very virulent type of influenza and must be moved at once to a hopsital where the nuns can look after him. He cannot possibly be looked after here.'

Sir William then said a few words to the doctor who nodded his head.

'He thinks that Ronnie's mother should be sent for. We must make all arrangements. The doctor will go straight off to see the Mother Superior. He will fetch Ronnie in about an hour,' and turning to the tutor he said, 'The doctor will give you a prescription to get made up, and you, Richard, must stay with Ronnie. You must not leave him for a moment. I will go straight back to the Embassy and send off a telegram to Lady Wentmore. She could be here by tomorrow evening. There is no time to waste.' He strode out of the room.

Richard watched him as he went down the stairs. The hotel proprietor and his wife stood staring upwards. He said a few words to them, ignoring their noisy exclamations.

Richard returned to Ronnie's room. He found that Ronnie had pushed the bedclothes back and was trying to get to his feet.

'Marie,' he said, 'I must see her——'

Richard pushed him back into bed and covered him up. 'Try and sleep,' he said. 'They will be taking you to the hospital soon.'

'Why can't I stay here?'

'Because you can't be properly looked after.'

Ronnie closed his eyes and whispered, 'You must go and see her. You *must*.' His breathing was more difficult. 'You must go tonight,' his voice was urgent, 'and see her and tell her I am ill, but directly I am better, I will come—you must.' His breathing grew more difficult.

'Yes, of course I'll go,' said Richard, 'but only if you will keep quiet and lie still.' Ronnie closed his eyes.

After Ronnie had been taken away to the hospital, Richard descended the stairs and asked for his bill. The hotel proprietor was profuse in his protestation of his sorrow about *ce pauvre milord*.

Richard turned away to go upstairs. He had some time to spare before he started on his very unwelcome errand. He had no desire to see the play in which Marie was acting again, but he decided that he would go in for the last act.

He heard steps on the staircase behind him and was given a letter. He looked at the signature. It was Harriet Warren. He read,

'Dear Richard,

'My husband, who is exceedingly busy, asks me to write and say that we both hope that you will come and take breakfast with us tomorrow morning. He asks me also to say that he thinks that Mr. Murphy should go home tomorrow, he can do no good here, and is only costing Lady Wentmore money. We are so deeply sorry for Ronnie and for your anxieties about him, but he is in good hands now.'

Richard went into the tutor's bedroom. Mr. Murphy was sitting reading by the light of two candles. Richard told him of the contents of Harriet's letter.

'You can be of no use here. Lady Wentmore will be coming. The Ambassador has telegraphed to her.'

The look of uncertainty vanished from Mr. Murphy's face. 'Then I will pack at once,' he said, and opening a cupboard door dragged out a shabby Gladstone bag. 'I fear she will think all that has happened is my fault.'

'No, of course not,' said Richard, 'you couldn't have prevented this. Ronnie is very headstrong.'

'I shall write from my lodgings in London to her ladyship.'

Richard sat in his room which seemed to become darker and colder as the hands of his watch moved slowly round. He put on his hat and went to the theatre. He scrutinised Marie closely all through the last act of the play. Her acting seemed to have a livelier quality and more finesse about it, and her slyness was accentuated.

He went behind the stage, tipped the man he met lavishly, and was awarded a look of amusement.

He walked along to the dressing-room and knocked. There was no answer. He walked in and saw Marie in the encircling arms of a short and stocky Frenchman. Marie gave a little shriek when she saw him. He closed the door. She took two steps towards him. 'What do you want?' she said.

Richard had composed his speech in careful French before he came. 'My cousin is ill, very ill indeed, he cannot come to see you.'

The Frenchman flushed with anger.

'What is this? Who is this young man?'

Marie poured out a torrent of words which Richard barely understood. The words *milord anglais* occurred over and over again.

The Frenchman replied in equally torrential French.

'Milord want me to marry him.'

'Marry him, you are under my protection. You will marry no one else.

'In that case,' said Richard, 'there is no more to be said.' He turned round, opened and slammed the door, ran through the dark passages and drew a deep breath of air when he reached the street.

30

RICHARD spent most of the next day at the Embassy. He sat dazed and miserable, trying to read; but he could not concentrate. He was summoned to tea and found Harriet alone. A message had come from the doctor to say that Ronnie was still just holding his own but no more.

Harriet questioned Richard about his life at Oxford and his father. 'I remember your mother,' she said. 'I saw her once or twice. She was beautiful—always the most beautiful person in the room. Your father must miss her all the time.'

'Yes, he does, he's always sad now. The house just goes on but it's deadly still and quiet. He can't seem to rouse himself.'

'Well, you must marry and bring some life into the Priory, mustn't you?' she said with a smile.

'I want to marry,' said Richard, the words coming out in a rush, and he told Harriet of his engagement, his father's disapproval and Mr. Barrington's reluctance.

Harriet sat looking quietly at him. He drew the photograph of Rachel out of his pocket and gave it to Harriet, who studied it for several minutes. Then she smiled at him.

'It looks as if you had made a good choice,' she said. 'She looks so serene and charming, and what fine eyes and wide brow. I think you are lucky, Richard.'

'Yes, I am lucky if I can overcome all this fimily opposition. By the way, it's supposed to be a secret.'

'I won't mention it to a soul, you are quite safe with me, but don't be daunted by opposition. She's the right person for you.'

'I am certain of that,' said Richard.

At that moment Sir William came in. He looked grave.

'Is it,' said Richard, 'bad news?'

'No,' said the Ambassador, 'not altogether. I have just had a note from the doctor. Ronnie is still holding his own, not more, but he thinks that is a good sign. He will come round this evening. You will dine with us and be here when Victoria comes. Now one thing we must settle, or rather two things. What do I tell his mother, and who is to tell Ronnie about this Marie? You will be back in Oxford. He cannot of course be told anything till he is recovering. What do you think, Harriet?'

'I imagine that his mother will be thinking of nothing but her anxiety for his health. I would suggest that you advise her to ask him no questions and not to speak of this affair unless he speaks to her about it.'

'Go on, my love,' said Sir William, 'please.'

Harriet smiled at him. 'As regards telling Ronnie, he must know the truth when he is strong enough to hear it. Otherwise he will go again to the theatre. I believe the kindest thing is to tell him straight out without giving him any hope at all that he can start again with this actress. Make him feel, I mean, that it is all finished. He will be sad and furious, and I fear angry with you, William, for giving him this news. But some day he will be grateful.'

'You are right as usual,' said Sir William, 'although I doubt his ever being grateful to me.' He was silent for a moment. 'The whole thing was nonsense from the start,' he said. 'I understand he wanted to marry her.'

'Yes, he did,' said Richard. 'He told me he thought they could live abroad.'

'The French are a hard headed and logical people,' said Sir William. 'This woman might have been temporarily attracted to the idea of being in London society as Milady Wentmore, but not to living obscurely abroad. For one thing she would never wish to leave Paris, no Frenchwoman does, or to give up her career as an actress. She knew that and was just playing with Ronnie and taking presents and money. This Frenchman you saw in her dressing room is the kind of rich protector that she needs. Well, if and when Ronnie gets well I must address myself to this.'

During dinner Lady Wentmore arrived. She was ushered into the dining room. The channel crossing had been both cold and rough, and she was torn with anxiety, but her face was set in lines of an iron composure. She looked as if years had added themselves to her age, but only her eyes, red-rimmed and sleepless, showed her feelings.

At that moment the doctor was announced. 'The crisis is passed, he should live,' he announced.

Lady Wentmore's composure cracked and tears ran down her face. She dried her eyes but the tears welled up again.

'I am sorry to break down like this,' she said.

Richard averted his eyes from her face. Harriet went forward and put her arm round Victoria.

'Come upstairs,' she said, 'to your room.'

Lady Wentmore stood up very straight. 'Can I see him?' she asked.

The doctor shook his head. 'It would not be wise tonight. He is sleeping. Come tomorrow morning.'

She had barely noticed Richard when she came in, but as she left the room she nodded to him. 'Thank you for what you have tried to do,' she said.

31

RICHARD's cold had become worse. He not only coughed but he felt as he would have described it himself, pretty odd. His head ached and there was a queer feeling of heaviness in his limbs. The channel crossing was uncomfortable and rough and stormy, like that endured by Ronnie's mother the day before. The journey to London seemed interminable. He drove to Paddington, found an empty carriage, stretched himself full length on the seat and fell into a deep sleep haunted by nightmares. As they were nearing Oxford he woke up and recalled that the train went on after Oxford by slow stages to the newly built junction at Dashbury, nine miles from the Priory.

Suddenly he felt a distaste for the idea of his small cold bedroom at Oxford and of lying there feverish and ill, so he stayed in the train, which stopped at several wayside stations before Dashbury Junction.

When he reached the Priory the house was silent and in darkness. He rapped on the door and rang the bell. It seemed an eternity till the door was unbolted. The figure of Johnson stood lit up by the lamplight in the hall.

'Mr. Richard!' he exclaimed, startled. Richard stumbled over the door step and nearly fell, to be caught and steadied by the butler. At that moment Sir Edward came out into the hall.

'Good heavens, Dick, you here? What's the matter? I didn't expect you.'

'I came home. I'm not feeling well,' said Richard as he collapsed on a leather chair beside the hall table.

A period of intense activity ensued of which afterwards Richard remembered little. He vaguely thought that he was helped upstairs, that someone was on their knees lighting a fire in his room. Then he found himself among the grateful coolness of sheets, but soon felt no coolness only burning heat.

His father's disturbed features came and went and then he was alone for a while. He dozed and woke with a start when the familiar face of the family doctor bent over him. He turned his head away as he had no wish to be disturbed, and while the doctor felt his pulse and listened to his breathing, he wished him miles away.

The nightmares came back, dissolved and faded, and he fell into an uneasy sleep. When he woke the room was still dark. His father was sitting by the fire where a kettle stood with steam coming out of its spout through a cylinder of brown paper.

Richard reached out his hand for a glass of water. His father rose stiffly to his feet, and put it to his son's lips. Richard lay back on his pillows—the world seemed again to stand still and not to whirl round him. His eyes caught his leather wallet which had been laid on a table near his bed. He looked at it idly as from a long way off. Next to it lay a little leather case. He tried to focus his eyes on it and then shut them, then opened them again.

Something from a long way off seemed to come to him, bringing a kind of peace and re-assurance. He lay trying to think why this was and fell again into a fitful doze. Rachel seemed there in the room, she came towards him and he tried to reach her but she vanished. 'Rachel,' he cried out hoarsely, 'Rachel.'

The doctor came again and made a more thorough examination. He looked at Sir Edward.

'He must have had a hard time, was there much trouble there? He's got something on his mind.'

'Rachel,' muttered Richard, 'Rachel, please come closer.'

The doctor's eyes met Sir Edward's across the bed.

'A young lady,' said Sir Edward heavily, 'at Oxford. He wants to be engaged to her but . . .'

The doctor looked at him under bushy eyebrows. He had been a country practitioner for many years and knew a great deal about the vagaries of the human spirit in illness.

He moved towards the door. 'Come outside with me, please, Sir Edward,' he said. 'I will bring a sick nurse during the day. You must get some sleep, and he must be properly nursed. You are not well yourself and I do not want you to break down, and I should advise you—' he paused abruptly. 'Is this young lady free to come here?'

'Yes, I suppose so.'

'Can her mother come with her?'

'She has no mother,' Sir Edward said reluctantly, 'but there is a lady who looks after the household.'

'Well, I'll give you my advice, however little you want it. It is absolutely necessary to keep Richard from fretting. Remember you are not bound to take my advice, but I feel bound to give it.'

Sir Edward said, 'It will make a lot of talk.'

'Talk,' said the doctor wearily. 'The people round here will talk us into our graves. But there are things which matter more than idle talk.'

The two men were old friends and the doctor put his hand on Edward Gervase's shoulder.

'Send your man along to Oxford, there's a train this morning, and let him bring the ladies back. Well, I must be off; and mind you, the moment nurse is installed, you must go and rest, or you will be ill too. I shall come back when I've done my morning calls.'

Mr. Barrington was just leaving his house in Oxford when a cab drove up and a man got out and walked across the pavement. Mr. Barrington had no idea who he was. The man touched his hat.

'I'm from Sir Edward Gervase,' he said, and tendered a letter sealed with a coat of arms.

Mr. Barrington, who was in a hurry, frowned and read the letter which ran into two pages, his face lengthening visibly as he did so. It ran thus:

'I fear you will be surprised to get this letter but I am in great trouble and anxiety. My son Richard is gravely ill, he picked up this illness in Paris where he went to see his cousin, Ronald Wentmore. Ronald became ill in consequence of a neglected cold and he's in a serious condition in a hospital there. My son' (here the pen had spluttered a little) 'is very ill in bed and keeps asking to see your daughter and will not rest until he has done so, our doctor says. Our family doctor is a man in whose words I place great trust. I should be so much in your debt if Miss Barrington could come at once, if it is possible, and if Mrs. Cunningham could accompany her, and stay here at my house until Richard is on the road to recovery.

'I should be deeply in your debt if you would allow Miss Barrington to come at once, my anxiety is very great.

'I have sent my man with this letter, there is a train from Oxford this afternoon which reaches our Dashbury Junction at four o'clock, and I would send a carriage to meet the ladies. I should take it very kindly if you would telegraph to me. Please make any use of my man for messages that you wish.'

Mr. Barrington re-read the letter. He looked up and saw the man staring hard at him.

'Mr. Gervase is very ill?' he queried.

'Yes, sir, there's very little hope.'

'Well, you get rid of the cab and come into the house.'

Mr. Barrington called to Mrs. Cunningham who was upstairs. Then he pushed open the baize door which led to the kitchen.

'Please look after Sir Edward Gervase's man,' he said to Annie, then stood at the foot of the stairs until Mrs. Cunningham came slowly down. He handed her the letter.

'Where is Rachel?' he asked. 'What are we to do?'

'You cannot refuse this, Arthur,' said Mrs. Cunningham. 'The poor man seems distracted, and no wonder. No, this is something to which you cannot say no—it would be heartless to do so.'

Mr. Barrington pushed his spectacles up until they met his hair. He disliked the implication in her tone that he was lacking in proper feeling.

At that moment Rachel came in. Her father handed her the letter. She grew very white and her eyes filled with tears. 'We must go at once, please,' she said to her father.

'Very well,' he said.

'Come and pack your things,' said Louisa Cunningham and Mr. Barrington was left standing in the middle of the room. Presently he recollected himself and wrote out a telegram, explained to Sir Edward's man where to find the Post Office, and then put on his hat and went out.

32

ALL through the journey from Oxford to Dashbury Junction Rachel sat straight up in the railway carriage looking in front of her and saying nothing.

As they drove up the avenue Mrs. Cunningham gave Rachel's small cold hand a squeeze. It was a dark winter's afternoon, still and cold, and the Priory stood with the belt of tree behind it, their every twig motionless against the sky. The house looked forbidding and coldly grey. The front door was open and as the carriage stopped Sir Edward came down two stone steps, his hand stiffly outstretched.

Rachel looked up and their eyes met. 'How is he?' she asked.

Richard's father did not appear to be more than just aware of her. 'Will you come up and see Richard, or would you wish to rest after your journey?'

'I would like to see him,' said Rachel.

Sir Edward suddenly recalled his duties as host. He shook hands with Mrs. Cunningham and said formally, 'Would you care to go up to your room?'

'Thank you,' she replied.

'The housemaid will take you there.'

Rachel and her host made their way up the staircase from the hall in complete silence. Sir Edward opened a door in a passage at the top of the stairs and Rachel preceded him into a darkened room. A woman rose from the side of the bed in which Richard lay, his hair ruffled, his eyes closed.

Rachel approached the bed, sat down and took one of Richard's hands in hers.

He opened his eyes and stared at her. 'Rachel,' he said, 'Rachel, is it you?'

'Yes,' she said, 'it's me.'

Richard's hot hand gripped hers. He had spent the morning hours only half conscious. Objects loomed large before him, and when he tried to grasp them they vanished into thin air. When he held Rachel's small cold hand in his he felt that he had come back from a borderland of nightmare to something which was calm and real.

'You won't go?' he said.

'I will stay as long as you wish,' said Rachel steadily.

The nurse, who was hovering in the background, said to her, 'Mr. Gervase should not talk please, that is doctor's orders.'

Rachel heard what she said. 'Richard you mustn't talk, just hold on to me.' She laid her disengaged hand on his forehead and her touch soothed his restlessness. He shut his eyes and lay quiet.

The nurse put her finger to her lips and Sir Edward took the hint. The nurse came after him.

'I think, sir, that Miss Barrington should have something to eat. I should say a cup of soup would be best, she looks so pale.'

Sir Edward, who was much more accustomed to giving orders than to receiving them, said nothing, but made his way downstairs where he rang the bell in the library and ordered the soup to be taken up to Rachel.

The nurse found Rachel sitting in the same position with her eyes on Richard's face. He had fallen into a light doze and his breathing was easier.

When the soup arrived she brought it to Rachel, who shook her head. But the nurse, who stood no nonsense from anyone, put the cup to her lips. The hot liquid brought a little colour into Rachel's face and she smiled gratefully.

Richard shifted his position and gripped her hand more tightly. The nurse put a cushion behind Rachel's back and retreated to mend the fire.

The doctor arrived and stood for a moment regarding Rachel. She looked for a moment at him and then looked away, her eyes resting on Richard's face.

'Shall I go away?' she asked.

'No, wait a minute.'

The doctor sat down at the other side of the bed and looked at his patient for a few moments.

'I think you had better go now for a short time,' he said to Rachel.

She withdrew her hand from Richard's with difficulty. It felt stiff and cold and as if it didn't belong to her. Richard moved and pushed his hand towards her. Rachel rose to her feet.

'Go and get a short rest,' said the doctor, 'or I shall be having you as a patient, too.'

Sir Edward opened the door and led her along the passage which curved round the well of the staircase.

'You are next door to Mrs. Cunningham,' he said, and Rachel went into the bedroom. At that moment Mrs. Cunningham opened the door between the two rooms.

33

Mrs. Cunningham asked no questions but led Rachel to the washstand where a copper jug of hot water stood neatly covered with folded towels. 'Now wash your face and hands and I will comb your hair.'

Rachel obeyed mechanically.

'He was asleep,' she said, 'but the doctor woke him.'

'Well, if he could sleep that is something, come and I'll do your hair.'

This operation completed, Mrs. Cunningham said, 'Better sit by the fire, this room is full of draughts.' At that moment there came a knock on the door and the doctor entered. He smiled a little.

'Will you come please, young lady,' he said. 'Dick is calmer and his symptoms are less grave. He is asking for you.'

Rachel followed him out of the room, her heart beating.

Richard opened his eyes when she came in, and as she sat by his bedside he gripped her hand tightly, shut his eyes and drifted off into sleep.

At dinner Mrs. Cunningham felt tired and rather hungry and was disinclined to talk; as Sir Edward sat down heavily, she glanced fleetingly at the portraits round the walls, at the silver caldelabra and massive silver trays on the sideboard. Then she dropped her glance to her plate, while she sought for a topic of conversation.

'The doctor says that your son is a little better.'

'He is no worse, certainly.'

Silence fell on them both like a mantle, and the meal progressed in its ritual with the butler handing dishes at intervals.

'The weather has been good on the whole this winter,' remarked Louisa Cunningham, who felt she must break the silence.

'Eh, what's that you say?' said Sir Edward, whose mind was elsewhere.

'I said,' repeated Mrs. Cunningham, slowly and distinctly, 'that the weather has been good this winter.'

Sir Edward looked at her and roused to his duties as a host said, 'I am sorry, I was thinking about Richard. Yes, the weather hasn't been inclement.'

'I quite understand,' said Mrs. Cunningham, 'that you prefer not to talk. I do not care for talking much myself, and you are having a very anxious time. But your son is young, and young people can stand more than older ones.'

Sir Edward told her about Richard's arrival at night on the doorstep. 'He caught this from his cousin,' he added. 'These young men and their love affairs, they make endless trouble,' he added.

Mrs. Cunningham ignored this oblique reference to Rachel and rose to her feet.

'If you will excuse me,' she said, 'I will go back to my bedroom in case Rachel should want me.' She left the room, Sir Edward staring after her.

Mrs. Cunningham went upstairs. She looked through the communicating door into Rachel's bedroom and saw that it was empty. A thought struck her and she descended the stairs. She found Sir Edward restlessly pacing the floor in the library.

'Excuse me, please,' she said, 'but how often does the post go out? I wish to write to Mr. Barrington and tell him of our arrival here.'

'If you will put your letter on the hall table, it will go then tomorrow morning.'

She remounted the stairs, shut herself in her room and composed a letter.

She was awakened by the door opening after a discreet knock and saw the nurse standing in the doorway.

'I think Miss Barrington should rest,' she said, 'will you come and see her.'

Mrs. Cunningham leapt to her feet and followed the nurse along the passage. The curtains had been drawn in Richard's room and he looked calmer. He still held Rachel's hand.

Mrs. Cunningham approached the bed and he opened his

eyes and stared at her, recognition dawning in them. 'Rachel must have a rest,' she said.

'She won't go away?' he said.

'Rachel must rest,' said Mrs. Cunningham firmly. 'She can lie down and can be fetched at any moment from her room. Come, my dear.' She put her arm round the girl and drew her to her feet. Richard relinquished her hand.

Rachel swayed a little and walked like a sleep-walker to her room to be given food. Her hand was stiff and a little bruised. When she had been made to lie on her bed she fell into a profound sleep, holding her hand against her cheek.

34

IN the next few days Richard improved slowly but steadily and Rachel's heart lightened. She sat by his bedside and they talked a little, and at intervals, when she had retired to her room, Sir Edward came and sat at his son's bedside. But there was a constraint between them in their exchange of conversation and Richard's eyes constantly strayed towards the door.

When the doctor had pronounced Richard out of danger, Mrs. Cunningham said to Rachel, 'Now we must go home.' Poor lady, she had found the days interminably long. She had several times in the evening pleaded a headache and a tray was sent up into her bedroom. She felt certain that Sir Edward would be as relieved as she was to be spared a tête-à-tête dinner.

His manner to her was courteous but aloof, and she wished he would break down the wall of silence between them. She felt that she would enjoy telling him how little anxious Arthur Barrington was for his daughter to marry Richard. But he gave her no opening for this, and she felt unable to broach the subject. Her reserve and shyness stood in her way.

One afternoon the footman came in to say that the doctor would like to see Mrs. Cunningham.

Louisa followed him through the maze of passages and found the doctor alone in the library. He shook hands with her, and asked her to be seated. He stood with his back to the mantelpiece and before she had time to speak he said, 'Richard is on the high road to recovery. I am satisfied that he is out of danger. His father should be grateful to you both for coming so promptly. It pulled him round.'

Mrs. Cunningham looked at him, her expression lightening. 'Then can we go home to Oxford?' she said.

'There is no reason why you should stay if you do not wish to.'

'I have no desire to stay here,' said Mrs. Cunningham. 'I have my household duties and Mr. Barrington's comfort to see to.'

The doctor paused and looked at the carpet at his feet. 'Do I understand that Miss Rachel is engaged to Richard?'

'He wishes to be engaged to her.'

'And she?'

'She wishes it too, but Mr. Barrington is not at all anxious for it to happen, and Sir Edward, I can see, does not like it at all.'

The doctor found himself liking this little Scotswoman who sat so stiffly in her chair, and answered his questions with such brief good sense. 'There is one aspect of it,' he said, 'which you have perhaps not thought of. Richard by asking for the girl to come, has forced his father's hand. There is endless gossip in the village and speculation is rife. People here love to talk and discuss the affairs of the great house, and they are all asking why this unknown young lady has come here. I should think that possibly people in Oxford may be talking, too.'

'May be,' was Mrs. Cunningham's only comment.

'It all points, I fear, to my having a talk to Sir Edward and to Richard. I don't look forward to it. Will you talk to the girl?'

Mrs. Cunningham rose. 'Can we go home tomorrow?' she said.

'May we leave this until I have talked to Sir Edward?'

She nodded and said, 'I will go up to my room.'

35

WHEN Mrs. Cunningham reached her bedroom she found the door between her room and Rachel's ajar and saw that Rachel was sitting by the fire. She was holding something in her hand which sparkled in the lamp light. 'Richard bought it for me in Paris,' she said.

Louisa took it and looked at it. 'It's very pretty,' she said, 'but, Rachel, we can't stay here, we must go home to your father. It will be causing so much talk if we stay.'

'Poor Cousin Louisa, I have been selfish, it must be so dull and difficult for you here.'

'I don't mind dullness or difficulty, though I am not saying that there hasn't been both of these, but go we must.'

'Yes, I suppose we must,' she said slowly. 'Richard is going to speak to his father.'

There was a knock at the door and the doctor stood there in the lamplit passage.

'I want to talk to you both,' he said. 'I think it is easier to talk here than downstairs.'

He pulled an armchair forward for Mrs. Cunningham and seated himself on a higher chair.

'Well,' he said, 'I have talked to Sir Edward and to Dick.' He paused. 'Dick is determined to marry you, Miss Rachel, and I understand that you are as much in earnest about this as he is.'

'Yes, I am,' said Rachel.

'I have known Richard's father for many years,' said the doctor slowly. 'He is not an easy man to understand, his wife's sudden death has shattered his whole life and he has banked everything on Dick. He expected him to marry some time, but hoped it would be a few years hence, not as soon as this.'

He looked at Rachel who still sat without moving. He continued, obviously not finding his self-imposed task a light one, and getting no help from either of the two women. 'Miss Rachel I understand that your father is a very distinguished scholar whose name is known beyond the boundaries of his college, but he lives in a world quite different to this one. Richard is attracted to your world and interested in it, but he knows that it is a different way of life to that lived by a squire in the depths of the country. The Gervase family has produced men who both read and collected books. Dick perhaps takes after them. . . . do you think that you would be happy in this house? There is very little society here and very few neighbours, I mean.'

'I should be happy anywhere if I was with Richard,' said Rachel.

36

RICHARD was sitting up in bed, his mouth set tight and his eyes alert.

'Come in,' he said to Rachel. She approached his bed and sat down beside it. He took her hand.

'It's all right,' he said. 'My father's given his consent to our being engaged.'

'Does he like it?'

'Well, he said yes, anyhow. I'm so happy. You're happy too, aren't you?'

'Absolutely happy.'

'What about your own father?'

'Well, he can't say no if your father says yes.'

'The doctor says I can come down tonight for dinner,' said Richard, 'if I come up to bed directly afterwards. Won't that be nice? You haven't dined downstairs yet, have you?'

'No, I have been sent up a tray in my bedroom.'

'Poor darling, you have sat in this room hour after hour. You must be sick of it!' Rachel smiled and said nothing. 'Wear your brooch tonight.'

'Of course,' said Rachel.

At dinner that evening Richard, who was sustained by the happiness of having got his own way, talked gaily, and Rachel responded with smiles. Mrs. Cunningham also exerted herself to put in an occasional remark. She had arranged to go back to Oxford the following day. She could therefore afford to look happier.

Edward Gervase sat torn by his joy at seeing Richard (though thin and hollow-cheeked) restored to life, and the knowledge that Richard would no longer belong to him. Underneath everything there was a deep wound in his spirit.

Richard noticed little of this, he drank a glass of wine, and with his eyes bright he said to Rachel, 'Show my father your brooch I bought in Paris.'

Rachel detached it from her dress and handed it to Sir Edward.

'A pretty trifle,' he said, as he handed it back to her.

'I think it's beautiful,' said Rachel as she clasped it back on to her dress.

'I must give you a ring,' said Richard, then changed the subject and asked for news of Lady Wentmore and Ronnie.

'They are coming back in a day or two. Mary joined them in Paris.'

'How is Ronnie?'

'Better, but not well yet. He's had a bad time of it.'

Dinner was finished at last and they went into the library.

'You must go to bed now,' said his father, and Richard said a reluctant good-night.

Mrs. Cunningham also rose and asked at exactly what time she and Rachel should leave on the following day.

When Sir Edward had finished telling her she said, 'We must go and finish our packing.'

Sir Edward looked surprised.

'But the housemaid should do that.'

'We prefer to do our own,' said Louisa Cunningham. 'Good night and thank you all the same.'

Not until the train was running through low-lying fields did Mrs. Cunningham feel a lightening of her spirit. Rachel looked out of the window, her thoughts intent on Richard. He had wrung her hand when they parted.

'I shall write,' he said, 'and see you soon too.'

Mr. Barrington was at Oxford station to meet them. He enquired after Richard's health, but nothing more was said about the visit to the Priory. A glance at Rachel's happy face made him realise that something had happened which would have strong repercussions in the future.

Rachel went early to bed and her father and Louisa Cunningham sat together in the little drawing room. Mrs. Cunningham, who was mending a sheet, carelessly torn in her absence, told him about their time at the Priory. He listened in complete silence.

'So there we are, Arthur,' she concluded. 'Will you now give your consent to the engagement?'

'I don't see that I can do anything else, but I can't pretend to like it, or that my daughter should marry into a family on sufferance, and unwelcome . . . well, it's the last thing I ever expected to happen. Anyway term's almost over, and I am tempted to hope that Richard will stay at home.'

37

EMILY came in the next day. She was breathless and exclamatory, and to an accompaniment of 'Oh dear', 'You don't say so', she listened to Rachel's story.

'Well, you are a lucky girl to marry into a family like that.'

'I am marrying Richard, not his family.'

'Yes, but look what you will get, a country house some day and horses and carriages and servants and money to spend, and jewellery. Has he given you a handsome ring?'

'No, he's given me this brooch.'

'It's pretty,' said Emily, considering it, 'but you should have an engagement ring too. Your father and Mrs. Cunningham must be pleased at your making such a good marriage?'

'My father isn't pleased at all,' replied Rachel. 'He talked to me this morning about it. He thinks I shan't be able to manage the life in a big house. I know I shall probably be stupid about it and I do wish that Richard and I could live in a small house by ourselves.'

'When are you going to be married?'

'I don't know, nothing's settled about that. What about you?'

Emily's face closed up and she looked secretive.

'Oh, nothing much,' she said. Then she continued. 'I have an idea that father's going away, he's dropped some hints of business somewhere else. He doesn't say, and if Mamma or I ask him a question he either snaps our heads off or closes up like an oyster.'

'But what will you do if he does go off?'

'I don't know. Mamma and I will have to get rid of the house and live in lodgings.'

'Won't your aunt help you?'

'I doubt it very much. She may just a little with old clothes, but now I earn a bit with sewing.'

'Oh, Emily, perhaps I can help you now.'

'I do need help in all sorts of ways,' said Emily, and for once her voice was flat and rather sad, and Rachel noticed that her dress was not as neat as usual.

'Are you worried about something?' she asked.

'Yes, I am worried about lots of things,' replied Emily, 'but I'm not going to talk to you about my worries at this time. We are going to think about you. And now what about your trousseau? I'd like to help with that.'

'I don't know,' said Rachel. She smiled, talk of a trousseau seemed to bring her marriage nearer and to open up a vista of delight unthought of hitherto.

'I shall talk to Mrs. Cunningham about it,' said Emily, and she made her way downstairs to do so.

Mrs. Cunningham had privately given the subject a good deal of thought and she was pleased to talk about it to Emily. Rachel was marrying into a wealthy family, and she should not (if Louisa could help it) go to her new home inadequately supplied with shoes, dresses and underclothes. She and Emily had a satisfactory conversation. Emily would supply taste and skill and Louisa Cunningham would draw on her savings to pay for this. They were in agreement on many things—one of which was that Rachel's underclothes should be made of the finest materials and trimmed with real lace.

Arthur Barrington felt that the logic of events had defeated him. He made the best of the situation and showed no disapproval. He had made his protest, and now that Rachel's engagement to Richard was an accomplished fact he said no more. Only sometimes Rachel caught him looking at her with a kind of puzzled sadness. He would look quickly away and speak of casual matters.

Richard did not return to his college to finish his studies for he only slowly recovered his health. As he had no need to earn his living his father decided that he had better stay away from Oxford. Richard chafed at this decision but felt that he could not fight against it, as his father had given in about his engagement. He came to see Rachel some weeks later, having caught an early train from Dashbury Junction, and returned home in the evening. He did not seek out any of his friends, he knew that it would irritate him to listen to their cheerful gossip and to be given condolences on his ill-health.

Lady Wentmore and Mary usually came over on Christmas Day, but this year they stayed at home with Ronnie.

'I had better go over and see him' Richard said to his father.

'I shouldn't,' said Sir Edward, 'if I were you. I have heard from Victoria that he doesn't want to see you or to be reminded of Paris. She says he is very difficult, and she and Mary are having a hard time with him. I am very sorry for them both. He is not a good-tempered fellow at the best of times, and now he is really impossible.

Richard went off after Christmas to Oxford. He brought Rachel a small ruby ring.

'This belonged to my grandmother,' he said. 'I asked my father if I could have a ring for you, and he said of course you must have one.'

'Did he mind giving it to you?'

Richard looked embarrassed. 'He doesn't like parting with anything of my mother's, but there are a lot of family heirlooms you must have.'

'I don't really mind about jewellery,' she said. 'I've got a little of my mother's.'

'I don't believe you want anything for yourself.'

'Not now I don't,' she replied, 'except to be with you.'

When the New Year had passed Mrs. Cunningham spoke to Mr. Barrington. 'We must settle the date of the wedding,' she said. 'Rachel's trousseau, thanks to Emily's help, is well in hand. There is no use in putting it off, and a long engagement is trying to young people, especially as Richard's father makes it hard for him.'

'Very well,' said Mr. Barrington, 'I will write to Sir Edward. I had hoped to have heard from him about it, but he has not written to me.'

The wedding was fixed for the beginning of May and the intervening months passed in the jerky way of engagements, with chequered times of happiness, small misunderstandings, and revivals of confidence.

Rachel stood patiently while her dresses were being fitted and a dressmaker, her mouth dangerously filled with pins, progressed on her knees round the girl's still form.

Emily had retreated to London in the vacations but returned to stay with Rachel and to press forward with her trousseau. She showed more interest in it than Rachel felt able to do.

38

RICHARD had made one or two suggestions as to who should act as best man at the wedding. His cheerful cousin Roger was a possible choice, or Paul Sibley. But when he consulted his father Sir Edward said that he would like Ronnie Wentmore, and Richard agreed without enthusiasm to this.

Rachel was thankful that there was no question of Paul. She saw him from time to time and his manner showed no more than an ordinary friendliness. Their conversation in the wood might never have taken place. In fact she sometimes wondered if she had imagined the whole scene. But she well knew in her heart of hearts that she had not imagined it and that she would never forget the undertones of strain and longing in Paul's voice. Perhaps if he wanted to forget, she also must try and do so. In that short hour amongst the trees she had grown into a woman and Paul's voice, like a note in music, would return to sound in her ears. She had not told Richard of the incident; later when they were married she would do so.

She was glad that he was not going to be Richard's best man and also that he had told Richard he would probably be unable to come to the wedding. He had given no reason, and Richard had been too much absorbed in his own affairs to ask about it.

Rachel received a wedding present from Paul, a volume of Wordsworth's poems bound in red leather accompanied by a note, merely giving her his good wishes for her happiness. she replied, thanking him and assuring that it would always be one of her most prized possessions.

The wedding day dawned in an uncertain glory of sunshine, and with slate-coloured clouds against which all buildings were sharply outlined. But sunshine prevailed and when Rachel and her father drove to their parish church, the air was full of the scents and sounds of spring.

Rachel walking up the aisle on her father's arm saw only Richard. Then she noticed standing beside him a young man whose face she did not know, and as she moved her head to the right saw Sir Edward standing erect with two ladies beside him. To the left were Mrs. Cunningham and Emily and the Maxwells.

In a dream she handed her bouquet of flowers to Emily and the solemn words and promises of the marriage service flowed over her. She prounced the words, 'I will' clearly— more clearly than Richard.

Then she emerged from the church on Richard's arm, and as they drove back to her home he put his arm round her.

Mrs. Cunningham had put all her housewifery and cooking lore into a wedding breakfast which should surprise the guests by its excellence and variety. George Maxwell made a speech saying what he had to say with admirable brevity and Rachel went upstairs to change her dress.

Lucy Maxwell tried to talk easily to Lady Wentmore and her

daughter. She introduced the subject of her relations at Dashbury Park and this topic served its turn for a few moments. Mary hardly spoke, and when she did so replied in a civil monosyllable. Richard came towards her and they talked for a few minutes.

'She looks quite different talking to him,' Lucy thought. 'Like a statue come to life.' Lady Wentmore spoke to Richard, then turned away and went to speak to Sir Edward. They exchanged a few words and then both stood apart, tall, silent and somehow alien.

'They might make more effort,' was Lucy's indignant thought as she circulated among the guests. Ronnie Wentmore was talking to a group of Richard's friends. He looked a little sulky but was trying harder than his mother and sister to rise amiably to the occasion.

Soon it was all over. Rachel, followed by Mrs. Cunningham and Emily, came down the stairs; there was a shower of congratulations, exclamations. Rachel embraced her cousin and Emily and Lucy, and shook hands with her father-in-law and was embraced by her father, as he put her into the waiting carriage.

Mr. Barrington turned back into the house and encountered Lady Wentmore on the doorstep. As he escorted her to her carriage she remarked, 'A very pretty wedding.' She said nothing more and she seemed eager in a stately way to remove herself and her daughter as quickly as possible.

The guests departed, only Lucy remaining behind to help Mrs. Cunningham and Emily to clear up the remainder of the feast and to put the house back to normal. George, prompted by his wife, suggested taking Mr. Barrington for a walk.

When Lucy had left, Emily ran upstairs to fetch something she had forgotten. Rachel's little bedroom had a look of frozen tidiness, and a cupboard, empty of her clothes, stood with its door ajar. She peeped into the drawing-room and surprised Mrs. Cunningham with a pocket handkerchief to her eyes.

'Don't cry,' said Emily, 'she's happy.'

'Aye, she's happy now,' said Louisa, 'her world is full of light and sunshine, but what will it be in the future? She deserves the best of things.'

'Yes she does,' said Emily, 'but it's no good thinking too much about the future.'

39

THE honeymoon was spent at the seaside. The moody and uncertain weather had passed and there was an even brightness about the days which made expeditions easy to do. They talked together a great deal, or rather Richard talked and Rachel listened, and, leaning against his shoulder, watched the tide coming in or going out, her eyes on the curling waves.

'The sea never bothers about anything,' she said one day. 'It just goes on and on, always the same. I wish people were more like that.'

'But don't you like people to be different, to change and alter, it would be a bit dull if they were always just themselves?'

'Not if they were their nicest selves,' she replied.

'We've all got nasty bits in us I suppose,' said Richard, 'but the sea can be nasty too, it wrecks ships and drowns people.'

One day she asked him about his mother and father. Richard obviously chose his words carefully.

'My father's all right,' he said, 'but he always liked things his own way really, till my mother died, although he would have liked more children. I wasn't born till they had been married some years and I had no brothers or sisters. But she made life so cheerful and amusing for him and he lived the life he liked best. Now that she isn't there the house is so dull and he isn't well, and he gets into the dumps and goes on doing things just because he feels he must.'

'When you go home I expect he feels more cheerful?'

Richard frowned and tossed a pebble into the sea. 'Yes I think so,' he said. 'I mean I think when I'm there it does cheer him up a bit and he feels things are a bit more worth while. I try to take him out of himself and make him come fishing and riding with me. Unluckily we haven't any near neighbours except Cousin Victoria and Mary.'

'She is rather alarming,' said Rachel. 'Lady Wentmore I mean.'

'Yes, I suppose she does strike people like that. I'm so accustomed to her that I don't mind her, and Mary's a dear really.' Rachel who had seen Mary's frozen stiffness at her wedding, said nothing. 'I hope you'll make friends with Mary, she's a real country girl and can tell you lots about country things. I'm a bit sorry for her, she can't have much fun now that Ronnie's back, he's so bad-tempered and not very well, and Mary has to be patient with him. He won't see me because of what happened in Paris so I haven't been there, but I shall insist on going to the Chase now I'm married. Cousin Victoria will call on you and I shall take you over there. It's a lovely place.'

'I'm sure it is,' said Rachel with a slightly sinking heart. 'But it's not your fault, what happened in Paris.'

'No, it's not and Ronnie knows it too, but he's a moody sort of fellow.'

The honeymoon over they journeyed to London and later in the day to Dashbury Junction.

On the steps of the Priory Sir Edward stood. As the carriage drew up to the door he came forward and shook hands with Rachel. The butler and footman followed him and took some small bags, while the luggage cart which held the rest of their belongings drove round to the back of the house. The servants were lined up in the hall—in their different grades of service. Sir Edward gave all their names and Rachel shook hands with each one of them, conscious of their curious glances. Some of them had seen her when she came to the Priory during Richard's illness. But they had had no more than casual glimpses, as she had spent her time at Richard's bedside and in her own bedroom, looked after by Louisa Cunningham. In spite of her inward tremors she looked composed and if her hand was cold inside her glove they did not notice it.

She was conducted up to her bedroom by her father-in-law. It looked light and pleasant. 'I hope you like it,' said Sir Edward.

'It's beautiful,' said Rachel, as she looked round. Not every object in it had beauty but the general effect was harmonious and pleasing. The walls were decorated with pale water colours of Italy. The chintzes were in soft colours and the room held a scent of lavender. The large mahogany wardrobe would have contained the effects of a princess, Rachel thought, and she smiled.

'I'm glad you like it. I will leave you now. Richard's dressing room is through that door.'

Rachel walked to the window and stared first downwards at the terrace and then beyond at the trees, river and soft distances.

Richard came in and put his arm round her shoulders. 'Well, what do you think of it?'

'It's all so splendid,' she said.

This was not quite what Richard had expected her to say. 'Don't you feel it's homelike?' he asked.

'Yes of course I do,' she said and to her horror she felt a pricking of tears under her eyelids. She moved away.

'Shall I unpack now?' she said. There was a knock on the door and her boxes were brought in.

'No, leave your keys on the dressing table, that will be done for you. No, I'll ring for Janet.'

When Janet appeared in answer to Richard's tug at the long tapestried bell pull, Richard handed her Rachel's keys.

Rachel smiled uncertainly at her. She had never been unpacked for since she was a child when her cousin had performed this office for her.

They made their way down the curving staircase with its shallow steps into the hall and from there into the drawing-room. Its dust sheets and holland bags had been removed in honour of Richard's bride, and everything, ormulu, brass and walnut, shone with endless polishing. The pictures on the walls were speckless and the whole room had a slightly self-conscious air of being for once at its best, like a scene in a theatre when the curtain has just risen.

'Will you give us some tea?' said Sir Edward. He pulled out a chair and waited till Rachel had seated herself.

She gravely poured out the tea, her hands trembling. She took up a small silver tea strainer and then dropped it on to the silver tea tray where it fell with a clatter which seemed to her to ring noisily through the room. Then, wishing to put more hot water into the teapot, she pulled the embossed tea urn too sharply towards her and the teapot over-flowed. She glanced helplessly at Richard, who took the overflowing teapot from her and refilled the cups. Sir Edward was watching them with an inscrutable expression on his face.

'I'm so sorry,' she said.

'It doesn't matter in the least,' said Richard, 'mother always had trouble with that tea urn.'

'I don't remember it,' said Sir Edward under his breath.

Rachel ate a small piece of paper-thin bread and butter and Richard cut a cake and passed her a slice. She had felt hungry but her appetite vanished, quenched by the array of food spread out on the table and her sense of failure with the teapot and urn. The elaboration of the meal, although she was accustomed to good Scotch teas at home, overwhelmed her appetite.

'What would you like to do?' asked Sir Edward. 'I think you should see the house.'

'Yes, you saw nothing of it when you were here last,' said Richard quickly. 'I'll take her round, father, and tomorrow you must show her the pictures.'

The two young people walked first the length and breadth of the house and then up the stairs to the attics.

'We won't go into the kitchen part,' said Richard. 'Mrs. Crocker will be doing the dinner—you can see her in the morning.'

Rachel's spirits rose a little when they looked at the attics where Richard's rocking horse stood amongst a dressmaker's dummy, old trestles, battered chairs and tables. Then they descended a staircase which led to more and more bedrooms and then more staircases and on to the floor of Rachel's room.

'These are the best bedrooms for honoured guests.'

The end of the passage widened out and showed two doors.

'That's my mother's room,' said Richard. 'It's always kept locked except occasionally when the housemaids are allowed in. My father always kept it like that. He moved to this room when she died,' he said, indicating a door on the left of the passage, adding, 'I can't think why he chose it, it looks north and doesn't get the sun.'

Back in her own bedroom Rachel saw her own hairbrushes and little pin cushion on her dressing table. The room was the same as she had last seen it except for the fact that she realised that the large wardrobe and the massive chest of drawers must be full of her belongings. She peeped into the wardrobe which had appeared to have swallowed all her dresses with plenty of space left over.

The next few days passed in a daze for Rachel—a daze of alarm, interest and strangeness. She had visualised her married life as time spent with Richard and although they had their walks together visiting the gardens and the park and loitering beside the river, there was always someone who looked at her with frank or veiled curiosity. Gardeners, keepers and grooms greeted her with the countryman's reserve at every turn. They all belonged to families who had been for generations in the service of the Gervase family. Most of them had never moved from their small orbit of a few miles round the Priory and Oxford was only a name to them. London, though more distant, they had heard about and some had gone from the village to the great Exhibition at the Crystal Palace. This was still spoken of with awe and astonishment; but Oxford represented nothing to them at all.

In the house Rachel had interviewed Mrs. Crocker, the cook. This stout and motherly woman had seen from the way Rachel spoke to her, that the girl before her was alarmed and rather confused and had tried to put her at ease by showing her the array of shining pots and pans, the glistening jelly moulds. She led her into the dark cool larder where joints of meat stood guarded from flies by dome shaped covers. Mrs. Crocker presented Rachel with a slate framed in wood, on which were written out the list of the meals for the day.

'Will you order the meals each morning, Madam?' she asked.

'I don't know,' said Rachel.

'Sir Edward orders them now, but it doesn't, if I can say so, seem quite the thing for a gentleman to do.'

'Does Sir Edward wish me to do this?'

'Yes, he spoke of it this morning.'

'I had better ask him,' said Rachel.

She plucked up her courage and did so when Richard was in the room.

Sir Edward said curtly, 'Certainly I think you should do this.'

'Yes,' said Richard, 'Mrs. Crocker's a good soul. She will tell you all about things.' He smiled encouragingly at her.

40

MARRIAGE is an unknown country to those who are new to it, a country which abounds in surprises. Two newly married people seem to explore the heights of understanding with each other, and then fall into the depths of misunderstanding. And when the wife is placed in surroundings unfamiliar to herself, but taken for granted by the husband, the difficulties are apt to gain momentum. Rachel discovered this, and being sensitive her mind groped painfully amongst an annoying confusion of small things.

Richard was happily oblivious to most of this, and he tried at first not to be impatient with her. He found her one day in tears and enquired why she was crying. She told him of an accumulation of little things.

Mrs. Crocker was kind but did not readily welcome Rachel's timid suggestions about the daily menus. The girl had been taught simple cooking and the rules of economy by her cousin in Oxford, and it seemed to her that a great deal was wasted in the kitchen. The vast joints, shrouded by their covers under which they looked like greasy fossils, rapidly disappeared, to be replaced by others. Jellies and large cakes, of which little were eaten in the dining-room, vanished and were no more seen there. The morning visits to Mrs. Crocker were increasingly irksome.

The servants were supposedly at her beck and call. But she never wished to avail herself of their services. Her bedroom she kept with scrupulous tidiness, and finding that some of the drawers in her chest of drawers could be locked, she put away some of her childish treasures there, although she had a feeling that Janet the head housemaid resented this.

Her father-in-law's aloofness chilled her spirit. She could not hide from herself that she made no headway with him, and although he never uttered a word of criticism, she felt that he was watching her all the time and noting every slip she made from absentmindedness or of ignorance of his way of life. The picture of Lady Gervase smiled or pouted at her from each room. Tables were laden with the mementoes of her life, cushioned by money and social success.

Richard dismissed the question of waste with careless ease. 'There's bound to be a lot of waste in a house like this,' he said. 'You can't help it.'

'But ought we to waste food when so many people haven't got enough to eat?'

'There's nothing to be done about it,' he said with a touch of impatience. 'Mrs. Crocker's been here since before I was born. She's a good cook, and they are always a bit wasteful, and I'm sure Janet doesn't mind you locking up your things, you're only imagining that.'

The most patient of women dislike being told that they are only imagining things. Rachel dried her tears, feeling ruffled.

She said nothing about Sir Edward. This went too deep and he would surely come round if he saw that Richard was happy. Her talk ended by Richard telling her that she didn't go out enough and he took her in a pony chaise for a drive in the lanes.

The only person she felt at home with was the old head gardener. His parents had been long in the service of the Gervases, having migrated from the Border country of Scotland when he was a child. He clung fiercely to the idea of his native land (although he had only once revisited it) and had a contempt for the softer ways of the English countryside. He drove his under-gardeners with a zeal which defeated any efforts they might have made to slack in their labours, and he only remained on good terms with Mrs. Crocker because of the excellence of his garden produce. No one, she felt, could look askance at such fruit and vegetables, but she rarely praised him when the overflowing baskets were brought in from the garden.

He had heard that Louisa Cunningham came from Scotland and assumed that Rachel was touched at any rate with good sense. He welcomed her in a reserved way into the large greenhouses at one side of the walled garden. He liked silent people and he cut her a few flowers each time she came into the garden when he was working there, and when he was in another part of the garden Rachel would sit on a bench and dream, though dreaming was not easy now. There seemed somewhere to be a cutting edge of reality which shredded her thoughts.

One day, soon after they arrived at the Priory, Lady Wentmore and Mary were invited to come and pay their wedding call on Richard's bride. Sir Edward had waived the formality of an early afternoon call with cards left on Rachel, if she had happened to be out. Richard went to the front door to meet them and Rachel remained in the drawing room. She knew that this was an important moment in her life and she stood in an expectant pose hoping that her smile of welcome would not betray her inward nervousness.

Lady Wentmore came in with her hand outstretched. Mary followed her. Richard arrived a moment later talking to Ronnie Wentmore. He had been asked to come to the Priory by his mother. He was reluctant but his sister clinched the matter by saying, 'Don't be such an ass, Ronnie, you've got to meet Richard some time.'

This and a curiosity to see Rachel again had made him say grudgingly that he didn't mind coming.

The ladies sat down at the tea table and at that moment Sir Edward entered the room. Rachel suddenly realised that her elder visitor, under her mark of civil pleasure, was also in the grip of some emotion akin to nervousness. This steadied Rachel, who managed the business of the tea pot and the urn with complete composure.

Her small head was held high as she sat straight up while Lady Wentmore enquired after her father and her cousin with a slight air of condescension.

She was conscious of Richard's glance quickly averted as he turned his head to talk to Mary, of Sir Edward's steady refusal to look in her direction and of Ronnie's eyes openly fixed on her face. Mary talked to Richard and then looked down at her plate.

'Don't you think this is a beautiful room?'

'Yes indeed I do,' said Rachel.

'It must seem odd to you to be in such a large house, and this must be a great change for you after Oxford? How do you like the quiet of the country, Oxford seems such a bustling sort of place?'

'I love the country,' said Rachel.

'Do you ride?'

'No I haven't ever ridden but Richard will teach me, I hope.'

'Do you play croquet?'

'I don't play very well.'

'Well you must come and have a game with Mary, and lawn tennis, do you play that?'

'I never have.'

Rachel became increasingly uncomfortable during this questioning. She rose, and addressing her father-in-law said,

'Shall we go out of doors or into the drawing-room?' She turned to Lady Wentmore and said, 'Which would you like to do?'

'I should like to go out.'

They filed out of the room into the hall. The drawing-room door was open and Lady Wentmore remarked to Sir Edward, 'I must look in there, it's a long time since I saw this room. You've taken it out of its curl papers I see."

She stood on the threshold of the drawing room and surveyed it through her lorgnettes and then dropped them with an audible sigh: 'What happy times we used to have in here in Marian's time.'

The young people at Richard's suggestion went for a little walk, leaving their elders seated on the terrace.

Rachel found Ronnie beside her.

'How will you like it here?' he asked.

She was startled and showed it. 'Of course I like it, it's Richard's home and it's a lovely place.'

Ronnie took a look at the surrounding landscape. 'It's lovely all right,' he said, 'and the Chase, too, I suppose is considered lovely, but they are dead alive holes in my opinion. I want to get away and I'm going to. I'm going into a regiment.'

Rachel saw his unhappiness. 'You've been ill,' she said gently, 'and that makes people depressed. Do come over here sometimes.'

'Can I come and talk to you? I haven't much to say to Dick, and Cousin Edward freezes me up. I expect my mother freezes you up too, but you put a good face on it at tea.' He smiled at her with a slightly conspiratorial way.

'I felt rather nervous,' she said.

'You didn't look it. I watched you. I know my Mamma. She's a good hand at making people feel shy—but you and I can be friends. You won't get very far with Mary, she only cares for dogs and horses, but I've been about the world a bit and I should like to talk to you.'

Rachel looked at him a little helplessly. She had no wish to receive his confidences.

Richard and Mary turned towards them at that moment and they walked back to the house.

A day was fixed for them to go and see the Chase, and then Lady Wentmore asked for her carriage.

When they had been seen off Richard said, 'You did very well at tea. Cousin Victoria's pretty alarming when she asks questions.' He picked up a loose stone from the steps of the front door and threw it on to the path. They had both heard her remark about the drawing room but neither spoke of it, and they walked silently back into the house.

41

On a fine July day Rachel journeyed to Oxford to stay with her father. It was all so familiar and easy from the moment she stood on the platform of Dashbury Junction to the moment when she saw her father's tall figure on the platform at Oxford. There was no doubt of his pleasure in seeing her or of Louisa Cunningham's joy at her arrival, although they were neither of them given to hearty expressions of pleasure. She went up to her little bedroom. It looked just the same as when she had left it. Only she felt different.

There was a pleasantness to Rachel in seeing the small house where she had been born and brought up, with every object in it hallowed by a memory, often absurd enough, but familiar and somehow endearing. It was pleasant, too, to walk down a small flight of stairs snugly carpeted and not polished and slippery; also to sit in the little drawing-room after dinner and to hear the faint clop clop of the horses' hooves from the small evening traffic which passed the house.

Sitting in the garden the next morning she pondered. Richard and she were happy in their married relationship. She knew that he had fallen in love with her partly or largely because she represented in his mind a quietness and sympathy. The shock of his mother's death, his father's sorrow and gloom, and the sense of tension in the house had made him turn to her to give him the peace of mind he needed. She thought to herself that she was becoming irritable, that she laid too much stress on trifling annoyances, that each time she did so Richard was disappointed in her. He was unreasonable in this as he had unwittingly placed her in surroundings where trifles bulked very large in daily life. But unreasonable or not he was her husband and she must give him the help he needed. He went out a great deal and saw to many things that his father had let go owing to melancholy and ill-health. Sometimes she went with him to see an outlying farm or to look at a wood or plantation, and she earnestly tried to understand something of the rotation of crops, the condition of barns, the endless fret and complications of the landowner's position. Richard was touched by her efforts but was not good at explaining matters of that sort to her. She tried in a tentative way to ask Sir Edward about his properties, but he looked so much surprised that shyness descended on her like a cloud. She quickly realised that his wife had never taken any but a fleeting interest in their land, or in fact any interest at all, and he could see no reason why Rachel should do so.

'If you want to know about estate management ask Victoria Wentmore,' he said. 'She has it all at her finger ends.' But this was the last thing that Rachel wished to do. She could imagine Lady Wentmore's slightly contemptuous amusement if she asked her questions.

They had returned the visit to the Chase, and Rachel had been as much charmed by its beauty as repelled by her reception there. Lady Westmore showed her the lofty rooms politely but with cold perfunctoriness. Mary had made no friendly advance to her and Ronnie had shown her a marked attention which embarrassed her.

'I wish you would try and make friends with Mary,' said Richard on their return to the Priory.

'Well she doesn't give me much chance.'

'She's very shy.'

'Im rather shy too, Rachel had said.

Rachel's reflexions were broken into by the opening of the door at the back of the house, and a glad cry of 'Rachel' and Emily swept into the garden slamming the door behind her. After an embrace they settled down to talk.

'What are you doing out here alone? You looked as if you were brooding about something?'

'I'd got a bit of a headache and Cousin Louisa thought that some fresh air would do me good.'

Emily gave her one of her sharp glances, but had the tact to say no more.

'Tell me about yourself,' said Rachel, 'you said you wouldn't say anything just at the time of my wedding.'

'No I wasn't going to spoil anything for you then.' She sighed and smoothed out the fingers of her glove. 'I've had a bad time,' she said. 'My father's gone away and left us. He left a note and a little money to go on with, he said he'd got a job in the West country and would send us some more, but it's my belief that he won't come back ever.'

'What *are* you going to do?'

'Well I've persuaded mother to get rid of the house and to go into lodgings, cheap ones. She made an awful fuss about her sticks of furniture, she cried over every bit and piece of it, and the people who came to look over the things weren't very nice about them, but it's settled now. We've got another situation for the girl and now we're settled down I can earn quite a bit more with my sewing. Poor Mamma mopes and cries but in her heart of hearts she is glad to be rid of the house and of father, and I am trying to pay off the bills.'

'But you must let me help you,' said Rachel. 'My father gives me a little allowance and Richard too and I have heaps of clothes and there's nothing I want to buy.'

After a long discussion Emily agreed to a loan from Rachel to settle the bills. 'I shall repay it sometime,' she said.

'I shall give you some money now and send the rest when I get back to the Priory,' Rachel said.

Emily squeezed her hand. 'You are the most generous person I know,' she said.

'I'd do more than that for you,' Rachel replied. 'But is that all? You don't look well.'

Emily's gloves received another smoothing, she pulled at the fingers with impatient jerks. 'There is something else. I told you, didn't I, that I met a man one day in the street who picked up my bag and we talked and he asked me where I lived, waited for me and we walked round the square and then went and sat in the Park. We often met. Mamma didn't know, and she was too miserable anyway to notice what I was doing. She thought I was seeing Madame about my embroidery because she's given me lots more commissions and I've asked for more money. She didn't like it but her customers are very pleased with what I do so she had to . . . I said I should take my work somewhere else if she didn't pay better.'

There was a silence, during which Rachel looked anxiously at Emily whose eyes were now bent on the ground.

'Mamma went away leaving me alone with the girl. I let her go home for the night to her mother and I went off with him. I thought he was taking me to a small restaurant but he said he would give me dinner in his room instead.'

'But Emily—'

'Yes I know it was wrong, the whole thing was all wrong but I was feeling desperately depressed and wretched and didn't care what I did. You're a married woman now so you will understand better than when you were a girl.'

'Go on please,' said Rachel, 'and I'll try to understand.'

Emily clasped her hands tightly and bowed her head. 'If you don't understand nobody ever will,' she said. 'I stayed the night there and got back early the next morning. The girl hadn't come back and I had time to arrange everything as if I had slept at home the night before. She didn't suspect.'

'But Emily, this man, I don't know his name—'

'You won't ever know it,' interjected Emily.

Rachel continued, 'But surely he will marry you?'

'He can't. He's married already. I found that out after that night. I asked him if he was going to marry me and he showed me his wife's photograph. Then I rushed out of the house.'

'Oh, my poor Emily.' Rachel put her arms round her friend. 'I am so dreadfully sorry. Do you love him?'

'I might have perhaps, he was—he was someone who made you do what he wanted—no I don't love him, I hate him and I was terrified by what I had done.'

'Do you mean—'

'Yes, I thought I might be going to have a baby.'

Rachel clasped her more tightly.

'Well, it's all right. It didn't happen, but I shall never be the same person again.'

There was a pause then Rachel said, 'Could you try and forget it?'

Emily shuddered. 'I shall never do that,' she said, 'as long as I live, and the worst of it is . . .'

She burst into noisy sobbing, and then said with a little air of defiance, 'I've met someone else. I took to going into church near us, and I prayed for myself and I told the Lord of my repentance and I was a little comforted. I always knelt in the darkest part of the church, as I so often ended up by crying; well one day someone put a hand on my shoulder and I looked up and I saw it was the clergyman who took the services. I had liked the way he said the prayers, and his sermons were short and I liked them too. He looked at me with such kindness in his face and asked me if he could help me in any way. I must have looked a sight and with my face streaked with tears. The congregation had gone by then and he sat down in the pew by me and we talked and I said I was very unhappy, and he said very little, but somehow he comforted me.'

'You didn't tell him what had happened?'

'No I couldn't tell a gentleman and certainly not a clergyman, could I? I should have died of shame. I told him about father leaving us and our going into lodgings, and he said could he come and see Mamma and me, and I said yes if he didn't mind it all being so shabby. He smiled and said his life was lived among really poor people and shabbiness didn't worry him at all.'

'And did he come?'

'Yes he did and he was so kind to Mamma and his visit cheered her up and she asked him to come again, and I go regularly to church and he does come to see us.'

'Is he married?'

'No.'

'Could he want to marry you?'

'I think perhaps he might some day, but, Rachel, I couldn't marry him, not after what I've done.'

'But if he's so good and kind, he would understand.'

'Being good and kind and marrying someone who's done as wrong as I have are different things. He couldn't marry a sinful woman. But do you think I could keep silence if he asked me to marry him? No one knows about it—'

Rachel thought for several minutes. 'That would be founding your life on a falsehood,' she said, 'and you would live in fear of meeting this man again.'

'I know,' said Emily, 'I'm caught in a trap. Oh, Rachel, you would like him. He isn't good-looking, he's got an ugly face and he's short, not tall and handsome like Richard, but you feel somehow so happy when you are with him, and I would work so hard to try and help him.'

Rachel aghast at Emily's revelations, but swept along by her narrative, could say nothing but, 'Slip upstairs and wash your face and stay to luncheon here. You don't have to get back, do you?'

'No, I'm only down here to see you for two days. I'm camping with one or two of the servants and living on cats' meat.'

'Cat's meat, oh dear, how terrible.'

'Well, not really cats' meat, but odd scraps of cold stuff.'

'Well, spend the days here, we shall be so glad to have you and you can have proper meals anyhow.'

Rachel sat on in the garden, while Emily went upstairs. Her mind was in a turmoil of shock and unhappiness. Her own troubles seemed almost trifling compared to Emily's. She shivered although sunshine was warmly illuminating the little garden.

Paul came into the house in the afternoon. He had just finished his examinations but had not heard their result. He looked tired, but as usual he came into the room bringing with him a feeling of steady cheerfulness. Whatever thoughts were nagging at the back of his mind, he greeted Rachel with cordiality, remarking that it was a nice surprise to see her.

'What are you doing here, Paul, after term is over?' asked Louisa Cunningham.

'Just packing up my books and things, and waiting for my viva; it didn't seem worth while to go home.'

He spoke pleasantly to Emily and was invited to stay to tea and to await Mr. Barrington who had gone for a long country walk. He enquired after Richard.

Rachel said that he was well. The talk round the table went on and Rachel found herself enjoying it. Emily joined in and they laughed at jokes which were not in themselves very funny. There was an ease about the talk although Mrs. Cunningham was apt to prick any balloon of fancy with a short and sensible remark. But that made the young people laugh again and Rachel looked with blank astonishment at Emily.

'How can she be gay after all that's happened?' she thought. 'If it had happened to me I should have been crushed and wretched.'

It was not the moment to think of Emily's troubles, however, as the light cheerful talk went on. Paul was looking at Emily with amused eyes. He seemed to like her today. She was more subdued, had more charm of manner.

Rachel found herself wishing that this little tea party would go on. The summer evening was warm and still. She could see that the trees outside the window were barely stirring their leaves.

Mrs. Cunningham asked Paul about his plans. He said he was going home, and then to start in a barrister's chambers in London.

'I may be staying near Gervase Priory with a parson friend of my father's. Could I come over and see you?' he asked Rachel.

'Yes, please do,' said Rachel, 'just write to Richard. He will drive over and fetch you himself, and he will be so pleased to see you.'

'And I to see him too.'

Rachel smiled at him and saw Emily's eyes on her face.

'I wish I could ask her to stay,' she thought, but put the idea from her. She could imagine her father-in-law staring at the girl not knowing what to make of her and despising her for being a little Cockney, the sort of person he had never had before in his house.

The evening was hot and the soft soporific atmosphere of Oxford pressed down on the city.

Rachel felt listless and tired and was persuaded to go early to bed. There was a heaviness in her limbs and she woke with difficulty in the mornings feeling a little sick.

One evening Louisa Cunningham came up to her room with her. It was brilliantly light outside, one of the longest days of the year. After a look round the bedroom, Mrs. Cunningham paused and sat down in the armchair. She gave a slight cough. 'Rachel, you do not seem well. There is nothing worrying you is there?'

'I don't feel very well,' said Rachel. 'I feel tired and rather odd in the morning.'

'You must be going to have a child,' said Mrs. Cunningham, her voice calm and interested. 'That is quite right and I am very glad.'

Rachel's heart bear fast and she sat down abruptly on the bed feeling a little dizzy with joy and relief. So that was why she felt irritable and cross sometimes, and inclined to mind small slights and inquisitive looks. She had heard that women when their babies were coming were like that. Then she was flooded with joy. Joy at having Richard's child—how pleased he would be.

Louisa remarked, 'Naturally living in a house with those men you would not know about it, but you can talk to me. Long ago I had a child.'

'I never knew . . .'

'I never speak of it. No one but myself and old Jessie in Fife remembers it. It died at a few months old. Well, we'll forget this and think about you, but I can advise you.' There was a just perceptible pause and Louisa went on, 'I can speak of it now. I couldn't for years but that's all over. Now we must think about you. Have you thought of seeing the doctor?'

'No.'

'Well then you must see him at once. I liked him when Richard was ill, he had sense.' Mrs. Cunningham pronounced this as if it was spelled *saince*. Rachel knew it was her highest meed of praise. She fell asleep smiling happily.

42

THE day of Rachel's return Richard went to meet her at Dashbury Junction. The Junction, built amongst fields a year before, had a look of newness and strangeness. It was painted a sad colour, neither yellow nor grey. The only pretty thing about it was a plaque with an interlaced cypher bearing the date of its building. This was placed high up on the wall beside the footbridge. Richard was not interested in railway architecture, and he did not notice the curious effect of the roofing with its teeth like a portcullis about to be let down. He thought of it only as a necessary but hideous blot on the pastoral landscape, and useful as a place where you could arrive and depart.

Richard helped Rachel to alight and as they drove together through the lanes he asked her one or two questions about her time in Oxford. She told him that Paul might be staying somewhere near the Priory.

'He must come and stay with us,' said Richard. 'I believe my father would like him, everyone likes Paul.'

That evening in their bedroom she told Richard about her baby. He clasped her in his arms and he murmured after some time, 'My father will be pleased, especially if it's a son.'

Rachel felt a little chilled. 'Only if it's a son?'

'I shall be delighted whether it's a boy or a girl,' said Richard, 'all I want is for you to be all right.'

'Cousin Louisa says I must see the doctor.'

'I'll send for him tomorrow.'

'Couldn't I go and see him? It's somehow so public. I mean everyone will talk if he comes here.'

'Yes of course I'll take you over there tomorrow. Can I tell my father?'

'I wanted it to be just our secret. Please, please wait till I have seen the doctor.'

They drove the next day to the doctor's house and Richard left his wife while he drove the pony chaise round the lanes.

Rachel confronted the doctor and with hesitation and embarrassment told him why she had come. He tried to put her at her ease, asked her a few questions, gave her some simple instructions and then added, 'Well don't move furniture, or listen to the old wives' tales other women tell you about the bad times they had. Walk about and get as much fresh air as you can and don't worry. I will come and see you from time to time, or you can come here if you prefer it. You will be well looked after.'

Rachel's heart resumed its normal beat. The little room with its simple furniture seemed a haven of common sense and kindness.

Richard drove up to the door and the doctor smiled at him and nodded his head. 'I wish you both all luck,' he said. 'Your wife's all right; be careful of her but don't fidget her, and don't let anyone else upset her either.' He turned back into the house.

Sir Edward received the news of the expected baby with mixed feelings. He was pleased at the thought of an heir, another Gervase to carry on the line, and a slight annoyance that Rachel's child should inherit the stately property, money and all the perquisites of his position. He was uncomfortably aware that he was doing nothing to make Rachel's position in the house easier for her. At times she looked puzzled and strained. He told himself that she had married Richard, and that that should surely suffice to make her happy. She had got what she wanted and was therefore a very lucky girl. She needn't be so sensitive about things. He was aware that for Richard's sake she tried to please him, but only because he was her father-in-law and it was her duty. There was no affection in her attitude to him or in his to her, and he measured her up all the time to his wife and found her wanting in the qualities he admired. She was pretty, he saw that, but she had no dash or style and she brought no one to the house who had any social brilliance. He felt sure that the servants discussed this. Bedrooms empty of guests were swept and polished, Mrs. Crocker cooked elaborate meals for a small number of people, life went on and on. Richard and he had endless discussions about the estate, but Richard seemed rather restless. After they had pulled things round it would be time to find some other work for him to do. It might be a good thing for him to stand for Parliament, it was in the Gervase tradition and Rachel might be happier living part of the year in London. So his thoughts rambled on

Anyway, he would now try to show Rachel more consideration as the mother of a Gervase child. Logic of thought and fineness of perception were not in his character, and his features, fine drawn by sorrow and sleepless nights, were those of a man who (like an oak split by lightning) is hard put to it to thrust out green leaves in the spring.

He did not mention the matter of the expected baby to Rachel, but treated her with slightly more courtesy and care than hitherto. He compared her in his mind to his wife, who had made a great deal of her condition and had spent the months before Richard was born in a picturesque languor, lying on sofas and seeming glad to squeeze out every drop of the importance of her frail state of health, while Rachel took walks and continued to read and study.

She tried to put difficult and tiresome thoughts out of her mind. Richard was kind to her, if rather unaware of her daily difficulties, but at any rate he was always concerned that she should not overtire herself. Rachel was deeply unhappy about Emily. She sent her the money for paying her mother's debts and asked Richard if a hamper of vegetables and flowers could be sent from time to time to Mrs. Deering from the Priory gardens. This was arranged, and Macandrew, who usually disliked parting with any of his carefully tended flowers and fruit, was as gracious about this matter as it was in him to be. Rachel's baby had been discussed by the servants and commented on in the village. Curiosity was mounting and Rachel was conscious of a changed attitude in the people surrounding her. She disliked their furtive glances, but managed not to show this, and gained in dignity as the time went on.

Paul arrived one evening in the late summer, to be greeted by Richard at the Junction. They were so glad to see each other, to talk of Oxford and their friends, and Richard was sorry when the carriage turned in at the gates of the Priory.

When the butler asked Paul for his keys Paul confessed that he had mislaid them, but that as there was nothing valuable in his luggage it didn't matter, and they went in to see Sir Edward, laughing together.

Sir Edward looked up and saw his son's friend for the first time. Paul advanced and shook hands. His smile lit up the room and Sir Edward found himself smiling in return. There was something simple in Paul's approach to his fellow human beings so that they confided their troubles, often embarrassingly, to him. Sir Edward found himself talking to this thin shabbily dressed young man with an ease which surprised him.

Presently Richard and Paul mounted the stairs and a door opened and Rachel came on to the landing. Through a tall window the light of the late summer evening illuminated her and she looked at Paul in the brief moment before they greeted each other. Her face had matured into a different kind of beauty and her figure, more loosely draped, showed that she expected a child. They talked for a few moments, then separated to dress for dinner.

Richard said to his father, 'We must drink Paul's health, he has got a first.'

'Of course,' said Sir Edward, and they did so. Paul looked pleased but a little embarrassed.

'Was your Viva very difficult?' asked Richard.

'No, they only asked me one question because they couldn't read my handwriting. It is very bad, I'm afraid.'

Dinner went through, it seemed to Rachel, with unusual speed. Richard and Paul talked of their Oxford friends and Paul brought Sir Edward into the conversation, and he appeared to enjoy it. Rachel talked a little more than usual, and when she left the gentlemen to their port wine and retired into the drawing room, she felt as if a fresh breath of wind had blown into the house.

She took up her embroidery, averted her gaze from Lady Gervase's work table, and put in a few stitches. She sat on a wide window seat to catch the last gleams of light. One of the peacocks had flapped up into the cedar tree and was indulging in an occasional mournful screech, said by country people to herald rain. Her mind was in confusion. The heat of the day had tired her body, but her mind was refreshed by Paul's conversation. He had drawn her back into a world she understood, and now knew that she loved. The annoyances of her daily life fell away from her.

The peacocks proved unreliable weather prophets. There was only a small shower of rain the following morning and the day became fine and warm. Rachel went out to sit under the cedar tree where there was a round stone table on which books and papers could be spread. If touched by anything it gave out a ringing sound.

She settled herself in a chair and saw Paul walking towards her. He sat down on the other side of the table. 'What a beautiful place this is,' he said.

'Yes it is,' replied Rachel, her voice sounding a little lifeless. 'Richard looks very well I think.'

'Yes I think he is well, the out-of-door life suits him.'

'Do you miss Oxford?' he asked.

Rachel was startled. 'Yes, all the time,' she said. The admission forced out of her, she flushed and looked up into the branches of the old tree.

Paul moved restlessly in his chair and played a five finger exercise on the top of the table which gave forth some small hollow notes. He dared not ask her if she was happy. His love for her, which he had relegated to a room in his mind on which after her marriage he had shut the door firmly, came flooding back over him.

Rachel stopped studying a group of cones on a branch of the cedar tree and looked down on to the table. She was trembling a little.

Paul said, 'Oh, by the way, Sir Edward asked me to tell you that he has had a note from Lady Wentmore, she and her daughter are driving in this direction this afternoon and would like to look in about tea time to see you.'

'Oh dear,' said Rachel, 'I hate it when they come. They

don't like me and Lady Wentmore is so patronising, and I hate being patronised.'

'Well you've got three of us to protect you,' said Paul, smiling.

'Sir Edward doesn't protect me, and he and she just look at me and I drop something and make a silly remark.'

'But surely Richard—'

'No Richard doesn't help, he and Mary get on very well and talk to each other about the same things.' Rachel was very near to tears.

Paul said, 'Well, I'm sure Richard really means to help and I'll do my best.'

When the family carriage from the Chase drew up and the two ladies were ushered into the garden Rachel had recovered her composure. A cloth had been spread over the round stone table and the tea urn glittered in the sunshine.

Paul, to Rachel's astonishment, seemed to find Victoria Wentmore easy to talk to. He asked her opinion on the current political scene and enquired what she thought of various political personages. She became quite animated.

Sir Edward, though disclaiming any knowledge at first hand of London life and the doings of Cabinet Ministers, was interested, mainly because several of them had been at Eton with him, or at Oxford, or in the Brigade of Guards. Paul listened to his reminiscences and returned to a skilfully flattering interest in every remark of Lady Wentmore's, while Mary and Richard seemed amused by the anecdotes which Paul recalled of various august figures who had visited Oxford to receive honorary degrees. Rachel found herself drawn into the talk and quoted her father's conversation with a famous personage, whose replies to his questions had been disappointingly unintelligent and uninformed.

Paul laughed and a sense almost of hilarity prevailed. Rachel realised that he had turned this tea party into a pleasant occasion, rather than a penance, where the personal feelings of a group of people resulted in silence and remarks edged faintly by malice.

When the ladies took their leave and were escorted to their carriage Rachel and Paul sat on under the cedar and after the men servants had cleared the table, she said, 'Thank you so much, you made it all seem so easy, it's usually so difficult for me, and it was going to spoil a lovely day.'

'Well it's the bright day which brings the adders out, as Shakespeare has so well said,' remarked Paul, playing a little tune on the stone table with his long fingers. 'Not,' he added, 'that I should dream of comparing those two stately ladies to adders. I rather like Lady Wentmore, she said one or two very shrewd things about politics.'

'Oh Paul, if only you were always here,' said Rachel. In the silence that followed she realised what her remark implied. 'I mean,' she went on hurriedly, 'please come sometimes, you are such a help. You've cheered up my father-in-law quite a lot.'

At that moment they were joined by Richard. 'Come for a walk, Paul,' he said. 'Rachel, you must go and rest.'

Paul and Richard walked across the park, skirted the river and leaned their elbows on the top of a hump-backed bridge in companionable silence.

'It's nice having you here,' said Richard.

'It's nice being in such a beautiful place.'

'Oh it's beautiful all right, but land-owning's not much fun really, it's an endless bother about crops, bad harvests, grumbling farmers and so on and so on. My father has let things go a bit and our agents are old-fashioned and not much good, and I am trying to plug up a lot of holes—it's a fretting, restless sort of business. I envy you going into the law, that's a straightforward job.'

'You won't think so when you see me struggling as a briefless barrister.' There was a pause and Paul aimed a small stone off the parapet at a group of rushes by the river.

'Are you and Rachel going on living here with your father?'

'Why ever not?'

'Oh,' said Paul, aiming another stone at the rushes, 'I just thought perhaps you had a small house on the estate.'

'We have several,' said Richard frowning, 'but if we left the Priory my father would be bitterly hurt.'

'Wouldn't it be better for Rachel? Wouldn't she like a house of her own?'

Richard looked bewildered and a little cross. 'I can't see why,' he said stiffly.

'Well, my mother always says that every woman should have her own home which she can manage as she likes. She and my father have always been poor, but since the day when he was a curate they have always had their own house.'

'Rachel has got nothing to complain of,' said Richard sharply, 'she's never said anything to me.'

Paul realised that he must not pursue the subject any further.

43

RACHEL had written to tell Emily about her expected baby and had received in return a loving and congratulatory letter. Emily said little about herself, only mentioning that she was not returning to Oxford. She was busy with her sewing and in the evenings would make some clothes for Rachel's baby, and also make Rachel a pretty negligée garment to wear in her bedroom. She had evidently decided to say no more about her difficulties but had at the last moment put in a crumpled postscript before posting her letter—the stamp was crookedly stuck on to a soiled envelope. The postscript ran:

'I gave up going to church and then he came round to see us. Mamma was out and he asked me why I didn't come, and I burst into tears and he said he was sure that something was making me very unhappy, and I said yes and he said couldn't he help me and I said no but I have started going to church again sometimes.'

Rachel derived a small amount of comfort from this epistle, but she wondered unhappily what would be best for her friend. It was all such a mess. Her thoughts went round and round and she surprised herself by thinking if only Emily had told no one of her escapade (even herself), no one would have known. But Emily had in her character a fundamental honesty, she would always tell things, good or bad about herself regardless of consequences. If she married this clergyman, even if the other man never crossed her path again, it would come out some time. Emily could never keep a secret for a life time—so she mused.

Rachel had been to Oxford to stay with her father and she wanted very much to talk to Mrs. Cunningham, but forbore to do this, as she felt tied by her promise to Emily. She had never mentioned the subject to Richard. She had still not told him about Paul and what he had said to her that day in the wood. She had been on the point of doing so, when something stopped her. It was wiser unsaid. The friendship between the two men could be spoilt, and the day in the wood was best forgotten, though it was not forgotten by Paul. Something in his voice had held a deeper undertone than friendship, when he came to the Priory. She pushed the thought away.

Her father noticed the languor and fatigue and spoke of it to Louisa Cunningham. 'She looks tired,' he said, 'and she seems unlike herself, I think.'

'Women in her condition often do,' said Louisa, but she felt disquieted about Rachel herself.

'She needs some intellectual interest,' said Mr. Barrington. 'Living with that father-in-law of hers can't be very stimulating, and Richard, who is by no means stupid, seems to have thrown himself into his outdoor work of keeping the property going, but the conversation about it cannot be very enlivening. I will talk to her.'

He did so that evening. He asked her if there was nothing she could do in the way of cataloguing the library at the Priory.

'There must be work to be done there,' he said.

'I don't know if Sir Edward would like it,' said Rachel.

'Well if you get Richard to ask him surely he will. Or aren't there any old papers that you could look through and sort out? A family like the Gervases, must have interesting material and it would give you something to work on if you cannot get about much.'

Rachel received this idea reluctantly at first, then she agreed to consider it. This was more to please her father than because she expected anything to come of it.

Mr. Barrington travelled back to Dashbury Junction with his daughter and stayed at the Priory for a few days. He was at first oppressed by the house, the elaborate meals and the falling leaves from the trees. He was pacing up and down the terrace with Rachel who caught a leaf in her hand.

'They say that if you catch a falling leaf you have a happy year.'

'I earnestly hope that you will.'

Mr. Barrington was not a demanding guest. Richard and Rachel were so pleased to see him that Sir Edward could do nothing but show some kind of hospitable pleasure in his visit But he had not been able to think of much entertaining for his guest. The late autumn weather was blustering and cold, and the rain came down with a sullen determination at frequent intervals. The sun shone rarely and then retreated behind clouds.

It struck him that the library might provide something which, perhaps, would keep Mr. Barrington happy, or if not happy, at any rate occupied. 'Has Rachel taken a look at the books?' Mr. Barrington asked.

'Yes, I believe she has, I have seen her taking one or two out. She reads a great deal, Richard tells me.'

'I brought her up to read books and to care for the things of the mind,' said Mr. Barrington with a slight edge in his voice.

At that moment Rachel came into the room and Sir Edward rose to his feet. 'Please look at anything you like in the library,' he said as he left the room.

Mr. Barrington glanced at Rachel. 'Let's have a look round,' he said. He pulled a chair forward. 'You sit down,' he said, and he put a cushion at her back. 'I'll hand you anything I think would interest you.'

They passed a very happy morning together and at the end of it Mr. Barrington said, 'Well, there's a lot of interesting stuff here.' He pulled out a sheaf of papers which had been pushed between two tall eighteenth century volumes with tooled bindings. The letters were yellow with age and gritty to the touch. Mr. Barrington sat down at a table and started to decipher them.

At that moment the luncheon gong rang and Sir Edward came in. Mr. Barrington rose. 'We have had a most interesting morning,' he said. 'I have looked with Rachel at a great many of the books, and now we have found some papers. May we look at them together?'

'Please,' said Sir Edward, 'do look at any books or papers you like in this house. There are some in the attics in trunks, I will have them brought down here.'

━━━━ 44 ━━━━

MR. BARRINGTON departed for Oxford. He was pleased that he had discovered an interest for Rachel. She had brightened up, he thought, and had handled the books and papers with intelligence. He had promised to send her some history and reference volumes, and he foresaw for her a good deal of the sort of work he held to be the most rewarding.

Richard had been out shooting while his father-in-law was at the Priory and came in with a fresh colour which faded in the evenings. Mr. Barrington was not usually observant about the looks of his fellow men, but where Richard was concerned he observed him closely. He had had hopes of Richard as a moderately intelligent undergraduate, but somehow the deadening atmosphere of the Priory had turned him into a country squire with a perfectly good (Mr. Barrington admitted to himself that it was good) piece of land-owning work to do. But he was troubled about Rachel. He couldn't get her out of his mind. The pictures of Lady Gervase oppressed him, it was almost as if the house was haunted.

Rachel had asked whether Mrs. Cunningham could come to stay for Christmas. She had told Richard that she did not feel that she could manage the village Christmas tea and the Christmas treats without help.

'Wouldn't you like Cousin Victoria and Mary to come and help?' asked Richard.

'No, certainly not,' said Rachel stung into an uncharacteristic asperity. 'I don't want them, they'll only make me feel that I'm doing everything wrong, besides they've got their own Christmas festivities to do.'

Richard looked worried but agreed. He seemed unable to bring the Wentmores and Rachel together, and the future in that direction was dark. However, he thought to himself, when the baby was born Rachel would be easier to do with, and he asked his father whether Mrs. Cunningham could come.

Sir Edward agreed to this. He rather liked Mrs. Cunningham and he felt helpless about the Christmas parties. His wife had always made Christmas so cheerful, the house blazed with lights, a monster bunch of mistletoe hung in the hall and polished holly leaves lay on the top of all the pictures. He sighed: 'Yes, do let Rachel bring her cousin here and we will try to make it as cheerful as we can.'

The tone of his voice indicated no great hopes of this, but he had at any rate given his consent.

Rachel then asked if Emily could come and stay for a few days before Christmas and Richard looked mildly aghast at this.

'But why do you want her? I don't think . . .'

'What don't you think?'

'I mean I don't think my father and she would get on very well.'

'I'm asking her to be with me. I've never asked for anything before, and she's the only friend I've got,' and with that Rachel burst into a flood of tears and Richard consoled her as best he could. Then it suddenly occurred to him that his father had expressed a wish to go to London to his club and to visit an old friend who was ill at his London house.

'Look here,' he said, 'ask Emily to come and I'll take my father to London for two or three nights and you will have her all to yourself—would you like that?'

'Oh, that is a good idea. I will write to her and Cousin Louisa at once.'

Rachel's heart lightened. She and Emily could talk to their heart's content and then Cousin Lou would help her through Christmas and she could face the ordeal of the baby's birth in February with less apprehension.

The winter was a bad one. The roads were flooded in places and the whole country side smoked and reeked with damp. No one could visit anyone else in this weather and Rachel could hardly go out. She worked with determination at the books in the library and on the old papers which she had spread out on a table hoping that their musty smell and gritty surface would diminish by exposure to the air and the gentle dusting which she gave them. She felt heavy in body, but the work on the lives of long dead people who had had their joys and tragedies restored in some degree a sense of proportion.

Mrs. Cunningham and Emily both accepted the invitation and Rachel had pleasure in allotting their rooms and thinking of how to keep the draughts away as much as possible from Mrs. Cunningham's bedroom. The incessant winter rain had made the house damp, and the fires smoked. She must warn Cousin Lou to bring all her warmest clothes, thick shoes and galoshes, and she would see to it that Emily possessed at least a solid mackintosh. She sent her some money for this useful purpose—hoping that Emily would be sensible and not divert her present to buying a new dress or hat.

She met the house carpenter in the passage, he was grumbling to himself as he gazed at some patches of damp which had appeared on the wall. He looked cross and there was slime on his clothes and Rachel knew that he had just emerged from his daily inspection of the roof, or rather the many roofs which, like hills and deep valleys, were hard to climb, and where water collected and lay in stagnant lines.

As she passed along the passage she heard him muttering, 'It will be a bad day for the house if nothing is done.'

'Can I do anything?' she said.

'You can speak to Mr. Richard, mum,' he said, 'something's got to be done, Sir Edward won't do nothing.'

Rachel listened patiently to his rambling explanations, 'An old pipe has burst inside the house,' he said, 'but I can't get into her ladyship's bedroom, it's as much as my place is worth to ask for the key, but it's all getting worser and worser and I can't get at the pipe without going into her cupboards.'

Rachel said she would do what she could and went downstairs to find Richard. She explained to him what the carpenter had said.

Richard frowned. 'Yes I see,' he said. 'Well my father will have to lump it, that pipe must be put right or the whole place will be flooded. He'll hate it. He's never let that room be touched except very occasionally dusted. He keeps the key of it and the cupboard on his watch chain, but something must be done, and I will speak to him at once. Luckily we go off to London tomorrow, and if it's done while he is away he won't know so much about it. I'll go and try and make him see sense.'

45

THAT evening Rachel was sitting by her bedroom fire reading quietly. It was the hour in the day which she liked best. Richard usually came in and talked to her about all he had been doing in the day time and she valued their *tête-a-tête* and the nearness it brought them.

There was a knock on the door and when she had said 'Come in,' it opened, and Sir Edward entered the room.

Rachel smothered an exclamation of surprise. She looked at him. His face was furrowed by unhappy lines, and he sat down heavily into the arm chair on the opposite side of the fire.

'I want to ask you to do something for me,' he said.

Rachel looked at him. Her heart smote her, he seemed so strained and odd. 'Yes, certainly,' she said in her gentlest voice. 'What is it?'

'The damp which has collected on the roof is damaging the house. My house carpenter says a pipe is leaking in the cupboard in my wife's bedroom. It must be looked at and mended and I do not want the servants to look at my wife's belongings, her cupboard has been locked since she died. I could not endure the thought of looking through her clothes myself and I would not permit anyone else to do so. Her maid who had gone away became ill and died at the same time as my wife. I shouldn't have minded her looking through them. When Richard and I have gone off tomorrow by the early train could you go and look through the cupboard and take her clothes out of it? I do not wish to see them. You can dispose

M

of them as you wish. It would not, I think, be a heavy piece of work for you to do. You could take them into what used to be my dressing room and lay them out there.' He hesitated and stared into the fire. 'I shall be gone to London and shall try and forget about this. It is very painful to me.'

'Of course I will do it,' said Rachel warmly. 'I am so glad to be of use. I sometimes feel that you never let me help you.'

He looked at her with astonishment and then said, 'If you feel like this, I am sorry and I apologise. Perhaps in the future you can help me more. I should be glad of help.'

Rachel in her turn was astonished. 'I will try, indeed I will,' she said earnestly, and in the lamplit bedroom there came a sense of happiness and a sudden easing of strain.

Sir Edward rose and then handed Rachel a bunch of keys. 'Open anything which is locked.'

'And if I find any letters or papers,' she said, 'what shall I do with them?' she asked.

'You won't find any,' he said. 'My wife was not a letter writer.' He made it sound as if letter writing was a slightly degrading occupation. 'If you do, just tell Richard when he comes back, and he will destroy them. But you won't find any, I'm certain.' He paused at the door. 'Thank you, my dear,' he said.

Richard came in a few minutes later and Rachel told him about his father's visit.

Richard's face lit up. 'You don't know what a compliment to you this is. He has asked you to do something which he would never have asked any one else. Cousin Victoria once asked if she should look through my mother's things, and he said almost rudely, "Certainly not." I am pleased about this.'

'He was so sad and somehow pathetic,' said Rachel. 'I am so glad to do it.'

'It augurs well for the future if you and he can get on better,' said Richard. 'It will make me much happier.'

The Gervases, father and son, departed from Dashbury Junction by an early train and Rachel breakfasted in bed. When she had finished she rose and put on an old dress.

She walked along the passages to Lady Gervase's bedroom,

clasping the bunch of keys. One of them bore the legend on an ivory tag: 'Her Ladyship's Bedroom'. She entered the room which smelt musty. She went to the window and drew up the blind and opened the window. The weather had improved and wintry sunshine poured in through the panes. She managed to push the window up and a gust of air came in. She looked around the room and walked to the other side of the bed and pulled the curtains there. She glanced at the dressing table. Its legs were sheathed in a gaily patterned chintz. The gilding in the ornate looking glass was dull, the glass itself was covered by a sort of haze. Rachel caught a glimpse of her own face in it. The reflexion gave her a mortal pallor and look of pain. She shivered and looked away. She would have liked to look at all the objects in the room, but knew that this would be wasting time. Emily was arriving at tea-time that afternoon, and it was most necessary to get this job finished before she came. She laid the keys down on the sheeted bed.

The wind blowing into the room rattled the curtain rings. Rachel looked round her but nothing stirred in the room which seemed to have withdrawn into a death-like silence.

She found the key of the cupboard and opened the door. A smell of damp and decay came out of it. She saw that it was one of those vast and cavernous cupboards to be found in ancient houses which go back into the thickness of a wall.

A large array of clothes were hung on wooden pegs at its side and Rachel was disagreeably reminded of a Bluebeard's cupboard. Upon the floor were lines of shoes of every colour and shape, and hunting boots flanked by boxes which evidently contained hats. Rachel cautiously took a step forward and lifted down a dress which was hung by hooks on two wooden pegs. Moths fluttered out of it in a cloud, but she grasped its ample folds firmly in her hands and took the dress to the window and laid it over the sill. The skirts billowed out above the magnolia on the wall of the house, whose polished leaves made a faint clicking sound as they clashed together in the breeze. The moths vanished into the daylight and Rachel unhooked each dress, cape and cloak and laid them down in the window seat or upon the window sill. A remark of their cook at Oxford came back to her. 'Moths don't like to be hurried,' and she hoped that the air and sunshine would displease and disperse them.

Then she took up armfuls of shoes. They were stained with damp and mildew. They gave Rachel a pang of unhappiness, they were so small and pretty, suggesting dancing and frivolity while exhaling a smell of corruption. Then she pulled the boxes out of the cupboard. More moths flew out as she opened them and draggled bonnets and sodden ostrich feathers and artificial flowers came into the light of day. She worked quickly and methodically, her eyes becoming accustomed to the half darkness which lurked in the depths of the cupboard. It seemed to her hours before she had cleared everything out of it. Time had ceased to exist for her until she heard the strokes of twelve o'clock from the stable clock borne on the breeze into the room. This gave her another hour before the gong would summon her to a solitary luncheon.

She had managed to open the further window in the room and on the window seat she had heaped the shoes and hats. They made a deplorable looking mass of untidy muddle—perhaps when they had dried out something could be done about them.

Opening the cupboard door as wide as it would go, she sat down to consider what to do next. She would summon the house carpenter at once and he must deal with the damp which would soon be seeping in through the ceiling and walls. She must remove these things into what had been Sir Edward's dressing room. She unlocked the door of his old room and pulled up the blinds, opened the windows and then looked round. It was a man's room with sporting prints hung on the walls, but it was empty of any personal belongings. They must have been removed when her father-in-law went to occupy a bedroom at the other end of the house. She carried several dresses and two riding habits fretted with moth holes into the dressing-room and again heaped the window sills with hats. The wind caught some ostrich feathers on a hat and lifted them as if they had come to life.

Rachel looked into a mahogany chest of drawers. The clothes, though frail and yellowing, were dry and neatly folded between layers of discoloured paper. She closed the drawers with a sigh. She must return to them tomorrow. She dared not go on too long for fear of becoming exhausted. She sat down again panting a little and her ears caught a faint sound of a drip drip from the cupboard. She had put a box of matches into her pocket, and she brought it out and lit a candle which stood on the writing table. Grasping the heavy candle-stick in her hand, she stood on the threshold of the cupboard to see that she had left nothing there. There was a scuffling noise in the wainscoting and Rachel, who shared the fear of mice and rats common to her sex, recoiled for a moment. Then she stepped bravely through the door. She had done her work thoroughly and there were no clothes, hats or shoes left in the cupboard. But under a pipe in the far corner from which the dripping sound had come she saw a square object. She advanced holding the candlestick in front of her and discerned that it was a box. She picked it up and, clasping it in her arms, brought it into the bedroom. She had no key for it, but as she tried to open it the top of it came off in broken pieces and the contents spilled on to the table and the floor below. There were packets of letters, tied with what had been narrow blue ribbon which, frayed and torn, snapped as she looked at them as they fell on to the carpet. The box itself was made of leather with the Gervase arms stamped on its lid. The gilding of the arms was hardly discernible and as she grasped its side they fell to pieces and lay on the table.

Rachel stooped and picked up the letters. Apart from spots of mildew the letters had not yet been made illegible by damp. She remembered her father-in-law saying that if she found any letters they should be given to Richard. Well anyway that was something she need not think about. She had found on the floor of the cupboard a bag embroidered with an elaborate pattern in tapestry work. She looked inside it, the satin lining though damp had remained fairly clean and she took up the letters and found that it held them all—it also held the fragments of the box. She locked the bedroom door, leaving the windows open.

Back in her own room, which seemed alive with sunshine, she caught a glimpse of her face in the mirror and saw that it was streaked with dust, while a lock of hair hung down over her forehead.

She washed her face and hands, tidied her hair and rang the

bell and asked for some luncheon to be sent up to her. She wanted very little to eat as she had a headache. She put the tapestry bag away in a drawer—it was full of holes and the moths had traced on it a pattern of their own where they had eaten away the elaborate design of flowers and fruit.

46

RACHEL returned to Lady Gervase's room after her tray had been carried away. She found the house carpenter and another man in the depths of the cupboard. They were muttering to each other as they tried to locate the cause of the leakage of water. The bedroom had lost its sealed up look. The windows were open and a chill blast came in.

Rachel unlocked the door of Sir Edward's dressing-room and attacked the sorry heaps of clothes with determination. She shook each of the dresses out of the window. She then closed it and went out into the passage. She found Janet, duster in hand, hovering there, and caught a glimpse of intense curiosity on the housemaid's face. She gave orders that Lady Gervase's bedroom should be cleaned and said that the chests of drawers were not to be opened.

It occurred to her with a sense of relief as she walked along to her own bedroom that Emily would help her on the following day. Emily always liked looking at old clothes. Then she remembered the tapestry bag into which she had stuffed the letters, and she took it out of the drawer and looked at it when she got back to her room. She would dry it by the fire and then hand it to Richard when he returned, and also give him the ruined box.

As she lifted it out of the drawer she noticed that there was a slit in the bottom of the bag. As she grasped it to take it to the fireside several letters fell through on to the floor. Picking them up it occurred to her that it would be best to spread them out and lay them on a footstool to dry. They were stained with damp and creased at their corners, but if she laid them out flat they would be easier for Richard to read. So she smoothed out each letter and made a mounting pile of them on the footstool.

As she placed the last one on top of the pile her eyes caught a few lines written in a bold hand—

'We will meet at three o'clock. You are sure, aren't you, that E. does not suspect anything?' It was signed by an illegible initial.

The words at first did not penetrate into Rachel's brain. She pushed the footstool a little nearer to the fire and sat down in the armchair beside it. The fire was burning cheerfully and a small coal flew out of it. It landed on the floor by the footstool. She retrieved it with a shovel. As she turned round from doing this her eyes caught the words on the paper again, it was only about three lines. She lifted it up and looked at the one underneath.

It was dated Monday, and began 'Dearest M.' Rachel read on with growing repulsion as the sordid intrigue was revealed in one letter after another. She clutched the edge of the mantelpiece as her mind struggled with first incomprehension and then disbelief.

'Dearest M.' And Lady Gervase's name was Marian.

Louisa Cunningham had impressed on her when she was a child that it was in the highest degree dishonourable ever to read a letter not addressed to herself. She had never had any temptation to do so. But this was something quite outside the rules of her elders. Richard must never see these letters, they would destroy all his love for his mother. He would never, of course, mention them to his father. Rachel shuddered as she thought of the carefully preserved image of Marian Gervase, her perfection in every relation in life as built up by her husband and accepted as gospel by her son.

She sat down and stared at the large pile of letters. Then a thought struck her so forcibly that she gasped and almost choked. What a complete reversal of fortune it would be for her if she let Richard see the letters. All the slights she had endured, the daily feeling of her own inadequacy would cease. If he showed the letters to his father or his father even noticed a change in his attitude to his mother's memory and her much exalted virtues it would break his father's heart and spirits and would probably even hasten his death. The crashing of Marian from her pedestal would bring ruin and destruction to his mind.

In some French novel which she had found in the library she had read the phrase which as she remembered it, ran thus, 'Never handle idols: the gilding will come off in your hands.' She had unwittingly done this and was plunged into a sea of uncertainty. Her thoughts ran to and fro. Was it not perhaps better that Richard should know the truth rather than subscribe all his life to the legend of a false goddess? Was it not better, far better, for herself that the Gervases should not treat her as if she could never come up to the ideal of her mother-in-law? Or was she selfishly wanting a complete and final revenge? Then she thought of Edward Gervase's visit to her room and his slightly softened manner to her, and the way he had trusted her to look through his wife's belongings. But then if her position in the house was altered would not she and Richard have more happiness together and more understanding? Her thoughts whirled round and her eyes sought the clock which at that moment struck three strokes.

Emily's train was due at Dashbury Junction at a quarter to five, and Rachel had said she would drive there in the brougham and meet her. She rose up and carefully collected all the letters, put them back into her chest of drawers, turned the key on them and rang the bell. When Janet appeared she said, 'Have you cleaned her ladyship's bedroom?'

'We've done what we could, madam, but it needs more of a clean tomorrow.'

Rachel asked if the house carpenter had finished. Janet shook her head and replied, 'Oh no, he found the leak in the pipe but there might be another one somewhere, and he will have to come back several times. He says it's all in a shocking mess,' she added.

'I expect it is,' said Rachel, who felt suddenly very tired. 'I shall not be going to the station to meet Miss Deering,' she said, 'I am going to have a rest. Will you please ask Miss Deering to come straight up when she arrives and we will have tea up here.'

When Janet had gone Rachel took off her dress and put on the negligée Emily had made for her.

Janet's words 'a shocking mess' lingered in her mind—a shocking mess indeed.

Rachel lay down on the sofa at the foot of the bed and shut her eyes. Emily mustn't know. No, indeed, Emily must not know. She would put the whole matter out of her mind and talk about Emily's difficulties and let her roam over the house and look at Lady Gervase's clothes. That evening she must think of what could be done, when Emily had gone to bed. She tried to rest and still the beating of her heart. For the baby's sake she must keep calm. She tried to doze but found it impossible.

She rose up and opened the door and presently heard voices in the hall, a measured tread on the stairs as the butler, followed by Emily, came up on to the landing.

Emily was full of exclamations. What a handsome bedroom Rachel had got, how cold the journey had been, and how was Rachel? 'You look very pale,' she said.

'Everyone does who has a baby coming,' said Rachel calmly.

Emily seemed satisfied by this, but insisted on pouring out the tea when it came, as Rachel's hands were shaking. She cast some sharp glances at her friend.

'My hands always shake now,' said Rachel, trying airily to dismiss the subject.

Rachel told her about the clothes and Emily's eyes glistened. 'I love looking at clothes,' she said. 'You might find some of them useful later on. I expect they are made of good satins and laces.'

Rachel gave an involuntary shudder. 'I've got lots of clothes,' she said, 'but you must take anything you want. My father-in-law said I could dispose of them as I wished.'

Emily clasped her hands together smiling with delight.

'We can't look at them by lamplight,' said Rachel, 'but we will sort them out tomorrow morning after breakfast.'

She escorted Emily to her bedroom and was made happy for the moment by Emily's delight in its size and handsome appointments. One of the many portraits of Lady Gervase hung there. Emily stared at it and said,

'She looks lovely. You must find her hard to live up to.' She glanced at Rachel's white face and shapeless figure. 'I expect your father-in-law makes you feel all the time that there was never anyone who could come up to her.'

Rachel looked helplessly at the portrait which smiled down at her with the insolence of admired beauty.

'Yes,' she said, her voice sounding strange in her ears, 'he's always making me feel that, all the time.'

'It's a horrible shame,' said Emily, 'you're worth ten of her I'm sure. Don't you let them make you feel that you aren't heaps better than she was. I don't like the way she looks, she looks sly to me. Don't you think she was sly?'

'Don't let's talk about her,' said Rachel. 'You must tell me about yourself,' she added as she left the room.

She must get away from Emily's clear-sighted acuteness. Back in her own room she forced herself to tidy her hair and to change her dress. She composed her features and when Emily and she descended the stairs to the dining room and took their place at the table, she somehow managed to sustain a conversation suitable for the ears of the two menservants.

After the meal was over they sat one on each side of the library fire. Rachel felt that it would be easier to talk there. The thought of the letters and what she was to do with them she put resolutely out of her mind, and as resolutely listened to Emily's talk. She enquired after Mrs. Deering.

'She's better and happier now my father's away and the bills are paid with the money you gave me I even let her help me a little with my sewing and then . . .'

'Yes?' prompted Rachel.

'Then he, my clergyman friend, comes and she likes seeing him and she comes with me to church sometimes. She's sure he wants to marry me.'

'Do you think he does?'

'Yes,' Emily's face softened a little. 'I don't know what he sees in me. I think his life in the Vicarage is dull. It's such a dark house and his housekeeper is old and very deaf. He thinks I'm cheerful, I suppose. He hasn't any idea what I'm really like.'

'You would like to marry him?'

'Better than anything in the world,' said Emily. Her voice

took on a deeper tone and she looked for a moment older and vastly serious. Rachel stared into the fire. Emily had so often complained that life was dull. She had wanted things to happen of an exciting kind and Rachel had thought too that a little excitement would not come amiss—and now they both had something to hide. She wished herself back in her little bedroom at Oxford on a dull day where there was nothing but the daily routine of living.

'Rachel, you must go to bed, you look absolutely worn out,' exclaimed Emily. 'I think you ought to send for the doctor tomorrow, anyhow come along now.' She drew Rachel to her feet, and arm in arm they went upstairs.

47

ALONE in her room Rachel undressed and went to bed. Her brain was racing but she must try to think clearly what to do.

She piled up the pillows behind her and left a small lamp burning by her bed. The fire sent flickering lights into the room. She thought first about showing Richard the letters and then she wondered if he would dislike her for doing so. Innocent messengers with evil news often came to bad ends in historic times. The potentates to whom they brought the news sacrificed them to their own anger and disappointment.

No, Richard would not be angry with her, he would realise that she had done her best. He had tried to help her, even though he had been affected by his father's attitude towards her, and sometimes he had been impatient with her.

If only she could ask someone's advice. Her glance fell on some books on a table. The light caught a red leather bound volume—the book Paul had given her. If she could talk to Paul in her distress and indecision. Paul's steady judgment, his sympathy and his understanding of other people would help and sustain her; but Paul was far away in London and she must make up her mind what to do here and now.

She must put all thoughts of revenge out of her mind and get rid of these letters. She lay back wearily on her pillows. How had it all happened? Marian Gervase must have been very clever in conducting her intrigue with such complete secrecy. Why had she left the letters? That was a very risky thing to do. Then Rachel recalled all that she had heard about the maid. Marian Gervase evidently had the gift of inspiring devotion in certain people, and she must have been Marian's confidante in everything. Rachel tried to conjure up a picture of the woman. She saw her as soft-footed, silent, watchful, content to let her mistress deceive an employer in whose house she lived and whose wages she took. She must have had a key to the cupboard and left it with her mistress when she was called away to her sister, and Marian Gervase on that fine morning when she set off hunting had no inkling that she would never return alive. She must have left the key in her dressing-table drawer, where Sir Edward found it after her death. He had opened nothing in her room—merely shut it up in his desperate grief.

Rachel's thoughts ground on. She wondered what the lover was like? Was he dashing and light-hearted and volatile, a contrast in every way to her husband whose devotion was secure and commonplace, and one who loved admiration must have enjoyed the change and excitement of this love affair.

Rachel sat up in bed. 'I must stop thinking about her,' she said half aloud, 'or I shall be haunted by her too.'

She pushed the bed clothes away. The fire had sunk down but she could put more coals on. Then a thought struck her. The letters were written on thick paper and still damp. It would be hard to burn them for they would choke the fire with black fragments.

Janet, in making up the fire tomorrow morning, would wonder what Rachel had been doing, and it might certainly cross her mind that it was odd that Rachel should have burnt so many papers at one time. She might also wonder if they had been brought from Lady Gervase's room, and if so why this midnight burning?

No, that would not do. Servants in a big house watched with interest every move made by their masters and mistresses. She could not burn this pile of letters in her bedroom or in any of the downstairs rooms.

With the startling clarity which only comes in the night when everything is still she devised a plan. Tomorrow was Saturday and after mid-day there would be no one in the garden. Macandrew made bonfires of refuse which left a residue of hot ash which only smoked on sullenly. He called them smutch fires. Sir Edward had in her hearing said that Macandrew's bonfires were exceptionally well laid with wood, and that he kept a pile of sticks beside them with which he started them afresh. She rose and opened the drawers into which she had put the letters, took one of the newspapers which in Sir Edward's absence had been brought up to her room (otherwise they were laid on the library table for his inspection) and made a neat parcel tied securely with string. She closed the drawer and crept back to bed. She extinguished the lamp and though shivering with cold, the fire having gone out, she still thought and planned.

Emily was the difficulty. If Rachel said she wanted to go out she would insist on coming with her. Her only plan must be to tell Emily that she was going to have an afternoon rest and to ask Emily to look at Lady Gervase's clothes and to decide what she wanted to take back to London with her. Then she would slip out of the house and burn the letters and come back and lie down, and no one would be any the wiser.

There would be no risk of her being found out, and the letters, which she felt to be a pollution of her bedroom, would be something she must forget. No word would ever pass her lips about them and no slights or criticisms of her own behaviour must ever make her reveal what she had read—revenge of that kind was not for her. She closed her eyes and resolutely tried to sleep.

The next morning Emily glanced searchingly at her. 'Don't you think you had better have the doctor?' she said. 'You look dreadfully tired.'

Rachel said, as lightly as she could, 'The doctor said he would look in next week. Let's go and look at the clothes.'

Emily was obviously not satisfied by this answer, but was

silenced for the moment and they made their way to Sir Edward's bedroom.

'Could you open the window?' said Rachel.

Emily did so, letting in some thin sunshine with an icy blast of air.

'There was a hard frost last night,' said Rachel. She glanced out of the window. The trees were edged with white rime and there were icicles hanging from the fountain on the terrace.

'Mercy, what a waste,' said Emily, her eyes gleaming. 'All these lovely clothes. I can't understand your father-in-law letting them stay in that cupboard.'

'You would if you knew him,' said Rachel.

'Well, I suppose waste doesn't matter to rich people,' said Emily. 'Well now, Rachel, you sit down in that armchair. Look, you are shivering. Why don't you light the fire?' and before Rachel could say anything she took a box of matches from her pocket and applied it to the newspaper under the coals. It burnt sulkily, both paper and coals being damp, but soon Rachel could warm her hands at a blaze.

Meanwhile as Emily was vigorously shaking the dresses and riding habits out of the window more moths flew out. 'There's some lovely lace on this dress,' she said. 'You should have it, it's valuable.'

'I don't want any of it,' said Rachel with so much emphasis that Emily stared at her. Rachel added, 'Take anything you want, take it all back to London with you.'

'Do you really mean that?'

'Yes, every word of it.'

Emily's eyes glistened. 'Well,' she said, 'I would be glad to take the things, I don't deny. I know a woman who would give me something for them, there's such a lot of material in them I could cut out the stained and moth-eaten bits and she'd give me something for the stuff.' She held out a lovely black velvet dress. 'I could make a dress for Mamma out of this.'

Rachel surprisingly gave a hysterical giggle at the thought of Mrs. Deering decked out in Lady Gervase's finery.

Emily was paying no attention. She was trying on some shoes.

'They fit me,' she said. 'Isn't that splendid?'

'Yes, indeed.'

'I think I can clean them up and polish them. I have some cleaning stuff with me.'

'You don't need to clean your own boots here. They will be cleaned for you.'

'Well, I must say it's comfortable here,' said Emily. 'I've never been waited on before like this.'

'No, nor had I,' said Rachel, 'till I came here. Look, my dear, I think I had better have a rest this afternoon. Would you like to go on looking at these things?'

'Yes, I would, there's such a lot here, I haven't half done with looking at them.'

'Come along to my room at tea time,' said Rachel, 'but not before four o'clock, as I should like to have a good rest.'

48

DURING luncheon Rachel tried to be her most normal cheerful self. She knew that of all the people in her intimate circle Louisa Cunningham and Emily were the most impossible to deceive. Her nearly sleepless night had exhausted her and she longed for her pretended rest that afternoon.

Luncheon went on at a maddening stately pace, and afterwards Emily went back to look at and pack the clothes in a trunk which she had brought nearly empty with her. It held her own scanty wardrobe. She had brought the trunk with her to impress the servants at the Priory. A Gladstone bag would have looked insufficient for a country visit.

As Rachel was slowly mounting the stairs to her bedroom she heard a discreet cough behind her. She turned round and saw the butler mounting the stairs. He offered her a telegram on a salver. Her heart beat faster as she tore it open.

It was from Richard, saying that his father had not been well and that they were returning that evening. Rachel steadied herself by the banister of the staircase and gave the necessary directions for rugs and shawls and a foot-warmer to be put in the brougham and for a fire to be instantly lit in Sir Edward's bedroom. She wondered if she should send for the doctor, but as Richard had not mentioned it she did nothing about it.

'Oh dear,' she thought 'I had hoped I should have Emily to myself till Monday—with no one looking on to criticise her.'

The return of the two Gervases made her self-imposed task more urgent, and she felt a kind of madness seize her. She must get this done. Her body was getting more unwieldy as the days passed and Richard would not allow her to go out alone, and when she was in bed after the baby was born (or if she died) someone might find the letters. Reason and logic had fled from her mind and she had to fight hard against panic.

She found a bag into which the parcel of letters fitted neatly, and put on the cloak which she now daily wore and thick shoes. She cautiously opened her door. The house was still except for the ticking of a clock in the hall. Rachel descended the stairs and opened the front door. The icy freshness of the afternoon air made her gasp for a moment. Then, closing the front door as noiselessly as possible, she made her way along the terrace keeping close to the house. It was unlikely that anyone would see her—Emily would be too much absorbed in her task with Lady Gervase's clothes, and the servants were all at the back of the house.

She met no one and reached the green door of the kitchen garden. She had had to walk very slowly as the paving stones had frozen patches on them. The sky was a pale blue behind the motionless trees and there was a feeling of more frost coming in the evening.

Rachel carefully closed the door and made her way along a path which ran alongside a wall. She went past the greenhouses on her left and skirted vegetable beds where the cabbage stalks were brown and withered, until she reached the bonfire.

Macandrew had evidently made a bonfire that morning, a faint smoke rose from the heap of rubbish. Her face brightened. This would mean that there would be a residue of hot ashes on which she could place the parcel of letters.

She had brought newspapers with her. She took a stick from

the stack beside the fire, and cleared a few cabbage stalks from
the top of the pile of rubbish, and wrapped some of the newspapers round the parcel and ignited them. A blaze of flame and
smoke smote her face and she stepped hurriedly back. She
had not noticed a puddle which had a thin coating of ice
just behind where she was standing. Her foot slipped on it
and she fell heavily backwards, hitting her shoulder on a loose
stone.

Emily, who had been happily employed folding up dresses
and conveying them to her bedroom to put in the trunk,
returned for the shoes and boots, and glanced at her battered
watch, once the property of her father. She saw that it said
twenty to four, and she remembered that Rachel had told her
not to come to her room before four o'clock. She finished
packing the shoes into the trunk, then again glanced at the
clock on the mantelpiece. It said two minutes after the hour.

She went along to Rachel's bedroom and knocked at the
door. Her mind, intent on her afternoon's occupation with the
dresses and shoes, was in a slight daze, and she waited a few
minutes before she knocked again. There was no answer.

'She must be asleep,' thought Emily. She gently pushed the
door open and went into the room. She looked at the sofa at
the end of the bed and then at the bed itself. The afternoon
sun shone into the room which was chill and empty.

Rachel must have gone downstairs, she thought, but it's odd
because she said we should have tea brought up to her room.
She must have changed her mind. She went downstairs into
the library. There was no tea-table laid out there and no Rachel.
She began to feel uneasy and ran upstairs two steps at a time.
In Rachel's bedroom the cupboard door was slightly ajar. She
looked into it. Rachel's cloak was missing. She ran downstairs
and met the butler in the hall.

'Have you seen Mrs. Gervase?' she asked.

'No, miss,' he said, 'I think she is resting. She asked for tea
to be taken upstairs.'

'She's not upstairs,' said Emily. 'Please look everywhere.'
She snatched a coat which was hanging up on a peg and rushed
out of the house. The butler caught something of her alarm and
went out on to the terrace.

'Rachel, Rachel,' cried Emily, there was only silence.

She turned back and cried, 'Get everyone to go and look for Mrs. Gervase. She must have gone out and slipped down.'

The butler, who was not accustomed to take orders from anyone except Sir Edward, stared at her.

'Hurry,' said Emily. 'Please be as quick as you can. Get everybody to look.'

He saw the necessity of this from the urgency in her voice and presently every available person in the house ran out in different directions calling at the top of their voices. Some rooks rose from the trees cawing noisily. Emily ran fast. She tripped over a branch in the rose garden, tore her skirt and gashed her ankle, but she went on unheeding. She stopped for a moment to get her breath. Then she remembered the kitchen garden. Rachel often went there and sat on a garden seat and watched Macandrew at work. She wrenched the green door in the wall open and flew along the path, her breath coming in gasps. She saw Rachel lying on the ground by the bonfire, her eyes closed in her white face.

Emily's heart beat furiously. She rushed forward and tore off the coat she was wearing and laid it over Rachel. Then she started back along the path. She could hardly see or think, and she saw the burly figure of a man whom she recognised as Macandrew.

'What is it?' he said.

'Mrs. Gervase. She's lying beside the bonfire. She's had a fall.'

Macandrew wasted no time. He pushed past Emily, and when he reached Rachel he lifted her up in his massive arms. Emily came after him and as she caught up with him she saw that Rachel stirred a little in his arms.

'You go on to the house and send for the doctor,' he said.

Emily obeyed and found the butler returning from a fruitless quest in the garden.

'I've found her, she's had a fall in the kitchen garden. Send for the doctor at once.

She went into the house, rang a bell furiously, and ordered whoever she saw to bring hot water and make up the fire in Rachel's bedroom.

Macandrew laid Rachel on the bed. He stood looking down on her, his harsh face set in lines of anxiety and pity. Then he turned and left the room with a slow step. Emily undid Rachel's heavy shoes and chafed her cold feet and undressed her and laid a heated stone bottle in the bed. She prayed the most fervent prayers of her life that Rachel might not die or be badly hurt and that the doctor would come quickly.

Meanwhile all she could do was to keep her warm and quiet. There was a bustle throughout the whole household. A man had gone off at a gallop to fetch the doctor. Hot water was brought. The fire in the room was made up. The bed grew warm. What else could she do? She sent Janet to fetch a sheet which she tore methodically into strips in case bandages were needed.

Rachel's eyes were still shut but she gave a slight moan from time to time. Emily chafed her hands. Then she rang the bell and when Janet appeared she asked for a telegraph form. When it was brought she addressed it to Mrs. Cunningham and wrote, 'Come as quickly as you can. Rachel has had an accident.'

'Get this sent off at once and get a room ready for Mrs. Cunningham.'

Janet, who in common with the rest of the servants had found nothing hitherto to admire in Emily's slightly shabby clothes and unaristocratic manners, nevertheless obeyed quickly. The Priory servants understood authority when they met it, and Emily, her hair hanging in strands round her face and her dress disordered and her skirt torn, had a furious intensity which brooked no denial of her orders.

At last she heard a heavy step on the stairs and the doctor came in.

'What's all this?' he said, staring at Emily.

'She's had a fall in the kitchen garden by the bonfire and must have slipped and hurt herself.'

'What was she doing there alone?'

'I don't know,' said Emily. 'She told me she was going to rest but she went out alone and without telling me.'

He nodded and gently turned Rachel on her side while Emily watched him, her hands clasped. He took a strip of linen from her.

'She must have fallen on the point of her shoulder, there's a bruise coming up, but as far as I can see there are no bones broken. Her bonnet prevented her from hitting her head, I suppose.'

He went on with his work, wetting Rachel's lips with brandy. She opened her eyes for a moment. 'It hurts,' she said.

'Oh, thank God she's not dead,' cried Emily.

'Dead, no of course she's not dead, but it's the child I'm afraid for. This may bring it on. I sent the man from the Priory on to Dashbury for the nurse.' He gave Emily a sharp glance. 'What's your name?'

'Emily Deering,' she replied, 'I'm a friend of Rachel's.'

'Where's Richard?'

Emily told him that Richard and his father were returning that evening and that she had sent for Mrs. Cunningham.

'Well, Rachel must be kept absolutely quiet. Keep everyone out of the room till the nurse comes.' Then he looked more closely at Emily.

'You look as if you wanted my attention as well. There's blood on your skirt.'

Emily stooped and drew her skirt aside, there was a gash on her leg.

'I'll attend to this and what's more when I've bound it up, you are to go downstairs or order yourself some tea with a drop of brandy in it. Rachel will need all the help you can give her. I can stay here for another hour—go along now.'

Emily restored some order to her hair, changed her dress and limped downstairs. The butler was hovering in the hall.

'How is Mrs. Richard?' he asked, his voice strained with anxiety.

'She has hurt her shoulder,' said Emily. 'The doctor is staying with her for an hour. He says I must have tea with some brandy in it.'

She sat down in the library by the fire and tried to get warm. She had flung her coat over Rachel in the kitchen garden and had not noticed how the cold had caught at her in her thin dress. She shut her eyes and opened them again to find a tray being put on a table beside her and the butler saying, 'I should eat something first, miss, if I was you,' and he handed her a plateful of bread and butter.

After she had eaten and then drunk two cups of tea laced with brandy Emily made her way upstairs.

The doctor was sitting by the fire. 'You look better,' he said, 'that's good. I think I shall stay here for the night, and look at Sir Edward if he is not well, and I would like to keep a watch on this girl. I must send my gig home with a message. You stay here while I go downstairs and make arrangements.'

Emily sat very still, then rose and tiptoed to the bed. Rachel stirred. 'My shoulder hurts and I seem to hurt all over,' she said.

'Yes, you must have slipped on some ice and had a fall, just try and rest.'

Rachel's forehead wrinkled into a frown. 'Were the letters all right?' she said. 'I mean were they burnt?'

'Yes, yes,' said Emily soothingly, 'they are all right.'

'But you don't know,' persisted Rachel. 'Could you go and see first thing tomorrow morning, please, please go.'

'Yes, of course I will,' said Emily, 'I'll go early before people are about.'

Rachel seemed satisfied. 'Richard is coming back tonight. You will go early tomorrow morning, won't you?'

'Yes, I promise. Now try and sleep.' Deeply mystified she sat holding Rachel's hand.

Louisa Cunningham had received the telegram, and as usual she wasted no time in conjecture or exclamations. She looked at the timetable of the trains, ordered a fly and did her packing. Mr. Barrington was out. She left a note for him and made her way to the station, and only when she was seated in the train did she give rein to her anxiety.

When she arrived at Dashbury Junction she saw the Priory footman on the platform.

'How is Mrs. Gervase?' she asked.

'She's very bad, I think,' he said. 'The doctor's there and they've sent for the nurse.'

Emily was in the hall to meet her. The strain of the day had told on her and her tears flowed freely.

'Be calm, Emily,' said Mrs. Cunningham, 'we shall all need calmness to be of use to Rachel.'

49

WHEN Sir Edward and Richard arrived at the station they were told by the coachman that Rachel had had a fall. Richard, deeply anxious, swore under his breath at the slowness of the horses on their drive to the Priory. Sir Edward's rheumatism had increased in London. He had found the friend he went to see aged and fretful, and his visits to his club disappointing.

When he heard of Rachel's accident he felt a spasm of irritation. Why couldn't she look after herself better when she was to mother a Gervase.

When they arrived, Richard leapt out of the carriage. The servants looked harassed and mournful and Richard rushed upstairs after flinging down his coat and hat. He met Louisa Cunningham on the landing.

'How is she?' he said.

'Not very well,' she replied, 'but the doctor is here and he has sent for the nurse.' She grasped his sleeve. 'She must be kept completely quiet. Don't talk to her and don't stay long, and don't ask her about her fall.'

He nodded and went into the bedroom. Rachel was moving uncomfortably in the bed. She smiled at him a little anxiously. He asked her how she felt.

'Just a bit of pain here and there,' she said.

'Well, you are all right now,' he replied with a confidence he was far from feeling. 'I'm back and Mrs. Cunningham is here and the doctor, and the nurse will be coming. I hate you to be in pain.'

'And Emily, she's here too,' said Rachel.

He had forgotten Emily. 'She's somewhere about, I haven't seen her.'

'You will see that she's all right, won't you?'

'Of course I will.'

Privately he resolved to take Emily to task as to why she had not taken better care of Rachel. When he emerged from Rachel's room the passages seemed to be full of rustlings and low whispers.

The sudden advent of Mrs. Cunningham, the doctor, and the nurse, with Emily already there as a visitor, had meant endless preparations; fires had to be lit in rooms unused for a long space of time. Cans of hot water had to be taken upstairs; fresh linen to be put out. The servants were enjoying the unusual sense of drama pervading the house.

'It's like the time when her ladyship was brought back,' said Mrs. Crocker, and a shudder went round her audience.

Richard met Mrs. Cunningham in the passage. His face was set in lines of anxiety, he was so full of his own troubles that he did not notice how tired she looked.

There was a ring at the front door.

'I think I hear the nurse,' she said. A cold air came into the house and a small square figure dressed in grey entered the hall.

'You go down and meet her,' said Louisa. Poor boy, this will give him something to do, she thought, as she went back to Rachel's room.

Richard went to his father's room. Sir Edward had refused to go to bed and was sitting hunched up beside the fire.

'How is your wife?' he said.

'Not very well,' said Richard.

'I don't know how that friend of hers—dash it I can never remember her name—let this happen.'

'No, nor can I,' said Richard. 'The nurse is here and Mrs. Cunningham.'

'A pack of women,' said his father, and then looking at Richard's strained face he mumbled, 'I'm sorry, Dick. I'm glad to see them both. Let me know how Rachel gets on.'

Richard turned on his heel, leaving his father ashamed and unhappy.

Mrs. Cunningham, Richard and Emily had a meal together. Richard barely spoke. He had greeted Emily with curt abruptness. Mrs. Cunningham appeared not to notice this, and threw an occasional remark into the silence.

After dinner Emily said she would like to go up to her room

and Mrs. Cunningham said she would speak to the doctor. Richard was left alone. His eyes met his mother's smiling portrait and he pushed his port wine glass away, and he too mounted the stairs to Rachel's room.

He knocked and was admitted by the nurse. She had a wide mouth and small opaque eyes, but looked competent to deal with emergencies. He remembered that he had liked her when he was ill. The doctor was taking Rachel's pulse, she looked flushed and restless. He turned his head and said, 'You go downstairs and I'll come and see you presently.'

Richard walked to and fro in the library and presently the doctor came. 'Make up your mind to a bad night,' he said. 'I'm afraid her pains have begun. Her shoulder's better, the compresses on it have helped and the bruise on her side is coming out well.'

'Is the baby coming?'

'I think so, but I fear that the shock of the fall has brought it on. There's nothing you can do; just go and give her a kiss but don't talk to her, and go and see your father too, and tell him we're doing all we can. He had much better try and get some sleep. Then come back here and I'll come down from time to time or send nurse down to tell you how things are going.'

Richard found Sir Edward in bed. He gave his father the doctor's message and urged him to get some sleep. Sir Edward replied irritably that sleep for him was out of the question and Richard left the room quickly. He returned to the library. He unfastened the shutters of a window and peered into the night. The air was damp. The frost was breaking and there was a faint sound of dripping from the trees. He closed the shutters and flung himself into a deep armchair, and presently, in spite of his acute anxiety, he hovered on the borderland of sleep and then fell into a deep unconsciousness.

He was awakened by the sound of someone coming into the room. He started to his feet.

'What is it?' he cried.

'You've got a son.'

'How is she?' cried Richard.

'She's had a hard time,' said the doctor gravely, 'a very rough time, but she's been very brave. The child is small but has the right number of toes and fingers and its lungs seem all right.'

'A son,' said Richard. 'I must see her.'

'Only for a moment, she is exhausted. I shall stay with her while nurse looks after the baby.'

'I don't know why I slept,' stammered Richard.

'I am very glad you did, there was nothing you could do. Mrs. Cunningham was very helpful. She is a woman in a thousand, just did what she was told and was never in the way. Come along,' said the doctor.

Richard followed him into Rachel's room. She lay very quiet. As he approached the bed, she said, 'It's a boy. Are you pleased?'

'Utterly pleased if you're all right.'

The nurse came in with a bundle of flannel in her arms and offered Richard a glance at a minute red-faced object which let out a wail. It's tiny claws like a bird's moved feebly. Richard slipped a finger into one of them which tightened round it with surprising force.

'You must go,' said the doctor with a smile. 'Don't disturb your father, and go to bed yourself. There's not much of the night left. Go on now.'

Richard left reluctantly and flung himself fully dressed on his bed.

The following morning Emily woke later than she had meant to do. She had passed a miserably unhappy night. Excluded from the sickroom, she had tip-toed along the passage at intervals and given a faint tap on the door of Rachel's bedroom. Mrs. Cunningham had answered her tap and given her a brief nod or a smile. Even in her own anxiety about Rachel she could remember that Emily would be racked with fears.

When the baby was born Louisa came out of the room closing the door noiselessly behind her. She gave her the news and then said, 'Now go back to your room. You can do nothing here,' and Emily had taken her advice.

A hasty glance at her watch showed her that she had only an hour before appearing at breakfast. She dressed rapidly and slipped down the stairs. The front door had been unbolted and she went out into the morning. The skies were grey and lowering and everything was dripping with a fine rain. She had brought her umbrella and underneath its ample covering she scurried along. She turned the handle of the green door of the kitchen garden, it was slippery with wet and she walked cautiously along the path, her shoes getting muddier. She peeped from under her umbrella as she neared the bonfire and saw Macandrew, a sack thrown over his shoulders, staring down at it.

Hearing her footsteps he turned. 'I'm hearing that a son has been born,' he said, 'and how is she?'

'She's very tired but the doctor thinks she will be all right.'

He looked relieved. 'And what are you after doing here at this hour?'

Emily looked up at him, tilting her umbrella backwards.

'Mrs. Gervase was burning some papers,' she said, 'she asked me to see if they were burnt.'

She suddenly felt that she could trust this man. It was all so unexplained. Why had Rachel wanted to burn them? But if only she could tell her that they had gone up in flames, that was, for some mysterious reason, going to ease Rachel's mind.

Macandrew took up a forked stick from beside the bonfire and stirred the pile of dead matter. The letters had only been partially burnt.

'I shall go home and get some paper and dry sticks. The rain is stopping now. I will come back and see that every bit is burnt. If you would like to see me do it come into the green-house and wait.'

Emily sat down on the shaft of a wheelbarrow in the green-house, her heart pounding. Her head ached and her limbs were heavy with fatigue, but she felt too restless to sit still and walked back to the bonfire. Then she saw that two letters had been pushed under some heavy green rubbish and were intact. She lifted them off to put them among the half-burnt pile, but devouring curiosity made her glance at them.

Her eyes glistened. These were love letters, but whose? Then, with a shock, the whole thing fell into place. This was why Rachel had gone out by herself to burn these letters. She must have found them in Lady Gervase's room. Stunned she leant on her closed umbrella. Yes, this must have been why Rachel had gone out without her, pretending that she was going to have a rest. She didn't want Richard or his father to know of them, and had chosen this way of getting rid of them, and yet what a glorious revenge for her it would have been after having been made to feel inferior all the time to her mother-in-law. That was like Rachel, she would never take a mean revenge, and now she was suffering for her goodness. Anger boiled up in Emily's mind.

At this moment she heard footsteps on the path. She turned to see Macandrew with a bundle of firewood in his hand and some newspapers under his arm.

While her thoughts had been racing she had twisted the two letters together and poked them under the others. She would have liked to keep them to show to Richard and make him realise what had happened, but this would make nonsense of what Rachel had tried to do to shield him.

With great deliberation Macandrew re-lighted the fire and the letters burned with a steady glow. He stoked the flames until not one scrap of the letters remained unburned. Then he heaped some cabbage stalks on to the hot ash.

'That's fine,' he said. 'Now you can go back to the house.'

'You won't,' faltered Emily, 'mention all this to anyone?'

'Not to a living soul,' he said, 'not to my wife or anyone else.'

'Thank you,' said Emily. 'Thank you very much.'

He looked at her with something approaching benevolence and she wondered how much he knew, or guessed.

50

THE next morning, to Emily's surprise and dismay, Sir Edward limped into the dining-room. He said good-morning but otherwise addressed no remark to her. Richard came in with the doctor. He, too, greeted Emily with a cut nod. She stood uncertain whether to help herself from the silver dishes on the sideboard or just to sit and wait until she was helped to some food.

The doctor took her arm and led her to the sideboard. 'You must eat a good breakfast, you look as if you needed it.'

Richard, who had come to stand beside them, overheard his remark and helped her generously to the food.

'Well, Sir Edward,' said the doctor, 'you're a grandfather. The baby's small and puny, but he's all right as far as I can see.'

'I am glad to hear that he is all right. If it hadn't been for this unfortunate accident . . .' He looked sternly at Emily, whose hand shook as she handled her knife and fork.

'Well, accidents will happen,' said the doctor. 'By the way Miss Deering, Rachel wants to see you. You can talk to her but only for five minutes—no more, she is too exhausted to talk. Nurse will come and tell you when you can go up to see her. She will leave Mrs. Cunningham in charge.'

Richard, his forehead furrowed with worry, said nothing, and his father ate in silence. The doctor, after having eaten heartily, rose to his feet.

'Excuse me,' he said, 'I must go back to my patient.'

'Come in to the library,' said Richard to Emily.

When they walked into the room Emily sat down. Her head throbbed with pain and the strain of the last hours had exhausted her. Richard crossed to the mantelpiece and looked down on her. 'What I can't understand is why you let Rachel go out without you. You must have known that this wasn't safe.'

'I didn't know she was going out,' she said. 'She told me she was going to rest and asked me to sort out some things for her.'

'Then why did she go out?'

Emily's head throbbed more than ever. She felt incapable of thought. 'I expect she wanted some fresh air, perhaps it felt stuffy in the house,' she stammered.

'Then why didn't she call you to go out with her?' pursued Richard.

'I don't know,' said Emily.

'It was very thoughtless of her, she was endangering her own life and her child's.'

Emily stood up, anger mounting in her. 'You're not to criticise Rachel,' she cried. 'She's stood quite enough of that from your father, and as for your mother she wasn't fit to black Rachel's boots. You've never appreciated Rachel. She's the best person in the world. She's . . .' At that point Emily burst into a flood of hysterical tears.

'Emily, what is all this?' Mrs. Cunningham came into the the room. She put her arm round the girl's shoulder. 'Go upstairs,' she said, 'and wash your face, and when you are quite calm, but not before, go and see Rachel.'

Richard was staring after Emily. 'She said such things.'

'Never heed her,' said Mrs. Cunningham, 'she gets a wee bit over-wrought at times. We've all got to keep calm, Richard, to help our lassie upstairs.'

Richard assented, but his mind was not on what she was saying.

'I would recommend you to think only of Rachel and your boy at this moment,' said Mrs. Cunningham with severity. 'What Emily said in a moment of hysterics should not weigh with you.' She turned and was gone before he could protest.

About half an hour later Emily went along and knocked at Rachel's door. Mrs. Cunningham admitted her. Rachel looked strangely small and pale as Emily sat down beside her and took her hand. 'It's all right,' she said, 'the papers are burnt to ashes.'

'Oh, thank Heaven, my dear,' said Rachel.

'No one knows I went out,' continued Emily.

Rachel gave a satisfied sigh and shut her eyes. But when Emily went back to her own bedroom and applied eau de cologne to her throbbing temples she began to weep again. She had done no service to Rachel by losing her temper and saying what she had said about Richard's mother. In fact she had very nearly given away the secret that Rachel was so jealously guarding.

The door opened and Mrs. Cunningham entered. She looked at Emily's dejected figure and tear-stained face. 'Bathe your eyes in cold water,' she said, 'I want to talk to you.'

When Emily had obeyed this command with a sinking heart she sat down opposite Mrs. Cunningham who looked severely at her. 'I heard what you said about Richard's mother. Whatever possessed you to say such a thing?'

'I don't know,' said Emily, her tears beginning to flow again. 'I suppose I was so angry when Richard began criticising Rachel for going out alone that I lost my temper.'

'Tut tut,' said Louisa Cunningham, 'you shouldn't have done that. You went out this morning early too. I know, for I caught a glimpse of you as you went through the hall in your mackintosh. Better tell me the whole story, and we will see what we can do for the best.'

And between tearful gulps Emily told Mrs. Cunningham how Rachel had got rid of her in order to sort Lady Gervase's clothes, and how she had found Rachel lying unconscious by the bonfire; of Rachel's request to her to go and see if the letters were completely burnt, and of her own glance at two of the letters; her meeting with Macandrew, her headache and anger and her suspicions as to why Rachel had acted as she did.

Mrs. Cunningham sat in silence, her eyes on the carpet. 'Well,' she said, 'let's hope not much harm has been done. Macandrew is reliable and will say nothing. You had better stick to the story that Rachel had a sudden wish for fresh air and went for a walk alone, not willing to take you away from the work you were doing. Sir Edward is vexed with her at this moment for taking such a risk, but if the baby gets stronger he will forget this in time. As for Richard, I will remind him that you had had a great deal to bear in finding Rachel lying there and that you acted with great promptitude in sending for the doctor and myself, for which he should be grateful to you.' She paused. 'I will say that you had no sleep and that your headache was painful and that now you do not remember what you said.'

'But it was true,' said Emily sullenly.

'Probably. But if you say any more you will not be helping Rachel. She did for the best, if what you think is in fact true, and I should say that it is. I have never admired what I heard of Richard's mother, but if Rachel, who has hurt herself so much in trying to suppress the letters, wishes Sir Edward and his son shielded from the truth, well we must keep silence. Now wash your face, pull down the blinds and get on to your bed and sleep, and look cheerful and pleasant when you come downstairs, please.' She paused at the door. 'Rachel's father is coming today. It will be a help to have him.'

51

Mr. Barrington proved a steadying influence from the moment he arrived in the house. His face was drawn with anxiety about Rachel, but he maintained a complete composure. He visited her and held one of her hands in his own and he expressed great pleasure in her son's arrival, and then regarded his grandson with the interest he usually reserved for an ancient inscription which was hard to decipher. He added that he looked forward to teaching him Latin.

He asked no questions about Rachel's accident and devoted himself to talking at meal times to Sir Edward and Richard on the topics of the day. He was kind to Emily. She felt that she was only staying in the house on sufferance because Rachel had expressed a wish for her to remain at the Priory. The doctor had also said that he wished her to stay. Very little escaped his notice where his patients were concerned, and he had seen that after a few minutes talk with Emily, Rachel had looked happier and more at ease. She was getting slowly better and the pain in her shoulder had diminished. The baby also showed signs of improvement. The stamina which had upheld the Gervase who went with Richard Coeur de Lion to the Crusades and another ancestor who had served with the Black Prince had come down to this minute creature who fought for his existence every inch of the way and yelled loudly when his wants went unsatisfied.

Several days passed. The doctor went home and Rachel began to take pleasure in the baby.

Richard asked Rachel no questions about her fall but she felt that there was something between them. Something that someday would need an explanation. She pushed the thought away from her. She must concentrate on getting well herself and on her child's welfare.

One morning Richard came into her room dressed for riding. He told her he was going to one of their outlying farms.

'A ride will do you good,' said Rachel.

'Yes my head feels a bit muzzy,' he said.

'I'm afraid all this worry has done this,' said Rachel.

'Yes, it's been a worrying time, but you are better and the baby seems all right. Goodbye my love, I shall see you when I come back.'

He rode off leaving the household pursuing its many avocations. His horse pulled a little and was inclined to be frisky and restless, but settled down as the ride continued. The cold air and the sight of familiar landmarks of trees and fields steadied Richard's nerves as he rode on. He interviewed the farmer, received congratulations on the birth of his son, and turned for home.

His head ached a little. Ever since his concussion at Oxford these headaches had come back. He looked round the landscape which showed the austere beauty of winter, but held no promise of spring. Something which had been nagging at the back of his mind came uppermost in his thoughts. What had Emily meant by what she had said? He remembered her words about his mother. The recollection flashed across his mind of a chance remark he had overheard one of the servants make about her. He remembered the furious face of his mother's maid and how she had drawn him into her room and given him some sweetmeats. Then a scene long buried in his mind emerged from the recesses of his memory. When he was a schoolboy he had gone one day into the garden and coming round a hedge had found his mother and a tall good-looking man standing by the old sundial. They were laughing, with their heads very close together. When his mother caught sight of him she had beckoned him to come to her and had given him a message for someone in the stables. Later, just before her death, as he peered into the past he seemed to remember that she talked less but had ridden more recklessly than before.

He stopped the horse and stared at the heavy brown plough land beside him. Had she had a lover? His father could never have known or suspected this. Edward Gervase had loved his wife with a blind unquestioning devotion and trust and had made the rooms at the Priory into a shrine for her perfection after her death.

Gradually the truth dawned on him. Rachel had been asked to look at his mother's clothes. Supposing that she had found some letters, letters to or from some man. She had wanted to spare his father knowledge which would have blighted the rest of his life. But why hadn't she handed them to him to destroy? Then he saw the reason, she wanted to shield him as well, so she went out on her perilous expedition to burn them. If she had shown them to him she knew how hard it would be to go on living in the Priory and to hear his father exalt his dead wife to the skies.

A wave of tenderness for Rachel swept over him. She had done this for him. She had been slighted by his father and compared constantly to his mother to her own disadvantage; but she had not thought of herself, only of how she could spare them both pain and disillusion.

Dear Rachel, he would tell her when she was well again that he knew what she had tried to do, and between them they would make a better life together. His one wish was to get back quickly and see her, so he turned the horse's head and entered a wood which was a shorter way home. Narrow rides had been cut in it but the ground was rough and withered grasses grew high below the trees. The horse stumbled against a hidden tree stump, put its foot into a rabbit hole and flung Richard, who deep in thought was holding the reins loosely in his hands, over its shoulder. Richard fell, hitting his head on a tree trunk and lay in a crumpled heap his face upturned to the sky.

The horse, its leg jammed in the rabbit hole, let out a whinny of pain and a labourer walking along another of the rides heard this and lumbered slowly to the spot. He looked aghast at Richard's silent form, and then freed the horse's hoof with difficulty from the rabbit hole. He mounted it clumsily and rode off to the village.

52

WHEN the news came of Richard's death the whole house was stricken into a horrified silence. Sir Edward collapsed in his chair. Mr. Barrington stood as if turned to stone. Emily, sat shaking in a chair, for once silent in a kind of stupor.

Louisa Cunningham was the first to rouse herself, she put her hand on Sir Edward's shoulder, ordered some strong tea for him and held it to his lips. Then she said, 'Rachel must be told at once, she may wonder what is happening, that would be worse for her than being told straight out.'

'I will do it,' said Arthur Barrington, and mounted the stairs with a set face. It seemed to him that he had never walked up them so quickly. He would have given everything he possessed to have had more time to think of how to deal this blow to his beloved child. He knocked at the door.

'Come in,' called Rachel's voice. She was sitting up in bed. She said, 'Where's Richard? he's been out a long time?' Then she looked again and saw that her father's face had an ashen pallor.

'What is it?' she cried, 'are you not well?'

He moved slowly to the side of the bed, his steps uncertain like those of an old man. Then he straightened himself up to his full height and took her hand. 'Rachel, there has been an accident. Richard was thrown from his horse.'

'Is he hurt?' she said, wide-eyed with fear. Her father sat down beside her and slipped his arm beneath her shoulders.

'He is dead, my child, there is nothing I can say to soften this for you.'

He held her shaking form close to him. After a while she disengaged herself and stared at him dry eyed and white faced. 'I can't believe it,' she said.

'I wish with all my soul that it wasn't true,' he replied, and told her how it was thought that the tragedy had happened.

The tears streamed down her face with an even flow. He dried them awkwardly with his handkerchief but they flowed on again. After a while he said, 'Rachel you must be very brave and think of Richard's child and your poor father-in-law who is ill with grief.' She did not reply and after a pause he went on, 'When your mother died, not of an accident but of an illness, and left me with you to care for, I had to make terms with my sorrow and go on living when nothing in the world seemed worth while.'

Rachel collapsed on to the pillows, her eyes closed, and he saw that she had fainted. He summoned the nurse and then went downstairs. The doctor was bending over Sir Edward who shook like a man with a palsy.

Mr. Barrington's eyes met Louisa Cunningham's, and though no word passed between them she went upstairs to Rachel's room. The nurse was holding a smelling bottle under her nose and her eyes were opening.

She looked at Louisa and said, 'This isn't real is it? Richard can't be dead? I can't believe it.'

Mrs. Cunningham sat beside her all day in the darkened room. In the late afternoon the baby, who much preferred being fed by his mother to receiving cow's milk out of a bottle, kicked and fought and screamed loudly and then was violently sick.

'Bring him to me please,' said Rachel.

 53

THE weeks dragged on. Sir Edward, unable to rouse himself from his grief, had taken to his bed. Strangely enough he preferred seeing Mrs. Cunningham to anyone else. She hid her sadness and her anxiety for Rachel under a quiet demeanour

and her matter-of-fact acceptance of events soothed his restlessness. She was not in any way happy. Mr. Barrington had
to go to London on business about a book he was publishing
and then on to Oxford, and Louisa tried to crush down her
apprehensions that Annie was mishandling the kitchen range,
that the larder was not being properly cleaned and that in the
hurry of her departure to the Priory dust sheets had not been
put over the furniture, and that when Mr. Barrington returned
to Oxford his library fire would not be properly lit nor the
fire-irons and brass fender polished.

She was also going through the exhausting experience,
familiar to all who have had it, of supporting a beloved person
plunged in grief. Rachel was very still and silent. She smiled
rarely. Her only glimmer of pleasure was when she held her
son in her arms. He steadily put on weight and showed his
determination to fight the battle for existence as plainly as
ever. Rachel seemed totally uninterested in the comings and
goings in the house. She had not been allowed by the doctor
to go to Richard's funeral.

He had been popular in the surrounding country and the
church was full. Sir Edward had risen from his bed and stood,
a stricken figure of grief, in the front pew with Lady Wentmore
beside him.

Paul had come down from London and sat at the back of the
church. He spoke for a moment to Mrs. Cunningham as she
was leaving the churchyard. He looked pale and sad. 'There's
nothing I can say,' he said. 'How is Rachel?'

'She's being very brave,' said Louisa Cunningham. She would
have liked to talk to Paul, he was related to her Oxford world
and was the only man she knew in a crowd of unfamiliar faces.

'Let me know please if there is anything I can do to help,' he
said. 'I will come and see you when I come to Oxford. I shall
be there in a few weeks' time.'

Louisa felt a slight lightening of her heart. Could there
possibly be a gleam of hope in the future for Rachel? She
sternly suppressed this thought. This was not the time or the
place to think such things. Paul disappeared in the crowd
of mourners to catch his train back to London, and she took
her place in the carriage with Edward Gervase and Arthur
Barrington.

Emily's departure was fixed for a few days later. She was going up to London by the afternoon train. Rachel had been walking round her room aimlessly looking at one object after another. She felt a sensation of returning life and vitality. She unlocked a drawer in her chest of drawers and saw the broken remains of the box which had held Lady Gervase's letters.

The whole episode of the finding of the letters, her effort to get rid of them, the flame and smoke of the bonfire striking her face with choking force, then a blank of unconsciousness; the joy of her child's birth, her own illness, then Richard's death, played itself out before her eyes as she stood trembling and holding on to the opened drawer for support. It no longer mattered what she did with the ruined box, but she would like to get rid of it all the same.

Then a thought struck her—perhaps Emily would take it and rid her of it? She closed the drawer and walked to the window.

She was young and although she did not know it the tide of her grief was turning a little. There was so much that she would have to do. She must put her own sorrow aside and help her father-in-law and cherish Richard's son and keep the Priory and the estate going, which would mean learning about many unfamiliar things. Then her thought turned to Emily. She must give Emily some money and thank her for all she had done. Here was someone who needed help. If Richard's death had shattered her own happiness, she must rouse herself and try to help Emily to a better life. When Emily came in she lifted up her head and smiled.

She looks more like her old self, thought Emily.

Rachel took some sovereigns from her purse and slipped them into Emily's pocket. 'That's just to help you a bit,' she said.

Emily protested but in vain.

'Now, my dear,' said Rachel, 'I've been thinking about you. Your future is important and we must think about it.'

'I've tried not to fret about it,' said Emily. 'I've been thinking about you. I wrote and told Mamma all that has happened here and she will tell him, I'm sure.'

'Well you are going to think about it now,' said Rachel.

'Because I'm unhappy, you need not be unhappy too. Nothing would help me more than to see you settled in life.'

'I can't make up my mind what to do,' said Emily.

'You must tell him everything. If he loves you he'll forgive and forget it. Look, Emily, I thought I was doing for the best when I decided to burn those letters on the bonfire. I couldn't see straight. I might easily have kept them and perhaps at some future time shown them to Richard, and until then I think I would have been strong enough not to show by word or deed what I knew. It would have been difficult to bear because I was always being compared to her, but I could and would have kept completely silent. I know I could. Somehow, not feeling well, I think I was a little out of my mind. I felt at all costs I must burn the letters, get rid of them. I thought I might die when the baby came and they would be found. I only made myself ill and the baby came too early and Richard was wretchedly anxious. It may have been partly that which made him fall off his horse. When he came into my room he looked tired and said he felt muzzy in the head. I should have kept the letters even if I hated having them in my room. I told you a lie when I said I was going to have a rest and I knew I meant to go out. I shall always tell the truth after this.'

'You poor dear,' said Emily, 'but I saw Richard in the hall before he went out, he looked cheerful.' There was a silence. 'Anyway he never knew about the letters.'

Emily's conscience gave her a sharp prick. She knew that but for Mrs. Cunningham's interference she would have told Richard about his mother. But she closed her lips. Rachel should never hear of this if she could help it. Mrs. Cunningham would not speak of it and it would be forgotten.

'Would you like me to tell him?' said Rachel. 'I could go up to London and see him later on and I would explain what a wretched time you had had at home with your father leaving you and that it wasn't your fault really.'

Emily shook her head. 'No,' she said, 'I must face it myself and tell the truth to him, and risk my happiness. I shall think of you and remember how brave you have been.'

'I think perhaps you are right,' said Rachel, 'but I would have gladly done it.'

After Emily and Mrs. Cunningham had departed the house

settled into a quiet sadness. Sir Edward came downstairs and Rachel was his only companion. She found the task of cheering him a very hard one, but she applied herself to it. This was something she could do for Richard, something which needed all her tact, her kindness and her sympathy. At first she felt herself defeated by his long silences and utter lack of response to her efforts. But gradually he talked a little more to her and his face lightened when she came into the room. One evening, when she handed him his bedroom candle outside the door, he said, 'You are very good to me, my dear.'

'I would give anything I have to help you,' she replied. 'You do help me,' he said.

After a brief inspection of her son, Rachel went into her bedroom and indulged in a storm of tears. The future stretched interminably in front of her. She would be the mistress of a house, the orderer of food involving a daily argument with Mrs. Crocker. The management of the estate would inevitably come into her hands, and for a companion (except for occasional visits from her family) she would have a sick broken-hearted man and a small baby. It would take all her courage and all the unselfishness at her command to live as she would have to live. Her youth cried out against it. She dried her eyes and moved towards the bed and her eyes fell on the leather bound copy of Wordsworth which Paul had given her as a wedding present.

She opened it and read a few lines. Did Paul still love her? Was there anywhere any promise at all in life? Perhaps. But no, she mustn't even think about this in the privacy of her room. It would be disloyalty to Richard's memory to let the thought so much as creep into her mind.

But it persisted in returning, as thoughts do which have long been suppressed, and she sat on the edge of her bed thinking of Paul and their shared laughter and community of interests.

54

ON a March day Paul Sibley rang the bell at Mr. Barrington's house in Oxford. Mr. Barrington was out and Mrs. Cunningham was alone in the drawing room. She looked at Paul. He did not seem quite so thin, his face in repose had a kind of gravity, but he laughed at something she said and looked boyish again.

'How is Rachel?' he asked.

'She is getting on fairly well, I think,' said Louisa. 'The baby is a great joy to her and Sir Edward is much easier to do with. But its a dreary life for her shut away in a big house like that. Her father and I have her much on our minds. She is too young to be burdened with sorrow and responsibility.'

'Yes,' said Paul. He was frowning.

Mrs. Cunningham had taken up a piece of embroidery, and with deliberation selected a strand of bright red wool to put some stitches into the heart of a rose. Then she said, 'Paul, I thought you once liked Rachel very much. Would you ever think of asking her to marry you?'

Paul sat bolt upright in his chair. 'I have always loved her,' he said, 'from the first moment I saw her by your garden gate, but she loved Richard and not me. I had to accept that.'

Mrs. Cunningham put two stitches in to the heart of the rose. 'She certainly loved Richard,' she replied, 'but she was not all that happy with him. He could not see how difficult life was being for her, and now that he has gone there is nothing but unhappiness there for her.' She paused, 'Paul, I am going to ask you again, would you not think of asking Rachel to marry you? I believe you have so much in common and you could make her very happy.'

Paul rose to his feet and moved to the mantelpiece and looked down into the fire. 'But this is impossible,' he said.

'It was one thing to tell her I loved her when she was a penniless girl and I had nothing to offer her except the chance of getting on in my profession. But now, how could I ask her when she is a rich widow?'

'Paul,' said Mrs. Cunningham severely, 'you put far too much emphasis on money, like all English people.'

'I haven't noticed that Scotch people are completely indifferent to money,' said Paul with spirit.

'No, but they have more sense,' she replied. 'They are careful about money, but they know that there are other things that matter more.' She put another stitch in the rose.

'If you let money come between you and Rachel,' she said slowly, 'you will be a much more foolish man than I think you are. You will be throwing away her happiness and yours for the sake of a scruple, and some day you will make money on your own account.'

'But she doesn't love me.'

'I should not be too certain about that,' said Louisa contemplating the rose with her head on one side. 'Try and see.'

At that moment voices were heard in the hall, the door was opened and Rachel, a small figure draped in black, came in. She was smiling.

'I have come for the night,' she said. 'Sir Edward suddenly decided that he would go and stay at the Chase and I had no time to let you know.' She caught sight of Paul standing by the mantelpiece and drew in her breath sharply.

'I am delighted to see you,' said Mrs. Cunningham. 'Now I will go and arrange that your room is got ready.' Before she closed the door she turned and said, 'I think Paul has something to say to you, my dear.'

Epilogue

To those of my readers who have taken a kindly interest in the characters in this book I will add a few words.

Emily's mother died suddenly after sinking into a protracted illness, during which Emily nursed her with care and kindness.

The clergyman, of whom Emily had spoken to Rachel, was a constant visitor at their lodgings, and one day he found Emily in dire grief at her mother's sudden death. He put his arms consolingly round her and asked her to marry him. Emily, incoherent with bitter tears, sobbed in his arms and then told him her story.

He was for a few moments shocked and deeply saddened, but when she said, 'I didn't want to tell you, but I am never going to lie to you. Can you forgive me for what I have told you?' he said, 'Ask God to forgive you, and if you will marry me we will forget this and never speak or think of it again.' They were married very quietly, and if the parishioners thought Emily's clothes too fashionable for a parson's wife, they were won over by her warmth of heart and kindness.

Ronnie Wentmore came down to the Chase. He found his mother frowning over some papers. 'I've come to tell you that my regiment has been ordered abroad.' She looked at him with a desolate look on her face. 'Oh, dear,' she said, 'you will be going away for some time.' He nodded. 'I don't know for how long.'

She sighed and said, 'I hoped you would be able to come here more and perhaps think of marrying.'

Ronnie was silent for a moment. 'I had thought of it,' he said soberly. 'In fact I asked Rachel to marry me.'

'Rachel Gervase do you mean?'

'I don't know any other Rachel,' he replied. 'I know you've

always hated her because you thought she snatched Richard away from Mary. But don't worry, she refused me. She is marrying that chap Paul Sibley.'

His mother looked at him so piteously that he said in a softer tone, 'Don't worry too much about Mary. She and our cheerful cousin Roger have made friends in London. I'm not very fond of him myself, but he's got a nice hunting box in Leicestershire, and they can talk about horses and dogs all day long.'

He rose to leave the room.

'I've another idea, Mamma. Why don't you marry Cousin Edward and then you could discuss woods and boundaries to your hearts' content.'

'I never heard of such a preposterous idea,' said Lady Wentmore.

'It's not all that preposterous,' said Ronnie. 'He's lonely and so will you be when Mary marries and I'm abroad, but,' and he came up to the table where she was sitting, 'if you ever make things difficult for Rachel you will have me to reckon with when I come back home.'

With that he left the room.

Lady Wentmore sat on. She was crying silently. Then she dried her tears, reached for her quill pen, dipped it deep into the ink pot and wrote to her cousin Roger inviting him to stay at the Chase. She sealed it with a blob of sealing wax, then she wrote a short note to Sir Edward saying she would like to come over to luncheon at the Priory in two days time.

Tweedsmuir, Susan
  A stone in the pool.

Redwood Library and Athenaeum
NEWPORT, R. I.

Selections from the Rules

New fiction is issued for 7 days, new non-fiction for 14 days, and other books for 28 days with the privilege of renewal.

Books overdue are subject to a fine of 2 cents a day.

All injuries to books and all losses shall be made good to the satisfaction of the Librarian.

5 volumes may be taken at a time and only 5 on 1 share or subscription.